Readers love *Vice City*
by S.A. STOVALL

"A fantastic and intense read that deeply satisfied my love of gay fiction and noir. Buon appetito!"
—The Novel Approach

"This was a super intense, high energy story that kept me on the edge of my seat."
—Love Bytes

"I am a sucker for a hard hearted fella finding and fighting for love."
—Jessie G Books

"…it has a lot going for it. I'm more than interested in seeing what the next book brings."
—Joyfully Jay

By S.A. Stovall

VICE CITY
Vice City
Vice Enforcer

Published by DSP PUBLICATIONS
www.dsppublications.com

S.A. Stovall

VICE ENFORCER

DSP PUBLICATIONS

Published by

DSP Publications

5032 Capital Circle SW, Suite 2, PMB# 279, Tallahassee, FL 32305-7886 USA
www.dsppublications.com

Vice Enforcer
© 2018 S.A. Stovall.

Cover Art
© 2018 Aaron Anderson.
aaronbydesign55@gmail.com
Cover content is for illustrative purposes only and any person depicted on the cover is a model.

ISBN: 978-1-64080-123-3
Digital ISBN: 978-1-64080-124-0
Library of Congress Control Number: 2017916219
Published April 2018
v. 1.0

To Ann, for whom the book was written.
To John, for everything.
To Rose, for the wonderful global comments on *Vice City*.
To Evan, for being an amazing agent.
And finally, to everyone unnamed, thank you for your support.

S.A. Stovall

VICE ENFORCER

CHAPTER ONE

A LOT of crime happens around railroad tracks.

I've seen it a million times—from drug deals to gangbangers smuggling guns—which is why I get nervous when I step out of the car and spot the North Union Rail Yard off in the distance. There are entirely too many shadows moving between parked boxcars for 2:00 a.m. in the goddamn morning. No one should be here at this time of the day, at least not at this particular ramshackle rail yard.

My gut tells me I'm gonna regret snoopin' around.

"Stay close, boys," Shelby says. "And keep your voices down."

Shelby grunts as he pulls himself out of his tiny four-door Dodge Neon. He's old, perhaps in his late fifties, but not so old that getting out of a vehicle should be a struggle. The way he takes in ragged breaths betrays a chronic problem. I'm guessing emphysema, given how much the man smokes, but I've never asked. I have my own lung problems to worry about.

Davis rubs his hands together and slams the back door shut with a quick tap of his hip. The loud bang of the car door travels out into the empty night sky. A pair of crows flies off toward the moon.

"Goddammit, Davis," Shelby hisses. "What did I just say? Keep it down!"

"I am, but it's freakin' freezing," Davis replies with a warble and whine to his tone that eliminates all patience. I swear his voice assaults the tranquility of the night with each raspy syllable he chokes out his mouth. If we aren't caught within the next ten minutes, it'll be a miracle.

Shelby walks around to the trunk of his car and pops it open. "Pierce," he says, staring at me with a harsh look of seriousness. "Get over here."

I walk over, pulling my jacket close. It is rather cold.

"What is it?" I ask.

"Do you know how to handle a gun?"

I stifle a laugh. "Yeah, old man. I know how to handle a gun."

"Good. I'm gonna need you to cover me."

Shelby rummages through the contents of the trunk. After a moment he withdraws a pair of handguns—two .50 caliber Desert Eagles. They've only got a seven round capacity, but they have a lot of stopping power. No man ignores a bullet from a gun like that.

I take the weapon and check the magazine. The handgun is loaded and ready to go. Not the safest way to store the thing, but I don't have any room to talk. I keep a fully loaded handgun under my mattress at all times.

"This is in nice condition," I say, turning the heavy gun over in my hands. "You don't use it often."

"As it should be," Shelby says with a grunt. "But tonight is different. Tonight you earn your wings."

Davis flounces over and motions to the handguns. "What about me? I don't get one?"

"I've got two guns. That's it. You've got the camera, don'tcha? You'll be taking the pictures."

I wouldn't trust Davis with a can opener, but Shelby is the one in charge. Davis and I are here for the experience—to get our hours marked off on our time cards—and to learn from an active private investigator so that we can qualify for our own licenses. Shelby was the only PI who would take me due to my questionable background, and I assume that's the same story with Davis, though I've never asked. I try to avoid talking to the other man as much as possible.

"Do you think we're gonna run into trouble?" Davis asks, his gaze flitting around in frantic motions.

"We might," Shelby replies.

"Then I definitely need a gun."

"You've got no experience. You'd sooner shoot yourself than your attacker."

The harshness of the statement shuts Davis up. I tuck the Desert Eagle into my pants waistband and cover it with the flap of my jacket. The silence persists as Shelby withdraws a pair of night vision binoculars from the trunk.

He isn't messing around. He came prepared for *something*.

Shelby holds the device up to his eyes and squints through. The rail yard is about a thousand feet away, and several detached boxcars are parked along the tracks, waiting to be loaded or unloaded. It's difficult to see anything from the gravel parking lot, especially with my bum eye and a chain-link fence in the way. I stare regardless. There's definitely movement between the moonlight shadows. I doubt anyone in the rail yard can see us due to the poor lighting, but there's still plenty of time for Davis to bitch and moan his way into a confrontation.

"Pierce," Shelby says, handing me the binoculars. "What do you see?"

I lift the binoculars to match my gaze and adjust the zoom. The green and black of the lens allows for contrast in the darkest of shadows. I spot a handful of men milling around the rail yard until a small commercial van drives down the tracks and parks alongside a loaded boxcar. The hurried movements of the men, along with their constant need to glance over their shoulders, tell me they want this job done as fast as possible.

And they don't want anyone to know about it.

I hand the binoculars back to Shelby. The old man glances through and takes in the new information.

"Something big is going down," I drawl.

Davis crosses his arms over his chest and huffs. "Can you even see anything with those? Aren't you blind?"

I give the man a sideways glower before returning my attention to the rail yard. My left eye draws more attention than I like. The iris is clouded over, thanks to a cataract—not something a thirty-seven-year-old usually sports—and it leaves my vision impaired, but my right eye works fine. I'm not fucking blind.

"They're criminals of the worst kind," Shelby proclaims.

Davis grabs for the binoculars. Shelby gives them over, his long face set into a neutral expression as he mulls over the situation. He's a clever guy for his age, but sometimes it takes him a minute to analyze all the facts.

"They might just be railway workers," Davis mutters, staring at the rail yard, the device firmly pressed against his face. "We don't know they're engaged in criminal activity."

"Did you get a look at the two men standing around the rails?" I ask. "The two not doing anything? They're acting as lookouts. You don't do that when you're working a legit job. Not to mention they're all carrying guns."

"Guns?" Davis somehow presses the binoculars harder against his eye sockets. "Where?"

"Look for the shoulder holsters. You can catch sight of them if you pay attention."

"Fuck. They do have guns."

Davis lowers the binoculars, and his skin—already pale—shifts two shades whiter than before, giving him the appearance of a semisentient jar of mayonnaise. His trembles something fierce, and I suspect he doesn't handle stress well.

Fucking perfect. He's a liability. This isn't going to be my night.

Shelby takes back the binoculars and packs them away. He shuts the trunk with a gentle click and then motions to the fence. "C'mon, Pierce. We're gonna get closer. Davis, you stay a little ways behind us."

"What're we doing?" I ask.

Private investigators don't go in with guns blazing—they're investigators who gather evidence for courtroom attorneys or snoop on cheating spouses. I knew that before I joined Shelby's firm two months ago, and he's never done anything as reckless as running out to single-handedly catch criminals like he's got a Batman complex. What's this old man thinking?

"You're a tough guy," Shelby says, giving me the once-over. "Don't tell me you're frightened."

"You don't live as long as I have by rushing into things without a little background information. These aren't normal thugs. They're part of a bigger operation. That means they'll have more resources. And that means bigger, better guns, and backup plans. What do we got? A PI with asthma and myself."

"Hey," Davis snaps. "What the hell? You don't know what's going on here! Stop acting like you've pieced everything together. You know jack shit."

I shoot Davis another glare. "I've seen enough of this operation to recognize we're dealing with some sort of syndicate or organization. All the hallmarks are here. Arranged pickups. Armed enforcers. Remote locations. This isn't some two-bit crime. We're walking into someone's territory."

"I thought you said you worked at a lumber mill before this. Since when do lumber guys know anything about organized crime? Huh?"

A small piece of me wants to shut this idiot up by telling him that I ran as a mob enforcer for twenty years, but another piece of me—the rational and clear-thinking part—knows that's a terrible idea.

"Just trust me," I drawl. "I'd bet my life on it."

Shelby holds up a hand. "Enough of this. I didn't think these goons would show up tonight, but now that they're here, I'm not going to let them get away. We don't need to arrest them—all we need is irrefutable evidence. Faces. Pictures. Vehicles. Things that lead us back to the real men in charge. And if you two help me, I'll sign off on twelve months of your training."

Davis lifts both his eyebrows. "Twelve months? For one night's worth of work?" He doesn't take long to weigh the options. "Count me in."

Getting licensed as a private investigator in Illinois takes three years of experience before an applicant can even apply for the exam. Cutting a whole year off is a nice deal, but Shelby's desperation gives me pause. He's checked this rail yard for the last three nights running. He knew these thugs would be here eventually. Shelby's not telling us something.

Then again, if I did all my training by the book, I'd be forty years old by the time I'm licensed. Shaving a year off this monotony might be worth the risk.

I grit my teeth and exhale. "Fine. But we're keeping our distance. We aren't going to mess with these guys."

"Of course not," Shelby says. "We'll get in, get our evidence, and then call the police."

Davis breathes into his hands and glances around. "Why not call the cops right now?"

"The moment these guys hear the sirens, they'll take off. We can't have them leaving before we've got our evidence."

Shelby seems pretty obsessed with catching these guys red-handed. Whatever. "Let's get this over with," I say.

We cross the parking lot, creeping along the edge near the office building, until we reach the chain-link fence. I follow Shelby to one end, away from the locked gates leading to the rail yard. He's wearing a lot more than usual tonight, and he carries himself as though burdened. It's unusual, but before I can comment, the old man pushes in a part of the fence, revealing a portion that had been precut.

He planned this so far ahead of time, the entire area is prepped. That fact worries me more than anything else.

I step through the hole and slide into the moonlight shadows cast by the large steel freight containers waiting for pickup. Shelby wipes a profuse amount of sweat from his forehead before continuing forward. His breathing is strained, like he's trying to keep it quiet, and we slow our pace.

Davis dawdles behind. He fumbles with his digital camera, dividing his attention.

The rail yard is massive. There are five full tracks for trains, two parking lots for trucks, one parking lot for employees, two loading and unloading docking stations, a storage area, and a two-story office near the gates. To my surprise, there are no lights illuminating the equipment—which is standard practice to deter thieves—but I suspect our thug friends have something to do with the darkness that engulfs the area like a thick blanket. We navigate our way closer to the men with uncertain steps, avoiding the areas bathed in moonlight, lest we get caught.

Once we reach a row of parked boxcars, I pull my handgun and press my back against the side of the car. Shelby does the same. Davis stops behind a stack of loaded crates a good fifty feet from us. Shelby attempts to motion him over, but Davis has eyes only for the camera. He's doing something with the damn thing, and I have the sudden urge to shoot the device out of his hands.

I've seen the man operate a smartphone, for fuck's sake, and those things have a hundred purposes. The digital camera has *one* function—to take pictures—yet somehow Davis treats it like a perplexing puzzle on par with a twelve-sided Rubik's Cube.

The crunch of boots on gravel gets me tense. Shelby stops motioning for Davis and holds his handgun close. I sneak a glance around the boxcar and pull back a second later.

Two goons walk along the other side of the tracks. I didn't see them when I originally glanced through the binoculars, but now that I know they're here, I get worried. How many guys are in this rail yard? Not only that, but farther down the track, near the van, ten guys are loading and unloading man-sized crates. They seem to be replacing cargo in one of the boxcars, but I didn't get a good enough look to say for sure.

What the fuck is going on here? Is this a drug deal? Are they smuggling guns?

The men work in silence and without flashlights. Even more evidence that they're professionals. Gangbangers are sloppy, since most of them are dropout kids or druggies, but high-level crime pays enough to hire bruisers with experience. And with the number of guys here, the work they're doing must pay bank.

I've seen enough of life on the streets to know that high-paying crime is cutthroat. If they find us, they'll kill us.

No questions. No loose ends.

I already regret agreeing to Shelby's deal. We aren't in a position to deal with merciless killers. The reality of the situation sends ice through my veins, and my heart rate doubles.

"This was a mistake," I mutter. "We need to head back."

Shelby shakes his head. "We're not leaving. They're not getting away this time."

This time? Fuck. The old man has a vendetta. He's probably not even thinking straight.

Davis fumbles and snaps a picture—a bright flash lighting-up-the-area kind of picture—and my once-pounding heart seizes up in dread.

Within the next two seconds, men with guns converge on Davis's location, four surrounding the crates Davis hid behind. Before I can get my bearings, the harsh crack of a handgun causes me to flinch. Davis hits the ground bleeding from a gaping chest wound while six more guys come circling round like sharks drawn to chum.

I know I can't handle ten trained bruisers with guns. During the commotion, I shuffle back around the boxcar and stand in line with the steel wheels. Shelby dashes in another direction, sliding behind a separate boxcar. I watch the continuing scene through the open car doors, careful not lean too far out.

One thug walks up to the mewling form of Davis and takes another shot, this time to the back of Davis's head.

They didn't even bother to ask questions.

Two other guys search Davis's still-warm corpse. I doubt they're looking for a quick buck, but they go straight for his wallet.

"Who is this guy?" the shooter asks, his tone heated despite his low volume.

The goon searching shakes his head. "I don't know." He leafs through the contents of the wallet. "His name is Mark Davis." He throws the contents to the dirt and picks up a small scrap of paper. "Look here. He's a private investigator."

"That's a temporary license. He's a PI in training."

The statement leaves unspoken words that the whole group picks up on. If there's a trainee, there has to be a trainer. The guy in charge—or at least the one acting like he's in charge—swings a hand around over his head.

"Search the whole yard," he commands. "Go in teams of two. Find the other one." He glances back over to the van. "Pack it up! We don't have any more time."

The sudden energetic movement fills the air like the buzz of angry bees. I grab the handholds on the side of the boxcar and pull myself up, stopping halfway to the top and waiting, hidden in the shadows. I have no idea how I'm going to get out of this shithole of a situation, but I'm not about to roll over and die either.

"This is the Joliet City Police," Shelby shouts from two boxcars away. His voice chills the flurry of movement. "We have you surrounded! Drop your weapons and place your hands on your head!"

What a brazen bluff. Not one that the thugs believe, however.

They hone in on Shelby's voice and jog over, spreading out to surround him. Two guys round the corner of my boxcar, their eyes widening the moment they spot my shadowy figure. The next half second is filled with the burst of handgun fire. My Desert Eagle has a kickback that hurts my wrist, but I shoot the first guy in the jaw and the second through the knee. Bullets strike the boxcar, one clipping the shell of my ear before stopping dead in the hard steel. I feel nothing through the surge of adrenaline.

"There's one here!" the guy with a busted knee yells, his voice half a scream of agony and half rage. He lifts his gun, and I shoot him again, this time hitting his gut. A bulletproof vest shields his soft belly from getting shredded, but not from the concussion. The tough bastard curls around his bruised stomach and rolls under the boxcar, a trail of bloody mud left in his wake.

I clamber up the last of the handrails and crouch down on the roof of the car, ducking out of sight.

I swear I don't even take two breaths before a flash of light and an intense *bang* fills the rail yard. I'm far enough from the radius of the explosion—and shielded by the steel frame of the car—that I'm not disorientated, but I've experienced enough stun grenades to know that everyone on the ground is blind and deaf. A mild ringing fills my ears as I dig out my cell phone from my jacket pocket.

Maybe it's because I've lived most of my life as a criminal, or maybe it's because I've known a lot of crooked cops, but I've never trusted the police. I don't call them. Instead I call the one person I trust, and the one person whose voice I want to hear if I'm about to die.

The phone rings. In the distance, I hear another round of gunfire. I don't know how Shelby pulls it off, but he's making two people feel like ten.

"Hello?" a groggy voice echoes from the speaker.

"Miles, I'm at the North Union Rail Yard," I say with an exhale, thankful he answered despite the hour.

"Pierce?" Alarm replaces all hint of sleep in Miles's voice. "What's going on? Are you okay?"

The next round of gunfire is closer than the last. I hang up the phone, unable to explain the situation in a coherent manner. He's a smart guy. He'll call the cops.

The harsh strike of bullets on steel is so close to my head that it hurts my ears. I roll away from the gunshots, my clothes soaking up the icy dew pooling on top of the boxcar. Shaken and uncertain of what I'm going to do, I glance around.

There's a boxcar parked ahead of mine. I stand and run for it, well aware I can't stay up long or else I'll get shot from men on the ground. I jump over the three-foot gap and slip on the landing. Before I can correct my footing, I slide to the edge of the boxcar and spot the two guys climbing up the handholds.

I shoot at them twice, knocking one guy down and jarring the other enough to cause him to fall.

God, I wish Miles were here. Having heard his voice reminds me that I'm alone in this struggle. I have no idea what Shelby is doing—or whether he's still alive—and it's looking less likely that I'll see the dawn.

Sirens in the distance cut through the night. Miles must have called them. I knew he would.

"Get to the van!" the lead thug yells. "We're out of time!"

The rush of men to the vehicle is a relief. I shift back to the center of the boxcar roof, keeping out of sight. If they flee, I might live through this.

Another round of gunfire reminds me that reality hates my guts. I take one glance at the yard and curse under my breath. Shelby fires at the van as it peels away, hitting the tires and the driver with a few precise shots. The vehicle careens off its course and crashes into one of the steel freight containers, smashing up the engine block.

Does the old codger *want* to die? It takes all my willpower to restrain myself from yelling, *Just let them go, you idiotic kook!*

The fool keeps firing, building ire like he doesn't care about his own well-being. When he runs out of ammo, he ejects his magazine and reloads within two quick seconds. He wields his weapon with the skill of an expert.

That doesn't protect him from getting shot, however.

Shelby takes three bullets—one to the ribs, one to the arm, one to the shoulder—and then collapses to the dirt in a pool of his own free-flowing blood. When thugs come to finish him off, I take wild potshots over the edge of the boxcar. The men scatter and take cover before returning fire. On my third shot, I hear the click of an empty clip. That's it. I'm spent.

"We're leaving!" someone yells.

The roar and rev of motorcycles fills the area. I knew they had a backup plan.

The men stop firing at me and Shelby and instead gather up whoever they can and take off. One thug runs by and spots the goon with the knee injury, curled up in the fetal position by the wheel of a boxcar. The thug takes one good look before leveling his handgun at the man's head and pulling the trigger.

No loose ends.

As the sirens grow louder, so do the men. They squeal out of the rail yard at full tilt, leaving through the opposite gate and driving down the dirt roads normally reserved for railway workers. The dirt they kick up leaves me coughing, but I'm not about to complain. This is a better outcome than what I would have bet on.

The moment I'm sure they're gone, I step down onto the handholds, rubbing at my bruised hip. Without the rush of danger, my body feels every injury.

Shelby isn't far from me, and I jog over to his side. To my surprise, he's still alive. I crouch down and examine him closer. Under his many layers, he's wearing a cheap bulletproof vest. The bullet meant for his ribs is half-buried in the protective equipment.

I grab the man's jacket and pull him up, rage building with every breath. "You wore a vest?" I ask, my voice on the rise. "And you didn't give me or Davis a warning as to what you were planning? You knew there would be danger! *You knew that—*"

"Pierce," he interjects. "Check the van. Make sure they're okay."

Incredulous, I shake him by the collar, watching blood pump from the open bullet hole in his arm. "Are you even listening to me, old man? You better start talking!"

"The van…." Shelby grunts and grits his teeth. His legs shake right before they give out. I let him fall to the dirt. He's in bad shape and starts coughing heavily into his hand. Phlegm and spittle coat his palm a few seconds into his outburst.

What a piece of shit. He's the instrument of Davis's death, and he almost killed me as well. What the fuck is in this van? Why does he care so much?

I turn on my heel and march over, anger once again masking my pain. It's dark, but the van is left broken in a spot of moonlight. I hustle to the back and lift the shutter door up, intent on finishing this as soon as possible. The crates are thrown around the back from the crash, some cracked open. I climb up into the back and walk over to the first broken container. I rip up the lid and spot a large refrigerator. No wonder it took those guys so long to haul these crates around.

Curiosity gets the best of me. I reach down and pop the door of the fridge container, half expecting to find drugs. The moment I get an eyeful of the contents, I jump back, stunned.

I've seen all sorts of things smuggled and traded, but… the sight of two people catches me off guard.

They're crammed in the container, eyes sunken in and their skin cold. There's no ice, but the fridge unit seems to keep the temperature set low. Their soft intakes of breath and warm exhales of mist tell me they're alive, but their weak posture and half-lidded expressions say they're heavily sedated. They don't acknowledge my presence.

I stare at the two jammed in the fridge and then pan my gaze around to the other crates. There are ten containers—do they have twenty people here? Goddamn sons of bitches.

They're wearing nothing but tags secured around their arms. I squint to read that each tiny scrap of paper lists their age, blood type, and a short medical history. Despite the darkness of the van, I can see the discoloration of bruises across all visible areas of their flesh. The raw smell of copper hints at the fresh blood sliding along the bottom of the fridge.

The cruelty of man knows no bounds.

I've seen a lot of guys die, and a lot of terrible things happen to good people, but this is a whole new shade of darkness I hadn't mentally prepared myself for. The tags tell me everything—the people are here to be harvested for organs or shipped off as sex things. It's sick and vile, and my stomach churns.

I've never felt more relieved to hear the approach of sirens. The cops pull into the rail yard parking lot with their blue and red lights sweeping over the area. I hope they can help. Someone needs to bring these kids to a hospital, and fast.

Shelby's actions suddenly make a strange amount of sense. But how did he know what was going down tonight?

CHAPTER TWO

Like a hospital or a morgue, it's never a good sign to see a busy police station.

I glance around, nervous, and keep my hands deep inside my jacket pockets. The Joliet City Police Department swarms with uniformed officers, news reporters, and wide-eyed looky-loos who squeezed themselves into the front lobby. I stand behind the service counter, eyeing the front door and waiting like they told me to, but I'll take any chance to leave that comes my way. No good can come from me being here.

A man pushes his way through the crowd and walks straight up to the main counter. I'd recognize Miles no matter what, even in his hasty morning dress of sweatpants and a black wifebeater. Seeing him takes some of the weight off my shoulders.

"Pierce," he says the moment he spots me. "You're okay!"

"Yeah," I reply.

"I've been calling you for hours! I didn't know which precinct they'd take you to. Why didn't you answer?"

I don't much care for phones. I pull mine out of my pocket and see thirty-one missed calls, three text messages, and ten voicemails. I give Miles a sardonic half smile. "I was a little busy."

Without talking to the officer behind the counter, Miles effortlessly leaps over and closes the distance between us. Reporters protest and balk, and the officer in charge holds up a hand and shouts, "Hey!"

"He's with us," I say, giving him a dismissive wave of my hand. "From the PI firm."

That's not true, but I don't care.

Miles wraps his arms around me in a tight embrace, catching me off guard and causing me to tense. We're chest-to-chest, his chin resting on my shoulder, before I regain my senses enough to shove him away. The officer behind the front counter gives me a *You lying sack of shit* glance that punctuates the whole scene.

"Not here," I growl, my volume low but my tone heated. "Not in the middle of all this."

"I've been worried about you."

"Everything is fine."

"The reporters are calling you all heroes. They say you saved twenty people."

Goddammit. I don't want recognition of any kind. "We should avoid them and their cameras as much as possible."

Miles steps closer, leaving only inches between us. He stares at me with his dark hard-set eyes. I take in a short breath and exhale. The whole police department is filled with sounds of ringing phones, furious typing, and agitated people. It doesn't help me relax.

"Not here," I repeat. I hate this place. Nothing about a police department makes me feel safe.

"Why don't we leave?"

"Music to my ears. Let's get outta here before—"

A woman in a tight pencil skirt waves her hand near my face, cutting me off. "Sir?" she says, no patience in her tone. "The lieutenant will see you now." She's holding a mug of coffee but doesn't offer it—she keeps it close, like a precious object.

I hold back a sigh of irritation and return my attention to Miles. "I need to answer some questions. I'll be right back. Then we're leaving."

Miles replies with a curt nod, and I turn to follow the woman. The bustle of the station creates a white noise that drowns out footsteps and low-level thought. We're at the lieutenant's door before I know it, and I glance over my shoulder, unable to catch sight of Miles.

The secretary opens a door labeled *Lieutenant Rhett Walker* and ushers me into the office. I step in and the lady follows, a smile widening across her face, before speaking in a singsong voice.

"Hello, Lieutenant Walker. Here's the private investigator you asked for."

The man standing behind the desk is hunched over, reading a stack of papers, but offers a quick nod. "Thank you, Monica. Keep trying to get ahold of Deputy Chief Charleston. I need to speak with him as soon as possible."

"Of course! Right away." She walks over to the cluttered desk and holds up the mug of coffee with both hands. "It's early. I thought you might need a pick-me-up." She places it on the corner of the desk and continues, "I added some milk and cinnamon, just like you like it."

The lieutenant stops what he's doing and straightens his posture. And now I understand what this lady is so wet in the panties for.

Lieutenant Walker is a solid guy—taller and more muscular than I am, that's for sure—and he holds himself with a confidence you can't fake. His styled black hair and striking green eyes add together to make for a perfect model, and he wears his uniform like he was born for it. I wouldn't be surprised to hear he has the whole female population riding his nuts.

I stare longer than I should.

"Thank you, Monica," Lieutenant Walker says, a distant disinterest to his voice. "I appreciate your forethought."

She smiles wider, if that's even possible, and then backs out of the room, waving as she goes. I stifle a chuckle. The lust is thick. I can only imagine the things she does when they're alone.

"And thank you for waiting," the lieutenant says, drawing me out of my musings. "Are you Michael Shelby?"

I shake my head and stay close to the door. "I'm—" *Nicholas Pierce* is what I want to say, but that was my name before my new identity. It takes me half a second to remember my new, much less appealing name. "—I'm Percy Adams."

Percy Adams.

What a terrible name.

I didn't have much of a choice, though, and Percy is at least *mildly* similar to Pierce, so much so that most people assume it's my nickname rather than my given surname. I try not to think of it often, which might be why I almost forgot it.

The lieutenant walks around the desk and gives me an odd scrutinizing look. "You're Shelby's trainee?"

"Yeah," I reply. "What of it?"

My terse tone must not go over well with him, because he crosses his arms and regards me with a harsh seriousness. "What were you doing trespassing on private property?"

"You'll have to ask Shelby. I don't decide what cases we work on."

"What did he say to you last night when you went to the North Union Rail Yard?"

"He said, 'Hey, you want a paycheck? We're going to the North Union Rail Yard.' Then I got in the car. The end."

Lieutenant Walker narrows his eyes. "My investigators say there's evidence that you, Shelby, and his other trainee, confirmed dead earlier this morning, broke into the rail yard. Why don't you tell me a little about that?"

I force a laugh and shrug. "What is this? Shouldn't you be a little more concerned with the kidnapping and trafficking? Who gives a fuck about trespassing? You really think a district attorney is going to prosecute hero detectives after they saved twenty people? I don't think so."

"This isn't about the trespassing," he says, his fingers gripping into his arms, his knuckles turning white. "This is about the fact that Shelby has been involved in *three* separate instances of breaking the law in conjunction with this very same criminal activity. I'd like to know what's going on and how Shelby got his information."

"That makes one of us," I drawl.

Lieutenant Walker lets out a long exhale and walks over to me. He relaxes a bit, dropping his crossed arms, and meets my gaze. "A man died tonight. This isn't a laughing matter. Next time it could be you or Shelby."

"Shit happens."

He grits his teeth. "You don't care at all?"

"I don't wanna die, if that's what you're asking."

"But you'll do whatever is asked of you—so long as you get a paycheck."

I let my silence do the talking.

I know it's a lowlife mentality, but it's not like I have many options. I dropped out of high school, my mother is in prison, and my father killed himself drinking and driving. Not to mention my résumé includes a laundry list of corpses under the "references" portion. I can already hear the callbacks.

Lieutenant Walker opens his mouth to speak but then stops and stares. I lift an eyebrow.

"Have you ever been to the City of Noimore?" he asks.

"Never," I reply, probably a bit too hasty.

"Not once? It's a major metropolitan area. Most people drive through it when they take a trip to Chicago."

"I'm not most people."

He stares a bit longer. "How long has your eye been like that?"

I turn away. "It just happened."

"Hm."

I don't like the way he asks these questions. He starts to ask another, but the door to the office swings open and hits me in the arm. I hadn't even realized how far I had leaned away from him until this moment. The guy gets me on edge.

"Lieutenant Walker," Monica says, poking her head in and smiling. "I have Deputy Chief Charleston on the line for you. He says he isn't going to wait long."

The lieutenant mulls over the comment while running a hand down his face. He looks tired—and stressed—and eventually lets out a long sigh. "Wait here," he tells me. "I need to ask you a few more questions. I'll be right back."

He steps out of the office with Monica, leaving me alone with all his paperwork.

The commotion of a busy department filters into the room and creates a dull backdrop to an otherwise still environment. I glance around and smirk. The guy must be some sort of straightlaced white knight. He has a picture of himself becoming an Eagle Scout, right next to a picture of his police work at a local elementary school—not to mention all the handwritten cards from kiddies thanking him for his time—and on a shelf behind his desk, I catch sight of an ISBA Law Enforcement Award for a search-and-rescue operation during a major fire in downtown Joliet.

Well, la-dee-da. I wouldn't be surprised to hear he has an ego three times the size of the moon.

Curiosity gets the best of me, and I amble around the side of his desk to get a better look at his paperwork. I sift through mountains of personal files on the rescued individuals and take note that they're all under the age of twenty-five. Kids that young shouldn't be victims of crimes this heinous.

I freeze when I see a few case files labeled "Noimore."

I know that city like the back of my hand, and lately it's become a heart of darkness for the region, pumping the lifeblood of crime into the surrounding territory with a steady pulse. Once it was run by the Vice family mob; now it's tearing itself apart with turf wars and new emerging gangs. I'm sure some of the Vice family still holds power there—if anything, I'm sure Jeremy Vice is out of jail—but that only adds to the chaos of an already hostile environment.

Jeremy Vice.

Even thinking about the man gets me uneasy. I left the mob because I wanted out, but I had to fake my own death because Jeremy kept me as a tortured dog. He really did a number on me for the few months I worked under him. I swear he broke a piece of me—a piece of confidence I once had—and I can't bring myself to dwell on it too long.

I hope to God I never have to go back to Noimore ever again.

And what's a Joliet cop doing with another city's criminal records? Again, I can't help myself. I flip open the Noimore files and leaf through the information.

Everything stacks up pretty quick. The Illinois State Police want city police departments to work together to stop the recent uptick in human trafficking. Still… I don't like that cops in this area are involved with Noimore criminal records.

I catch my breath the moment I spot *my* file. It's open on his desk, like that asshole lieutenant had just been reading up on it. I yank it over and scan the information, my heartbeat threatening to drown out all other sound.

It doesn't have my name or picture, but it lists my appearance, profession, and suspected crimes. Vice family top enforcer. Suspected of murder, racketeering, extortion, possession of illegal firearms—the list is extensive and rather accurate.

Tall Caucasian man. Midthirties. Dark brown hair. One eye discolored. But everything else is flat wrong. My blood type, my fingerprints—everything. Big Man Vice had lots of connections in the Noimore Police Department back when I worked for him. They made sure misinformation was the only information the cops ever got.

My date of death was recorded eight months back, the night I escaped Noimore and got away from Jeremy.

I allow my panic to wane as the facts settle in. I'm officially dead. There's no way anyone's going to be able to link me to my past. As long as I don't give them the opportunity.

I graze my left eyelid and curse under my breath. I have a few distinguishing marks, and that golden boy lieutenant picked up on one fast. With a sigh, I pull up my left sleeve and examine the stark black text of the tattoo I have along my forearm. It reads: VICE HOUND. A gift Jeremy etched into my skin so that I'd always remember who *owned me*.

Maybe my bum eye alone can't pin me, but I'm sure even a simpleton could put one and two together after reading this file and seeing my tattoo.

Before the lieutenant comes back, I shut all the case files, leaving mine open like I found it, and exit his office.

Time to leave.

I step around officers rushing to and fro and head straight for the front lobby where I left Miles. I stutter-step to a halt the moment I catch sight of Lieutenant Walker chatting it up, right before the front counter. He's speaking to Miles, of all people, and the two laugh and smile like they know each other.

When the lieutenant turns to leave, I walk around one of the many occupied desks, keeping my back to the man as I make my way to the front. Police officers give me odd sideways glances, and I flash my PI trainee license to placate them.

I walk up behind Miles and grab him by the upper arm. "Let's go," I mutter.

"Pierce," he says, glancing over his shoulder. "If you want to avoid the press, we should exit some other way."

"Fine."

We head through the police department, following the Exit signs. In a long hall past the bathroom, where a few officers are congregating, I turn to Miles and frown. "You know that guy? The lieutenant talking to you?"

"Rhett?" Miles asks, lifting an eyebrow. "Yeah. He's an instructor at my police academy. Why?"

"Did you call him *Rhett*? You're on a first-name basis with the man?"

"He said that's what we should call him on the first day of class. Is something wrong?"

"I don't like him."

We exit out a side door into the police vehicle parking lot, and the predawn darkness is the only thing to greet us. It's been a long night. All I want is to get home. We cross the lot and enter the visitor parking away from the crowds.

When it starts sprinkling, Miles jogs ahead and unlocks the car. I walk over to the passenger side and crank open the heavy door with a bit of effort. Our clunker came cheap, but that's the only good thing you can say about it. It's silver, with a black driver-side door, and it's some foreign model of a two-door town car that I don't recognize.

I miss my old vehicle—she served me well for years—but I had to leave everything behind when I "died." I think I mourn the car most of all.

Miles starts up the engine and pulls out of the parking lot. The city of Joliet is quieter than Noimore, and I already feel sleep taking hold.

Our radio has two stations: white noise and static. Instead I listen to the gentle patter of rain on the windshield.

"I thought you weren't going to do this anymore," Miles says, his gaze set to the road and his voice neutral.

"Sometimes PIs get into some shit. Comes with the territory."

"Not gunfights. I never expected to get a phone call in the middle of the night and hear bullets whizzing by."

I exhale and lean back. What I wouldn't give for a cigarette. "It's a job."

"You know this isn't like working for the mob, right? You don't have to do whatever Shelby tells you to do. You can say no."

I don't answer.

What's he trying to say? That I should act like a coward and duck out if a situation looks too hairy? Fighting guys is the one thing I know I'm good at. He shouldn't fret so much.

"Listen," he says with a sigh. "I was worried, okay? I'd prefer if stuff like this didn't happen anymore. I don't want to see you hurt."

"I'm a grown-ass man, and I can take care of myself. I've done it for longer than you've been alive."

He doesn't say anything else after that. Probably for the best. What're we even arguing about?

The drive continues in silence. When the dawn breaks, it cuts through the thin storm clouds and ends the drizzle. The peaceful streets of Joliet are quiet at this time of the day, and it honestly relaxes me. Despite having argued with Miles, knowing he's in the car with me is a comfort. I don't have much in this world besides him, literally and figuratively. He's one of the few people who know who I am and who I trust.

Our home sits on the edge of town, in a small collection of one-story houses grouped together like a suburb but treated like a dump. Chain-link fences are the norm, abandoned houses are commonplace, and the sidewalk is cracked more than the broken windows. Some homes are pleasant—well-loved jewels in a pit of soot—but they're the exception, not the rule.

Miles pulls the car into our slanted driveway and parks. I step out, walk over the brown grass of our lawn, and unlock the front door. He follows me in and locks the deadbolt after.

The pale morning light isn't strong enough to pierce the thick curtains over the windows. Our place is dark. I like it that way. I like my business private, and I'd prefer not to see anyone else's either.

Miles walks up behind me and wraps his arms around my midsection. He pulls me close and licks my neck—his erection painfully obvious through his sweatpants.

He nibbles my ear and murmurs, "I'm sorry, Pierce. I can't stand the thought of losing you again." He unbuttons my shirt and runs his hands along my stomach and chest, his hot breath accelerating with each passing moment.

"I've got your back," I say, enjoying the feel of his desperation. "I'm not going to leave you because of some thugs in a rail yard."

"Mind if I go to bed with you?" he whispers.

"Get in there and wait for me," I command. "I'm going to take a shower first."

"All right."

He lets go of me and complies with my demand.

After the firefight in the rail yard, I would have killed to have Miles for a round of sexual escapades, but waiting three hours in a crowded police department put an end to that thrill ride fantasy like Travis put an end to Old Yeller. Miles, on the other hand, is still young and horny— he'll be twenty-one next week—and I swear he's never satisfied. After a hot shower, I should be good to go again.

I walk into the bathroom and shed my jacket and shirt. Once I click on the lights, I'm greeted with the dull, soul-crushing gray the room is decorated in. I swear it looks more like a prison cell. I've seen seedy motels with better accommodations.

I turn on the water in the shower stall and strip off the rest of my clothing. Right as everything gets lukewarm, I slide in and exhale, allowing the water to take away any excess stress. The heat does wonders for my sore body.

The shower stall clicks open and I flinch back, startled by Miles's sudden appearance. He steps into the stream of water, unapologetically pressing up against me and pinning me to the tiled wall.

Jesus Christ. I forget how good-looking this kid is from time to time. Maybe I'm taking him for granted, but I swear I don't think I saw him fully until this moment. Long workout days and eating right— coupled with a youthful metabolism—have transformed him from a lithe tween into a chiseled man. He's not overtly bulky, but his honeyed skin hugs muscles enough to see definition.

Miles runs his black hair under the water, allowing it to slick back before pressing his mouth against mine. His need is infectious. He laps his tongue across mine, and he bites my lip.

"I'm sorry," he mutters before licking my jawline. "I couldn't wait."

I chuckle. Fine by me.

The shower stall isn't built for two people, but Miles doesn't want to separate more than a few inches at a time, so it makes little difference. He kisses my neck and trails his lips down to my chest. I lean back into the corner and spread my legs enough for him to get in between. His hands run the length of my slick body as he gets down on his knees.

I weave my fingers through his wet hair, and he practically purrs, desperate for contact.

"Play with yourself," I say between husky breaths.

I'm hard. I've been hard ever since Miles stepped into the stall with me. But the swelling gets painful when he stares up at me with an intense yet playful look. He slides his tongue along my length, and I have to brace my feet against the walls in order to prevent myself from collapsing. The running water only adds to the sensation, and I shudder, caught off guard by the pleasure.

I twist my hand into a fist, pulling on his hair and forcing him close. "Enough games," I growl. "Take me in your mouth."

Miles is usually compliant, but when he wraps his mouth around me this time, it's slow and featherlight. He glances up at me, giving me the same look as before.

If we weren't in this narrow-ass stall, I would throw him down and fuck him, but as it stands, I'm too caught up in the gratification to walk. Instead I hold him close and buck with my hips, eager to feel the tight grip of his throat. He's strong enough to resist and holds back from giving me what I want.

I tilt my head back and let my jaw go lax, allowing water to brush along my lips and tongue. I close my eyes and continue thrusting, my mind consumed by the need for relief. Miles picks up his pace, moaning once or twice from his own handiwork.

The heat from the shower couples with the heat of Miles's mouth to create a hot potency that I haven't experienced in a while. I hear my own moans echoing throughout the bathroom, but I'm so lost to the moment I don't remember making them.

Miles sucks hard and groans, his orgasm evident in his stiff posture and trembling grip on my hip. The tension in my body builds to the point it's unbearable before releasing in one powerful moment. I seize up and unload my seed into Miles's mouth—which he swallows—before sliding down the wall of the shower into a sitting position, Miles kneeling between my thighs.

I take a few seconds to breathe. Miles laughs and leans his head into my shoulder.

"You taste good," he says.

"Fantastic," I reply between pants.

He scoots forward and braces himself over me, the water blocked by his body as he locks lips with mine. Despite having just come, I feel his semihard cock pressed against my leg.

Miles breaks our kiss and stares at me, his gaze a little too hungry for someone who should be satisfied. He looms over me, leering like he enjoys what he sees.

"Pierce," he whispers, his tone low, "I wanna fuck you."

I grit my teeth. "No."

"Afraid you'll enjoy it?"

"I'm not into it. Now get up."

Miles stands and holds out a hand. I take it and he pulls me up, but my legs threaten to buckle. He leans me against the wall and hands the shampoo over, content to go about his routine of washing as though that's what we had been doing the entire time.

"Do you think you'll ever want to try it again?" he asks, soap running down his sculpted body like he's in a goddamn commercial. "Being the bottom, I mean."

I'm open with my staring, and Miles seems to enjoy it. He's got a tattoo on his leg—a phoenix done in solid black, with the tail starting at the knee and the wings ending on his hip. It's a nice design. Nicer on him.

I stop myself in order to wash. "What's got you into this all of a sudden?"

"Well… I want to know what it feels like."

I glance over and meet his gaze. I keep forgetting I'm the only one he's ever been with. A small piece of me feels guilty, like I'm limiting his possibilities, but another piece of me knows I don't want to give him up. But I'm not in the right frame of mind to talk about it.

My phone rings, the beeps muffled by my pants pocket. I step out of the shower, dripping water all over the floor, and amble over to my slacks. In one quick motion, I scoop up my clothing and dig out my phone.

Shelby.

I let the thing go to voicemail. I'm not in the right frame of mind to talk to him either.

Miles turns off the shower, and I glance over my shoulder at him. "We'll discuss this some other time."

CHAPTER THREE

THE MIDAFTERNOON sun is marred only by the occasional cloud overhead. The fleeting shadows are nice. I loathe working in the harshness of unabated light.

And I also loathe this fucking garden.

I throw down my hand spade and glare at the myriad of dead plants scattered throughout my elevated garden box. Seven and half months ago, when we moved into this shithole, I decided I would try my hand at domestic life. Gardening seemed easy then. I even bought a goddamn book on the subject.

But nothing works. It's like the Grim Reaper himself toiled over the soil before I started planting.

That's not entirely true. One single radish is still alive.

I lean over it and graze the green leaves with the tips of my fingers. The thing feels limp. I glance through my gardening book, attempting to find a solution. Maybe I can save this one sad-sack radish. Then I can say I wasn't a complete failure.

I find a passage about caring for plants midgrowth. It reads: *talking to your plants is one surefire way to perk them up!*

Talk to the plants? What do you say to a plant?

"Grow, you little piece of shit," I say. "Don't you wanna live? Fucking act like it."

I swear the radish wilts a little more the moment I'm done talking.

Miles opens the back sliding glass door and steps out into our backyard. He's dressed in his police academy uniform—some shiny black shoes, dark blue cargo pants, and a tight matching T-shirt. He looks like a cop already, in part due to all the rigorous training he's gone through to make sure he can pass all the obstacle course tests.

"Pierce," he says as he approaches. "I'm going to go pick up Jayden and Lacy from their tutoring lesson." He glances from me to the garden box. "Who were you talking to?"

"The last of my sanity," I quip. "Is that all you wanted to tell me?"

"Yeah. I'll be back in a little bit."

I nod.

Miles walks over and kisses me. I don't protest, but it's not like our backyard is a bastion of privacy. There are missing fence boards on all sides, sometimes multiple in a row. I can see into each neighbor's yard, and I'm sure they can do the same.

"Why're you in uniform?" I ask him as he turns back for the house.

"I went to the shooting range this morning."

"Hm."

Miles disappears inside, leaving me with my failed attempt at a simple life.

I'm not in the mood for company.

Jayden and Lacy, Miles's siblings, are the sole reason we didn't leave Illinois after I broke away from the mob. Miles wants to help his brother get back on track with his life, and he also wants to get to know his sister more than not at all. They're also the reason why we rent a shitty house and use a junker as our vehicle of choice.

We'll get better things once we're away from here. Well, that's the plan, at least. I didn't leave the mob poor. I took half a million dollars in savings when I left—which is what we live on now. That'll keep us going for a while without worry, but not forever.

I return my attention to the dead vegetation and sigh. A small piece of me worries. If I can't make this simple hobby work, what chance do I have of making a life for myself once the money runs out?

"Stop crowding them together."

I snap my attention to the sound of the scratchy voice. Our neighbor, some old crone, stands on the other side of the fence, staring through the missing fence boards. Her sunbaked face scrunches into a long frown. Given the heavy age lines and sagging skin, I'd say she's somewhere in her seventies.

I ignore her and start the process of ripping up all the dead produce. After a few moments, she clears her throat. I stop and return my gaze to her, this time glaring.

"The soil isn't ready for planting yet," she says in the tone of a disapproving grump.

I'm not in the mood for this bullshit. "Did I ask for your input? Keep to your own business, Grandma."

She answers with a huff and holds both her hands on the small of her back. "I've been forced to watch you muddle in the mud for months now. If this isn't a cry for help, I don't know what is."

Everybody's a goddamn critic.

With a long exhale, I stand and brush the dirt off my slacks. "I can do this on my own."

"Not at the rate you're going."

"What does it matter, you old hag?" I snap, throwing up a dismissive wave of my hand. "You'll be dead in a couple days anyway."

She replies with another huff and then turns away. I wait, watching her hobble into her house before once again returning to my graveyard.

My phone rings. I groan and answer the thing, way more irritated than I should be with each new distraction.

"What is it?" I ask, half yelling.

"Pierce?"

I recognize Shelby's voice, and I take a deep, calming breath. "Yeah. It's me."

"I've been callin' you. Have you gotten any of my messages?"

"I saw. I've been busy."

"What're you doing?"

"Pulling up weeds."

"Stop that. I need your help."

I focus more of my attention on the conversation. "What's wrong?"

"I can't talk about it right now," he replies, his voice barely above a whisper. "You need to come see me. I want you to work on something."

"Aren't you in the hospital?" I ask. I figured I wouldn't be working for the next few weeks while Shelby recovers, but I guess I got that wrong.

"Yes. The hospital. Come see me in the hospital."

"I'll be there shortly."

"No!" he says, stepping on the end of my statement. "Not now. Later tonight. Around 8:00 p.m."

The hell? What's this guy's problem? "Why?" I ask.

"I'll tell you when you get here."

Shelby hangs up the phone before I get my two cents in. Whatever. My level of giving a damn is pretty low. I stoop down to the garden box and pull a plastic baggie out from the wood paneling. It's got a pack of cigarettes and a lighter—they're the last of my old habit—and I take out a smoke and light it up.

After one long inhale, tranquility settles over the ramshackle neighborhood. Maybe I should drink more to compensate for not smoking. Obviously I get irritable without something coursing through my system.

Now that I feel more like myself, I kneel back down and snatch up my spade. It doesn't take me long to tear through all the plant corpses, and I toss them onto the dead grass of the backyard. I keep the little survivor. The radish is tenacious and doesn't give up. Reminds me of Miles.

I pick up a packet of spinach seeds, and right before I throw them into their furrows, I stop. I'm crowding them? The soil isn't right? I need to talk to them? Plants are needy sons of bitches.

The back sliding door opens and closes with a slam. The sound gets me on edge, and I grab for the pistol I keep in my gardening tool box—but I roll my eyes and release my grip the moment I see who it is.

Jayden Devonport, Miles's brother, saunters out of the house with his thumbs through the belt loops of his school slacks. He has a smug grin about him, like he's thought of something clever, but I return to my task rather than engage him in conversation. The kid's nothing more than a dumpster fire masquerading as a person.

"Well, well," he drawls. "Look who's been neutered."

"Well, well," I repeat in a mocking tone. "Look who finally got out of rehab."

"Is this what you do now? Play the part of a retired geriatric?"

Yup. Still a dumpster fire. I wish Miles would cut him loose and stop worrying about him. He had the perfect opportunity to let him die when Jayden got shot ten months ago, but maybe I'm just an asshole. I don't care if Jayden graduates or not. Hell, if Jayden started choking to death *right this instant*, I might pretend I didn't notice.

"You're even starting to look the part," Jayden continues. "Do you see those white hairs?"

I exhale a long line of smoke and stand. Jayden takes a step back toward the house. I glance over and chortle. The kid's put on some weight. Once upon a time, he and Miles looked like twins. I guess the rehab center didn't require Jayden to exercise often—his green-and-tan school uniform hugs his protruding midsection a little too tight. The kid even has a pencil-line beard to hide the fact he's losing any noticeable jawline.

"Nice facial hair," I say. "Did your boyfriend draw that on for you?"

"Hey," Jayden barks, indignant. Then he takes a moment to mull over my comment and gets red in the face. "And that's not even a joke a faggot like you can make! *You're* the one suckin' dick!"

I walk up to him and pat him on the cheek. Jayden stumbles back, startled, almost like he's afraid I'll follow it up with a left hook. I laugh and continue into the house without another word. The kid never had much courage—he's two nuts short of a ball sac, and I wouldn't be surprised to hear he still wets the bed at night.

Miles and his sister are at the kitchen table. Lacy, unlike Jayden, isn't a thorn in my side, but I know her about as well as I know the female orgasm. She sits, prim and proper, with her long black hair straight to the middle of her back. Her nose is buried in a book as Miles prepares her homework across the tiny table.

"You're smoking?" Miles asks.

I forgot I even had the damn cigarette. I take one last drag and toss it into the sink. "Just when things get stressful."

"Why not take another nicotine patch?"

"Fuck it. I hate wearin' 'em."

Jayden ambles in and takes a seat at the table, his face stuck in a frown. He grabs the TV remote and turns on the tiny set located on the far counter. The news starts up—it's the only channel I watch—and I get tense the moment I see a picture of the North Union Rail Yard.

"—and authorities say some of the kidnappers are still at large," the newswoman says, her voice filled with a showman's flair. "The private investigators on the case, from Shelby's Private Investigations, have yet to comment, but local sketch artists have drawn up representations of the criminals found at the scene. All information should be directed to the Joliet City Police hotline, or directed to your nearest precinct."

A photo of the police department flashes on the screen, raising my heart rate. I'm in the picture, walking into the station. Luckily for me, my back is to the photographer.

"Pierce?" Miles says, staring at me rather than the TV. "What's wrong? You don't look well."

I grab the controller from Jayden and switch off the television. "I don't need any fame," I state. I don't want my picture all over the news—what if one of my old associates sees me?—and I certainly don't want those kidnappers to know I'm one of the guys who busted their operation. They weren't small-time. Even if they know Shelby's PI firm is behind the investigation, that doesn't link me. But they might deal with Shelby like they dealt with Davis.

"You don't think there's a chance I'll be taken, do you?" Lacy asks, turning to Miles.

Miles offers a shrug. "Just stay close. I'm sure you'll be fine."

"Way to cheer her up," Jayden interjects.

I walk over to the table and lean my weight on the back of a flimsy chair. "You don't have to worry," I tell Lacy. "They don't target girls like you."

Jayden glares. "Why? Because she's part Asian?"

I shake my head and offer the kid a sneer. "Do you think scumbags like them give a shit about your racial makeup? No. They want easy targets. Not kids who go to prep school—who have people around them at all times—or kids who have parents who would contact the authorities within minutes of their child's disappearance."

"Then who do they go after?"

"Teenagers hooked on drugs. Runaways. Prostitutes. People who don't have someone who cares about where they are. It's easier to drag some homeless druggie off the street than it is to raid a school with cameras and walls. You and your sister aren't in danger."

Jayden sits up straight. "*Me* and Lacy? You think those guys would try to take someone like me?"

"Maybe to harvest your fat organs."

"Tsk. Fuck you."

Miles gives me a half-lidded stare, and I stifle my chuckles. Then I remember Shelby's phone call.

"You want to go with me to the hospital later?" I ask Miles.

He nods. "Sure."

"Good, because I have business to take care of."

I DON'T like hospitals. All I can think about is catching a cold or disease from someone else nearby, like the air is filled with sickness and each breath gets me closer to infection. And it's not like you can physically fight or shoot a sickness—which is how I've handled everything else trying to kill me in my life.

The Joliet Saint Joseph Medical Center, however, is clean and quiet. The place doesn't seem to get much traffic, or maybe it's because the building is huge.

"You worried someone will recognize you?" Miles asks as we walk down the wide corridors of the fourth story. "Is that why the news bothered you?"

"Yeah," I reply, keeping my voice low. "Some cop already asked me too many questions. If some goon came looking for me, it would only add to my problems."

"And you think guys will come calling for Shelby?"

"I'm willing to put money on it. If he dies in this hospital it won't be an accident, no matter what the papers say."

The nurses and technicians give us quick glowers. It is 7:53 p.m. and visiting hours end at 8:00 p.m. I'm sure none of them want random people mucking up their jobs by getting in the way.

I walk by a mirror and slow for a moment to get a better look at my hair. I don't have many white hairs, just a few at my temples. That's normal. Completely reasonable for my age.

"Checkin' yourself out?" Miles asks with a chuckle.

"I'm not so narcissistic," I say, turning away from the mirror and continuing along with Miles.

"Worried about your appearance? You shouldn't. You're a good-lookin' man."

Worried about getting old is what I want to say, but I keep it to myself. Nobody wants to hear a guy talk about regretting how he spent his youth. That bullshit is for daytime dramas or sappy, emotionally manipulative memoirs.

"Hey," Miles says, tapping me with his elbow. "Look. Rhett is here."

I glance ahead and freeze. Lieutenant Walker stands in front of Shelby's room, his gaze on a file filled with paperwork. Miles hustles over before I can stop him.

"Hey, instructor!"

The lieutenant glances up from his work and smiles a perfect white smile. "Miles," he says, a pleasant surprise to his tone. "How are you?"

"Excellent." Miles stands next to the man and places his hands in his pockets. "What're you doing here in the hospital?"

"I came to speak to the private investigator linked to my special assignment."

"Shelby?"

"That's right. Do you know him?"

"We're here to see him as well."

"We?"

Miles motions me over with jerk of his head. I hesitate—half tempted to leave and come back once this guy is gone—but the lieutenant sees me before I can make a break for it. His sudden tense stance and hard gaze tell me that he remembers who I am.

Fucking perfect.

I walk over to Miles and give the other guy a curt nod.

"This is my boyfriend, Pierce," Miles announces, patting me on the shoulder.

I cringe at the word *boyfriend*. That's not the terminology I'm used to. Nobody in the Vice family mob wanted to hear about men having boyfriends *or* girlfriends. You had your bitches and your hoes, your fuck toys, your flings—admitting you had an emotional attachment to someone was unacceptable. It was weak. It invited trouble.

Lieutenant Walker glances from Miles to me, and then back to Miles, looking at him like he's seeing him in a whole new light. "Miles, you never told me about…. Well, I didn't know this about you."

Miles lifts an eyebrow. "Is this a problem?"

"No," Lieutenant Walker says, fast enough that he practically cuts off Miles's question. "Of course not. You've just never mentioned him before."

"I'm pretty sure I have."

"Trust me," the lieutenant replies with a one-sided smile. "I would have remembered if you had."

The way he says that irritates me. I know what he wants. I can see it in the way he looks over Miles with renewed interest. My dislike for the man only intensifies as he pats Miles's upper arm.

"You scored a hundred percent on your last test. I mean, not that that's unusual, but with your new score, you've solidified yourself as top in your class."

Miles rubs at his neck, a slight flush to his face. "Thank you."

"I expect great things from you in the future."

"I don't know what to say. That's a real honor coming from you."

I'm not into this.

I throw an arm over Miles's shoulders and pull him back a few feet. "Sorry, Lieutenant," I drawl. "We're pressed for time."

"Call me Rhett," he says, narrowing his gaze as he meets mine. "And I'm sure we'll be seeing more of each other in the future."

I really don't like the way he says that. Without any further commentary, I guide Miles over to the appropriate hospital door. Before I open it, Miles pulls me close.

"Hey," he says under his breath. "Do you mind if I stay out here while you talk to Shelby? I want to ask Rhett a few questions about academy stuff."

"Why?" I ask, my tone curt.

"I don't usually see him outside of class. Plus, he's a really important and accomplished police officer. I have a lot of questions that I think he could—"

"Fine," I snap. "Don't take long."

Miles tilts his head like he wants to ask a question, but I slam into Shelby's room without giving him the opportunity. It's probably for the best that Miles talks to Rhett without me. Rhett's distracted by Miles now, but that might not be the case once he's thinking straight, and then he'll want to question me.

And what kind of name is Rhett? Everything about the man—every little thing—gets under my skin.

"Pierce!"

I turn to find Shelby sitting in a hospital bed. Despite wearing a bulletproof vest, he still took a considerable amount of damage in the rail yard. He doesn't look half-bad, though. He sits up on his own, and his skin isn't pale or drained of blood. Besides the bandages, he looks fine. Doctors can work miracles.

"Thank you for coming," Shelby continues as he waves me over to the side of his bed. "I need someone I can trust."

I walk over and exhale. The sterile room is soaked in cleaning chemicals that burn my nose. "You don't have anyone else you can trust? What about your wife?"

"We divorced twenty years ago."

His ring finger is still adorned with a gold band. I always thought he was married, but I guess he hasn't moved on.

"What do you want?" I ask.

Shelby motions me closer. I lean down. "I need you to go to my office," he mutters. "And I need you to continue this case."

"What case?"

"The case we were working on. These scumbags can't be allowed to go free. I'm so close."

"Are you talking about the human traffickers?"

"Of course. Who else would I be talking about?"

"No," I say. "I'm not going to do that. Do you remember what happened *just a few days ago*? This is a suicide case. Leave it to the police."

"I can't," Shelby hisses. He grabs the collar of my jacket and pulls me closer—to the point his two-day-old stubble scratches my ear. "They're in on it."

"What?" I ask.

"The police. Not all of them. But *some* of them. Enough that I can't trust them. I gave them information in the past, and they let those villains get away. Not anymore."

I laugh once and shake my head. "So you want me to continue investigating an entire organization of murderous human traffickers, *and* you want me to go against a corrupt police force, all while you sit here in a hospital, warming your feet with an electric blanket? What kind of fool do you take me for, old man?"

"That's why I needed more evidence," Shelby mutters, his voice heated. "I need to figure out who's behind all this, so I know who it's safe to leak it to. Anything to bring them all down."

I say nothing. His crazy mission will get him killed for sure.

"I'll make you a deal," Shelby says, staring me straight in the eye. "Help me do this and I'll sign off on all your training. All of it. All three years. You could strike out on your own or work with some larger firm if you want. What do you say, Pierce? Will you help me?"

CHAPTER FOUR

THIS IS a terrible idea. I'm one guy, not an army or a member of some greater organization I can call upon for aid.

Then again, all he wants is irrefutable evidence. I don't have to fight anyone or do anything too risky. I'm a pretty accurate judge when it comes to questionable situations. Plus, it would eliminate the long years of training before I can work on my own—away from idiots like Davis— and under no one else's authority.

And, *if* Shelby is right about the cops, who else is going to help those kids get back to their lives? But the how the hell did *I* become their last line of defense? There's got to be other, more altruistic people out there who would help them. Right?

"Just evidence?" I ask.

"Just evidence," Shelby repeats. "Nothing more."

"Credit for three years?"

"Credit for three years."

I run a hand through my hair and sigh. "Fine."

Shelby smiles. "Good." He claps once, a liveliness to his mannerisms unbefitting an injured old man. He grimaces right after, though, and rubs at his shoulder, like he forgot he's wounded.

"Listen," he says, "go to the office and get the keys out of my desk. Open the bottom drawer of my filing cabinet. I have all my information tucked away there. Get it, and check all the locations I have marked."

"All right."

"And you need to stay on them." Shelby holds up a finger. "They don't keep strict schedules."

"Yeah, I understand. They'd be a lot fucking easier to track if they had a set weekly schedule of illicit activity."

"I knew you were a man I could turn to. You have this look about you. Like you know your way around a dark alley."

"Tsk." I step away from his hospital bed and shrug. "Don't die before I get you what you need," I say. "Your face has been all over the news."

"I'll keep it in mind."

With another long exhale—to clear out the terrible chemicals burning in my nose—I exit the hospital room and step out into the corridor. Miles leans against the wall, Rhett nowhere in sight, and I walk up to him. The place has thinned out, and I glance at my watch. 8:05 p.m. We should be leaving.

"Pierce," Miles says as he pushes away from the wall. He gets close and lowers his voice. "Look over there."

I follow his gaze to the far end of the hall. The only people walking around now are nurses, technicians, and the occasional doctor. But one guy stands out like a sore thumb. He's dressed in a thick, puffy jacket—perfect for concealing all sorts of objects—and he glances over at Shelby's door like he's waiting for us to leave.

"How long has he been there?" I whisper. I take Miles by the shoulder and lead him away like we're set to leave.

"He's been there since we arrived," Miles replies.

I never saw him. I can thank my terrible vision for that fact. I'm glad Miles is here to make up for my weakness, but a piece of me curses my diminished perceptions. I glance over my shoulder and spot the man ambling toward Shelby's door, his hand tucked inside his jacket.

"We're gonna turn around and question this guy," I say to Miles. "Got that?"

"Sure."

We both stop and turn. The jacketed man doesn't like that. He freezes in place, and when Miles and I head straight for him, he takes a step back. I pick up my pace—he's only thirty or so feet away—but that agitates the man more than I thought it would. He turns on his heel and hustles away. When a nurse walks in front of his path, he throws her to the side and starts running.

I dash forward, Miles by my side, and I sidestep the poor woman on the ground, gathering her fallen paperwork.

"Hey!" a nurse at the nursing station shouts. "No running!"

I ignore the scolding and continue. Our suspicious man dives around a corner, and Miles sprints to catch up, passing me in the process. Despite the fact there are fewer people than before, the halls are filled with empty stretchers, chairs, nurses doing their work, and medical equipment.

Miles navigates through the hall like he's running an obstacle course.

I slam my shin on the corner of a metal chair and curse aloud.

When I round the corner, I see Miles frantically glancing down a four-way intersection of hallways. I jog over and grab his shoulder.

"Where'd he go?" Miles asks.

"It doesn't matter," I say with a huffed breath. "He's going to try to leave. Take the elevator. I'll take the stairs."

Miles nods and hops off, rushing toward his destination without glancing back. After a moment of reflection, I roll my eyes. What was I thinking? *I* should have taken the elevator. I take a deep breath and head for the stairwell.

The cold shaft of switchback stairs is dim and uninviting. I leap down several steps at a time, passing a handful of people in the process, but my shin throbs with a dull ache by the time I reach the bottom. I take a moment to rub my leg before exiting the stairwell and glancing around.

My unfamiliarity with the hospital hinders me. I search for the exits, but I don't see any.

"Sir?" a nurse says as she walks up to me. "Visiting hours are over."

"Have you seen a man wearing a large jacket?" I ask.

"Lots of people are wearing jackets."

I give her a sideways glower. She returns my look with a sneer.

"I'm going to have to ask you to leave," she says.

Miles jogs down the hall toward me. When he gets close, I take him by the arm. The nurse ushers us to the front of the building. Miles gives me a questioning glance, and I shake my head. "I didn't see him," I mutter.

"Neither did I," Miles replies.

"I told you Shelby might not live through his stay here."

"What're we going to do about it?"

I grit my teeth. I want to say *call the police*, but the fact that a questionable character was already here tells me that Shelby might be right. The police may be in on this operation. The police know where Shelby is. How did that goon? Was he told?

"I can talk to Rhett," Miles says, "and tell him about the incident."

I offer a dismissive wave of my hand as we step outside into the fluorescent lighting of the parking lot. "Sure. And I'll tell Shelby to sleep with one eye open."

MILES PARKS our clunker in our driveway. The glow of the moon illuminates our otherwise dark neighborhood, and I step from the vehicle with a new appreciation for the surroundings. The dead grass, thin shrubs, and chain-link fences have an odd twilight charm when half-lit and half-buried in shadow. Then again, I've always preferred the night.

"What did Shelby want to talk to you about?" Miles asks as he steps out of the car and shuts his door.

"He wants me to continue his case."

"The one with the kidnappers?"

"Yeah."

Miles waits as I walk around the back of the car before he asks, in a low voice, "What did you say?"

"I said I would."

He furrows his brow and crosses his arms over his chest. I stop once I'm next to him—I know he has something to say—and I shake out my bruised leg. The seconds drag. It's cold out. I glare.

"Out with it," I demand.

Miles stares at the concrete. "This is a dangerous case. I said I didn't want you to go throwing yourself into gunfights all the time."

I don't respond.

"You couldn't be bothered to ask me before you said yes?" he asks, returning his gaze to mine. He looks more hurt than angry. I can't stand the guilt.

"I told you I'm capable of taking care of myself," I say, terse. I take one step toward the house, but Miles grabs my forearm and pulls me back. I whip around, tense and out of patience, half-cocked for a fight.

"Pierce, listen." He leans back against the side of the car. "I'm not trying to tell you what to do. I just want you to think about your own safety, ya know? You've been a little off since we moved in together. Since you came back to me after Jeremy."

"I told you I'm not gonna talk about it."

"That's fine."

"Then why bring it up?" I step up even closer to him and glare. "Do you have something else to say? Get it out of your system now, if you do. I don't want to hear about it later."

"I do have something to say."

I'm a little taken aback by his confidence, but I let him speak his piece.

Miles pushes off the car, and we stand inches apart, his conviction as visible as his foggy breath. "I'm going to help you."

"Help me?" I repeat, confused for half a moment. "No."

"I'm not asking. I made a decision."

"This isn't a game. Those thugs are out for blood."

"I'm a grown-ass man," Miles states, mimicking my own words. "I'm capable of taking care of myself."

I shake my head. "You have your classes."

"Only four hours a day. I think I can manage."

What a smartass. He has an answer like he's been mulling over this whole thing in his head.

"And," he continues, "I think this is a noble cause. One worth the risk."

"I agreed to do it because Shelby will sign off on my experience if I do," I say, clearing this up before it becomes an issue later. "I didn't do it to help anyone."

"But helping people will be incidental."

"Sure."

"I know you thought about them. And even if you didn't, I don't see how this isn't worth doing."

I want to shake Miles and force him to realize I'm not a good guy. I'm not like him. I'm sure, in his mind, I'm a grump with a heart of gold, doing this all for the poor victims of some heinous crime, but that's not the reality. Why does he try to paint me in colors I just don't have?

Miles leans forward and kisses me. It surprises me for a moment, and I attempt to take a step back, but he reaches his hand up and grabs the back of my neck, keeping me close. His actions aren't filled with urgency or need—his tongue slides along my lip in one slow, soft motion, and his other hand wraps around my waist.

When he breaks away, he doesn't go far, speaking to my cheek more than anything else. "You saved me once," he murmurs. "I wouldn't even have a life if it weren't for you. I think it would be fitting if I paid it forward. I got your back, Pierce."

"Fine," I whisper. It only makes sense that we'd do this together.

Miles presses his mouth against mine again, nibbling on my lip and gripping my jacket to pull my whole body close. His affections cool me down, and I relax against him. It's odd having someone care about my physical and emotional well-being at all times. I hate thinking I have to take him into consideration or else I'm hurting him—I never had to worry about that before, and the habit doesn't come naturally.

"I'm sorry," I mutter once Miles breaks for air.

He chuckles. "Did you just apologize? That's not like you."

I grit my teeth. "What do you want from me?" I snap. "I realized I made a mistake, okay? You're the one fuckin' apologizing all the time. I figured it would be what you want, and—"

Miles cuts off my tirade with a quick kiss. I know my blood pressure rose a slight degree during my rant, but it goes back down the moment I realize I lost my shit for no damn good reason. Maybe Miles is right. Maybe I am a little off.

"It's cold," Miles says. "Let's go inside."

I nod.

We step apart, and I already lament our separation. The entire walk into the house, all I can think about is how simultaneously glad I am that Miles will be with me for the investigation and bothered that he might get hurt doing so. It's a confusing state to be in.

The darkness of the living room makes it difficult to see, but Miles's mannerisms identify him as much as his appearance. He rubs at his neck—an unconscious habit that betrays the fact he's thinking over something. I throw myself down on the couch, never bothering to flip on the lights, and Miles follows suit.

I go to say something, but Miles leans into me and resumes our kissing, silencing all my comments. Again, his actions are slow, and he pushes me against the armrest like he's asking me to comply through nonverbal means. I'm not normally into this pussyfooting around before having sex, but for some reason I don't mind it much right now, with Miles.

I slide fully onto my back, and he throws a leg over, straddling me. He's hot—temperature-wise, though he's also easy on the eyes—and I enjoy the way he presses down against me, his heat spreading to my body like wildfire. Soon it turns to grinding, sending urgency through my system. I want him.

Miles grabs my wrists and pins them above my head, leaning his weight on them like he means it. "I've been thinking about this for a while now, Pierce," he says, his tone husky. He gets close and licks my ear before whispering, "There's a lot I'd like to try. A lot I'd like to do to you."

Anyone with a half-functioning ear could hear the raw need in his voice. It's enough to get me in the mood to hear him out. "What's got you hot and bothered?"

"What if I—"

A door opens and closes.

I forgot his damn siblings were here. I should pay more attention when Miles asks for favors. Looking after his siblings while his mother and her boy toy take a vacation is something I should've wholesale rejected.

Miles sighs and then murmurs into my ear, "We should stop."

"Put a bullet through Jayden's head and let's keep going," I reply.

"Miles?"

The feminine voice of Miles's eleven-year-old sister echoes throughout the living room. He jumps off me and stands before the light floods our tiny living room. I roll off the couch, adjusting my pants before standing. I swear kids have a radar for activities they can ruin with their mere presence.

"What's up?" Miles asks, his voice faltering.

Lacy shifts her attention to me and then back to Miles. "Mom said you weren't supposed to do any of this in front of us."

"I know. I'm sorry."

"I'm done with my homework."

"Tonight's?"

"All of it."

"The whole week's worth?" Miles balks. "Is that all you've been doing the entire evening"

"Jayden's hogging the TV, and you weren't here to do anything about it."

Miles gives me an apologetic glance before walking over to his sister. "Right. I'll talk to Jayden." He guides her out of the living room, through the tiny kitchen, and into the hallway that connects the two bedrooms and the sole bathroom.

His mother somehow gets to dictate what I can and cannot do in my own home? What a load of bullshit.

I go to walk around the coffee table—some cheap thing with sharp corners and a glass center—and I slam my bruised shin against the edge. Instant rage and pain block my judgment. I kick the thing over and take a minor amount of satisfaction in the smash of glass that follows. Fucking coffee table shouldn't have messed with me.

"Pierce?"

Miles jogs down the hall and stops when he sees the mess. Glass shards are scattered across the hardwood of the living room floor. Jayden and Lacy look on from the hall, confusion written all over their faces.

"What's wrong?" Miles asks.

"I didn't like our coffee table," I intone.

Maybe I'm stressed about this case. I'll be better when it's over.

CHAPTER FIVE

THE EARLY morning sunlight glares off the windshields of passing cars and assaults my eyes. Shelby's office isn't far, so I don't suffer long, but every intense shine reminds me why I hate the daytime.

Miles pulls the clunker into a parking spot and stops the engine. The vehicle coughs and hacks like a stage IV cancer patient. It won't be long before it dies.

Shelby's office is a modern space situated on the second floor of a two-story building. It doesn't have an interior wall, just floor-to-ceiling windows that look in on the office lobby. I unlock the glass door and enter with Miles close behind. The secretary isn't in—and I doubt she'll be in while Shelby is in the hospital—so I head straight back for Shelby's personal office.

I unlock his door and step into a cluttered mess of paperwork and food containers. The stale smell makes me think some of those containers still have food in them, but I'm not about to clean the place. Instead I walk over to his file cabinet and kneel down to the bottom drawer.

"This is how your boss works?" Miles asks, glancing around. He runs a finger over a four-foot-tall stack of boxes. "Some of this stuff has dust on it."

"He's a PI, not a maid. Who gives a shit if there's dust?"

"I dunno. Seems unorganized for this line of work."

Even the bottom drawer is locked. I flip through my key ring, examining each key Shelby gave me when I started working here, and realize I don't have one for the drawer. Of course not. He said it was in his desk. I stand and walk over to the solid oak desk parked at the back of the room. The chair sags in the middle of the seat, no doubt from carrying Shelby's substantial weight for more than a few years. I don't sit on it. Instead I rummage through the desk in search of a key.

"Wow."

I turn to Miles. He's staring at a wall covered in pictures and printouts. I return to my work. "What is it?"

"This guy is obsessed with Noimore. And kidnappings."

I lift an eyebrow but keep my eyes on the task at hand. "What's that supposed to mean?"

"I mean he has a lot of information and statistics on kidnap victims out of Noimore. As in, it's bordering on the obsessive. I'd go so far as to say it's unhealthy."

"He gets paid to investigate stuff like that. Why are you surprised?"

Miles doesn't answer. I glance back at him and see his attention is drawn to one article in particular. I let him read, unconcerned about Shelby's past cases. Fortunately for me, I find a key ring in the bottom drawer of his desk. I return to the filing cabinet and unlock it.

The jam-packed cluster of paperwork surprises me. It's difficult to open the drawer all the way, as the papers get caught on the sides and the bottom of the drawer above. I pull out the most recent file—the one closest to the handle—and open it up.

Like Shelby said, he has a list of locations. Six, to be specific, but I catch my breath when I look over the addresses.

Noimore. All but one of them.

I exhale and half crumple the paper in frustration. I never wanted to go back there. Ever. Maybe it once held fond memories for me, but after leaving the Vice family mob, I've had a different feeling about the place. It's a nightmare. A terrible reminder of my time with Jeremy and how I almost lost everything I give a shit about.

And what if my old acquaintances see me? Right now they think I'm dead. But if they knew… if they found me… what would they do? Jeremy Vice once risked everything to keep me at his side—his Vice Hound—but there are people out there who would pay to kill me all over again. If I go to Noimore, I risk dragging that all back to my new life here in Joliet.

Miles places a hand on my shoulder, and I jump up, my heart pounding. I reach for a gun I didn't bring, and it takes me a moment to take in even breaths. I think Jeremy left more than a tattoo on my arm—it's hard to focus sometimes when I think of life under him.

"Pierce?" Miles asks, looking me over. "What's wrong?"

"Nothing."

"I don't believe you."

"Nothing I can change," I snap. Better to just bury these thoughts and put them to rest.

"He wants you to go to Noimore," Miles says, his face emotionless. "Doesn't he?"

I hand over the list of locations. Miles gives it a quick glance and hands it back, his hard eyes set in understanding.

While he mulls over the situation, I pull out an armful of files from the bottom cabinet drawer and then shut it. I should probably read up on all of Shelby's investigations into this matter. Maybe I can find out how he got all this information in the first place.

"One of these locations is here in Joliet," Miles says.

"It's the North Union Rail Yard. They won't be returning there. Ever."

"You know you don't have to do this, right? You can go work for a different PI and earn your experience the hard way."

"Is that what you think I should do?"

Miles looks at me in confusion. I narrow my eyes.

"Isn't that what you want?" I ask, holding back my sardonic tone. "You want me to ask you what you think?"

"Y-yeah," he mutters. He rubs the back of his neck. After a long moment, his eyes locked on the floor, he replies, "We should at least try. We can turn back if it gets too dangerous. Unless you don't think you can handle it."

I know he doesn't mean it like a challenge, but I can't help getting defiantly angry.

"We should get familiar with these places," I say. "We'll go there now, in the day, when we're less likely to have problems, and then I'll decide."

"So long as we can get back before 5:00 p.m. That's when Jayden and Lacy need to be picked up from school."

Tsk. I forgot it was Monday. And how did I get the restrictions of a soccer mom's schedule?

"Fine. Let's go."

I exit the office and stop when I see someone waiting outside the glass front door. It's some asshole in a suit—an attorney, no doubt—and the man's frown deepens the moment he sees me.

"Let me in," the attorney demands, his voice half-muffled by the door.

Miles looks to me and I nod. He goes to open the door, and the attorney flounces in with flared nostrils.

"Where is Shelby?" he asks, glancing around. "I need that witness statement."

The prissy whine of his voice irritates me. "Which case?" I ask.

"*The People vs. McMillian.* Are you a PI at this firm? Do *you* know where my last witness statement is? I need it before Wednesday!"

The case name rings a bell, and I remember Shelby was going to get to it the morning after the rail yard incident. He must have forgotten.

"I'll handle it," I say. "Which witness do you need?"

He half stomps his foot and huffs. The man has a suit and posture that says *Yeah, you can kick my ass, but my father will sue.* I don't think he's told no often enough. And judging by his flashy cuff links, his pompous attitude works for him.

The attorney opens his briefcase and hands over a sheet of paper. I look at the address and read it three times before I believe what I'm seeing. It's our neighbor. The grouchy woman who pestered me about my garden.

I look at the charges in the case. Voluntary manslaughter. Interesting.

"I'll take care of this before Wednesday."

"You better," the attorney snaps.

"Now get out. I'm closing up shop."

I KEEP my jacket close and the collar propped up. I recognize the sights like I recognize my reflection in the mirror. Everything about Noimore is second nature to me. I almost want to tell Miles where to turn and what to avoid, but I keep quiet. Instead I check that my shoulder holster and firearm are secure. You can never be too safe.

Lake Michigan glistens in the distance, far beyond the multistory buildings, slums, and suburbs of Noimore. During the day, there's a bustle of workers and businessmen going about their business. But after dusk—when it gets dark—the place shows its true colors. The law-abiding denizens keep to themselves.

I spot a ramshackle hotel and tap Miles on the leg. His thigh is practically solid muscle—a thought I know I shouldn't have in the middle of a time-sensitive matter, but last night got me excited and I've yet to do anything about it. Miles doesn't seem to notice my hesitation. He turns to me, keeping one eye on the road.

"What is it?"

"Stop there. On the side of the road."

"In front of the hotel?"

"Yeah."

Trash fills the gutters, and the tires of our vehicle squish through it as Miles pulls up to the curb. Even with the light of a full afternoon, I swear the sordid atmosphere mutes all color until everything is either drab brown or dull gray. I avoid stepping on anything brown as I get out of the car.

"Do you have a pair of sunglasses?" I ask.

Miles nods. He pulls a pair out of the pocket of his cargo pants and tosses them over. They scream *police*. Do the police buy a special brand? I don't know, but it looks like something a cop would wear. Too sleek and too tinted. Not what I want to sport in this neighborhood. I tuck them into my jacket and lean against the car. Miles stands by my side, confused but patient.

A girl exits out the front door of the hotel, in heels so thin and tall you'd think she stood on toothbrushes. She struts with a hip sway all the way up to our car, her improbable footwear not a hindrance but an ally in exaggerated movement.

"Are you two looking for some afternoon delight?" she asks, a sweetness to her tone unbefitting her profession.

"Hello, ma'am," Miles says, no doubt feeling the need to be polite. The girl cocks an eyebrow and giggles.

"Normally there are girls outside," I drawl, glancing around and finding the sidewalk suspiciously empty. Even the dark alleys and shady bus stops are free of homeless.

She straightens her little crop top. "Business has changed. Do you want somethin' or not?"

"It's my buddy's birthday soon. He's been complaining about needing new experiences."

"Oh?" She gives Miles the once-over, his honeyed skin a slight shade of red, and then she smiles. "Well, we need to go inside to discuss specifics."

Inside? That's never how it was before. But I nod regardless.

We walk inside, and the pieces of this mystery start coming together. The lobby has a nightclub's worth of activity, including a small bar and a cigarette stand. Ladies hang around in groups, watching the street through the smudged windows, while a handful of enforcers keep an eye on their girls.

But why inside? Only people who knew this place was a hot spot would stop for a frolic between the sheets—it drastically cuts down on business. Half the game is playing someone desperate or drunk, which would be impossible standing around inside and not on the streets in front of bars.

Our girl waves to one of the enforcers and heads up the stairs to the second story. Miles glues himself to my side.

"What're we doing?" he asks under his breath, panic in his voice.

"They aren't going to mess with us. Calm your tits."

"I don't want to be with, er—well, anyone but you. That's not what I meant by new experiences." When I don't respond, he grabs me by the arm. "And I'm in a police academy now. You know what'll get me kicked out and prevent you from getting a PI license? Solicitation charges."

"Relax," I snap. "It isn't solicitation until we agree to exchange money for sex. We're not guilty of anything. Yet."

"Still," Miles drawls, "this looks bad. We can't keep using your old tactics for information gathering."

"Follow my lead."

The woman stops and leans against the door, a smile across her thin face. "I don't do group things."

"I'm just here to watch," I say.

Miles purses his lips and flushes harder. It amuses me, in a curious way, that after all we've been through, he could retain some semblance of innocence.

The girl must find it amusing as well. She giggles, opens the door, and walks into a room that was decorated during the '70s. Green shag carpeting and faux wood paneling walls. The place will only be complete with a lava lamp. The queen-size bed, to my surprise, is made and neat. Classier than most whorehouses, I suppose.

"So," the girl begins, "if you're going to watch, I'm gonna charge extra."

I shut the door and lock it. "How much for a conversation?"

"Conversation? Whaddya mean?"

She sits on the edge of the bed and crosses her long legs. Miles stands in the shadow of the far corner, his arms folded tight against his chest. He doesn't look comfortable, that's for sure, and I walk over to the woman to handle the situation.

"I mean, I want to know what's going on here in Noimore. I'm sure a smart girl like you sees and hears a few interesting things."

The woman snorts. "Oh." She licks her lips as she mulls over my comment. "A hundred for a conversation."

"Fine." I pull the money from my wallet and toss it onto her lap. She collects it up and stuffs it into some hideaway shoe pocket.

"'Kay. What's up?"

"What do you know about the recent kidnappings?"

Her stiff posture and frown tell me she knows something—and that she's not in the mood to share. I pay attention as she scoots back on the bed and gets comfortable among the pillows.

"I don't know anything about kidnappings," she says, a forced disinterest in her voice.

"Bullshit."

"I don't."

"And I don't believe you. What's the point of paying you if you're not gonna talk?"

"I can't tell ya what I don't know."

"What's your name?" Miles interjects.

The woman hugs a pillow. "Kimmy. But what's that got to do with kidnappings?" She glares. "You better not be thinkin' of tryin' anything. Johnny and Luca will kick your guys' asses."

"Is that why you're inside?" I demand. "So that *Johnny and Luca* can stop thugs from pickin' up girls and never returning?"

Kimmy continues her glower. "What does it matter to you guys?"

"Listen, Kimmy…." Miles steps out of the corner and loosens his grip on his arms. He walks over to the bed and takes a seat on the side. "We're looking for the people who have gone missing. If you have any information, any at all, that would really help us out."

She regards him with a frown, but her brow furrows as she fidgets with her pillow. "You're looking for them?"

"Has anyone you know gone missing? A friend, maybe? Could you tell us what *anyone* was doing before they went missing?"

The mention of "a friend" gets Kimmy quiet. I glance over at Miles, and he gives me a knowing look, like *he's* got this situation handled and I can sit it out. I bite my tongue. Maybe his brand of charisma will get more info than my streetwise.

"No," Kimmy answers. "No one has gone missing."

Goddammit.

Maybe I should have tried to find someone I know. Then again, the moment anyone knows I'm back in town will be the moment I have to leave the state. Which means I'm stuck trying to convince random people to give me information—and what am I going to give them in exchange? Trust doesn't come easy when you live life next to gangbangers and thugs.

"What about the Vice family?" Miles asks, shifting gears completely. "Do you know anything about them?"

I hold my breath.

"I only know Jeremy," Kimmy says, tilting her head from side to side. "Him and his guys run the docks."

"When did he get out of jail?"

"Six months back, I think. He wasn't off the streets long."

"Are his guys running around town or causing trouble? Maybe you've seen them ask you, uh, fine young ladies to go with them places."

Kimmy laughs. She falls across the other pillow. "Us fine young ladies don't interest Jeremy. And he really doesn't leave the docks. He's, like, into shipping and trucks now. The Vice family doesn't even peddle guns anymore. Just boats and stuff."

Boats?

Miles and I exchange confused glances.

Since when did the Vice family do stuff with shipping? Then again, Jeremy never knew how to run an operation properly. Maybe he's making another fucking mistake.

Still—we probably could have figured that out on our own—this girl's information hasn't been worth the time or money. "Let's go," I say to Miles. "We have places to check out."

Kimmy snaps her fingers as Miles stands. We both turn to her, confused.

"I want three hundred more," she says. "For your privacy."

"What?" I snap.

"Unless you want me talkin' to all my girlfriends—and my clients—about how some Asian and a guy with a weird eye came asking questions about the Vice family."

Tsk. Clever bitch. She doesn't even know how hard she has me over a barrel. I *really* don't want that story getting out and around town. But I can't let her know that.

"I'll give you fifty," I say.

Miles whips his attention to me, like I shouldn't be blasé about the threat, but what else am I going to do? It's not like I could handle this situation as a thug. I'm a law-abiding citizen now.

"A hundred," she demands. "And you go out the back door. And pay for a movie."

Heh. She doesn't want to go back downstairs and needs some entertainment. I roll my eyes and open my wallet. "Fine," I state. "A hundred and twenty for your silence."

I go to toss the money when a crash echoes from the wall. I glance over and hear it again, and this time it shakes the wall-mounted TV. Then I hear a half scream and snap of noise—it tells me there's a tussle in the room next door.

"What's going on?" Miles asks in a hushed tone. He turns to me. "You don't think someone is being taken from this hotel, do you?"

Another slam against the wall confirms that it's not two people fucking on a bed. But lowlife kidnappers wouldn't be in the heart of a whorehouse trying to abduct women, would they? No. That's preposterous. They'd get caught in a heartbeat.

I turn my attention to Kimmy and see her staring at the shaking wall, her eyes wide. She obviously didn't expect whatever is happening.

Another slam, followed by a yell.

Miles pulls his gun, and I do the same. There's a chance some thug got greedy—maybe he thinks he can get away with it—I don't know, but now's as good a time as any to find out.

CHAPTER SIX

"Are you two cops?" Kimmy asks the moment we have our Colt .45 handguns up and ready. "Y-you have to tell me if you're cops!"

I ignore her inane demands and exit the room. Miles and I take positions on either side of the neighboring door. He nods to me, and I nod back. Before either of us goes kicking anything in, I reach for the handle and find it unlocked. I guess the element of surprise is on our side.

After I open the door, we rush inside. The room is near identical to the last, just flipped around, and we barge into the bedroom with our guns up.

A man with a trucker's physique—large gut, thick arms, thicker beard—stands over a guy with the exact opposite appearance, to the point he hits androgynous. But his bruises and bloody face are what I notice next.

"What the fuck?" the larger guy asks. He's topless, but he wears a natural shirt of hair like he's part grizzly.

"What's happening here?" Miles demands, never lowering his weapon.

The big guy puts his hands in the air and stumbles back. Is he drunk? One deep inhale tells me he's drunk. In the middle of the day? The man has hit more lows than one.

"You've been drinkin'," I state. "Maybe you should sit down."

"I'm not gonna sit down," he says, his speech more coherent than most drunks'. "I paid good money—hard-earned money—and then what do I go and find? I find me problems and more problems!"

Miles and I exchange perplexed glances. Maybe his speech is understandable, but it sure as fuck isn't coherent.

"Get out!" he bellows. "I paid, so I'm gonna get my money's worth!"

The man on the floor attempts to stand, but the larger guy cocks a fist like he's ready to dole out an ass-whoopin'. A piece of me wants to back out of the room—clearly this isn't a kidnapping—but another piece of me sees that this isn't a mutual agreement either. The guy on the floor looks to me and Miles with a silent plea, his shoulder-length hair half-clumped with blood across his face.

Before I make a decision, Miles takes a step forward. "You're not getting anything," he says. "You're leaving. Right now."

"I paid!"

"You're gonna pay more in blood if you don't get out of here."

"If you lay a hand on me, I'll call the cops."

Both Miles and I start laughing. The gut of the guy shakes as he whips his gaze between us. "You laughin'? You think this is funny?"

"Yeah, call the cops," I say, sarcastic in every regard. "Tell 'em you were trying to fuck some prostitute when two guys thought it got too rough, so they busted in to stop you. I'd love to see the look on their face when you tell 'em what a victim you are."

It takes a moment for the sluggish gears in this guy's brain to turn full circle. Realization dawns on him, and he stumbles around to collect his shirt. Miles stays tense and ready the entire time, watching the man's movements like it's all an act. I let the guy leave without another word and then tuck my firearm back into my shoulder holster.

Kimmy rushes into the room once the fat guy staggers down the hall.

"Are you okay, Nash?" she asks as she kneels down.

The guy nods. "Yeah…. Yeah, I'm fine now."

"What happened?"

Nash chuckles as he places a hand over his bruised eye and busted lip. "I think he thought I was… someone different."

"C'mon, get up. I'll take you to my room. I'm gonna get a movie."

"You're not hurt too bad, are you?" Miles asks as he walks over to help the kid up. "We could hear some stuff from the other room."

"I'll be fine." Nash gives Miles an odd sideways glance. "Are you guys cops?"

"No. We're just, uh, here for some answers."

Miles takes most of Nash's weight on his shoulder and helps the man all the way to Kimmy's room. Once inside, Miles sets him down and gets the remote for Kimmy, almost like he's caring for his two siblings. I wait by the door, ready to leave, but I don't hurry Miles. He can do whatever he damn well pleases.

"You sure you two don't need anything?" Miles asks.

Both Kimmy and Nash regard him with puzzled expressions and shake their heads. "No," Kimmy says. "We'll manage. I'll take care of Nash from here."

"Well, be safer in the future." Miles rubs at his neck before pulling out his wallet. He hands over a stack of cash—I suspect all five hundred he had on his person—before turning away, leaving the two to their movie.

I walk by his side down the hall and toward the stairs. "What was that?" I ask in a low voice. "You think they'll be useful to us in the future?"

"No," Miles intones. "I just…. Well, it got me thinking."

"What about?"

"I tried to be a prostitute once," he says with a chuckle.

We hit the stairs, and I give him half a smile. "Are you sayin' you've been with other guys than me?"

"No. No, that's not it. I *tried* to be a prostitute. One time." Miles exhales and avoids looking at me straight on. "A guy took me to a room, and, well, he got violent. He complained about something, I don't remember what, but I ran after he got a few hits in."

I remain silent as we walk out the back door to the hotel. The alleyway between buildings smells of trash and stagnant water. Even the rays of the afternoon sun avoid the narrow walkway, keeping the place dark.

"I was trying to make money," Miles says. "And I knew I wanted to be with a man, but that experience left me a little confused, to say the least. I went out onto the street to try again when some Vice family enforcers walked up on me. They asked me how I got my bruises, and I guess I wanted to sound tough—ya know, instead of pathetic—so I told them I got into a street fight."

"And?"

"And that's when they said they'd pay me to be a gun for them." Miles shrugs. "I needed the money for Jayden, so I went with it. You know the rest of the story from there. I guess Nash and Kimmy reminded me that things could be worse."

Hm. He's never told me that story before. I guess there's nothing too important in those facts, but still. I like knowing them.

"Hey," he whispers, "I'm the one always telling you stories from my past." Miles keeps his hands in his pockets. "You should tell me more about yourself. I want to know more about you."

"Maybe later," I say.

"Don't think I'll forget."

"Wait!" Kimmy's voice echoes down the alley.

Miles and I stop to turn. She jogs down to us, even in her crazy heels, and stops with a smile. I lift my eyebrow, wondering if she's going to try to extort some more cash.

"No thugs have been around here in a long time," she says, staring up at me. "It's the cops. They're crackin' down hard. We can't work the sides of the streets anymore, ya know? People aren't going missing. They're getting arrested and going to jail."

"The cops?" I repeat, mulling over the information. "They come around *here*?" That's unusual. They never did before.

"Yeah. The new deputy chief wants to put an end to crime in Noimore."

"An end, huh?"

"He's had his pigs arrest anyone and everyone. Even those homeless guys. For loitering. It's gettin' to the point that even some of the crooked cops are turning. Everyone's in jail."

I nod as I give her statements some thought. Crime *has* been going down lately. Well, everywhere but Noimore.

"I got a friend in jail too," Kimmy says. "She's been there for a few months now. I'm worried about her, but I don't want to go near the place." She taps the tips of her fingers together and says, "If you guys go there asking questions, can you tell Roslyn Applegate to call me? I just want to know when she's gettin' out."

Miles pulls out his phone and commits the information to the device's memory. "Of course. And thank you for telling us this."

Kimmy nods. "I hope it helps."

THE CAR ride home is far too long. Jayden's mouth-breathing buzzes over the sound of traffic. Even his little sister leans away from him, staring out the opposite window with a frown on her face.

I can't wait until they leave. I know Miles wants to spend his waking time with them, but it's hard to find a connection with two kids who either hate me or ignore me. At least when we get to the house, I can do my own damn thing and avoid them.

"Who's that?" Jayden asks, pointing forward.

I follow his gesture to a police vehicle parked outside our house. My chest seizes up, and my mouth gets dry. What the fuck are cops doing here?

Jayden leans onto the back of my seat and whispers, "Have they come to take you to the slammer, Pierce?" He gets way too much sadistic joy out of the situation. If I could, I'd turn around and break his face, but that's not an option.

Instead I zip up my jacket, concealing the gun still in its holster.

Miles parks behind the police vehicle, and a man steps out. I hold back a slew of curse words. If it isn't Lieutenant Rhett Walker. My favorite person.

I exit our clunker and hold the seat back so Jayden and Lacy can join their brother. Rhett saunters over with a pleasant smile on his face. Although I don't like seeing him, I doubt he's come here to arrest me, which is better than the alternative.

"Lacy, Jayden," Miles says. "Can you two wait in the house?"

Both his siblings nod and head for the front door, leaving me, Miles, and Rhett to the grandiose scenery that is our dilapidated neighborhood. None of our neighbors are out and about. I blame Rhett's presence.

"I'm sorry for dropping by unannounced," Rhett says. "But I wanted to talk you, Miles. Not on academy time."

Miles perks up. "Me, sir?"

"Yes. Not this weekend, but the weekend after, is the annual Blue Shield Gala."

"I've heard. It's a big deal."

"A very big deal," Rhett says with a wider smile. "It's a fund raiser, and the most important law enforcement personnel are there from all over Illinois, not just Joliet."

"Sounds amazing. But what about it?"

Rhett pats Miles on the arm. "Every year I take the top three students from the academy. You get to rub elbows with all the right people. It's a great way to start your career."

"Me?" Miles balks. "You want to take me?"

"Of course. You're top in the class. I'm inviting you, Barry, and Mina."

"Wow… I don't know what to say."

"Say yes," Rhett replies with a chuckle. "I'm sure you'll have a wonderful time. And I bet you look striking in a suit. First impressions with your fellow officers matter."

Miles crosses his arms and then uncrosses them, almost like he doesn't know what to do with himself. He turns to me and then furrows his brow. "Can Pierce attend?"

I freeze up and almost shout *Don't drag me into this*, but Miles got his damn sentence out. I don't want anything to do with some policeman's gala.

"Of course he can attend," Rhett says with a wave of his hand. "It'll be a great opportunity for him to meet your future coworkers." He stares at me for a moment, and his smile wanes into something else—a smirk, maybe? "How long have you two been together?"

"Almost a year now," Miles replies.

"Oh? Where did you meet?"

"On the Noimore docks, actually."

I catch my breath. Rhett smiles his same smirk. Does he remember I said I've never been to Noimore? I don't know, and I don't like where this is going.

"It's not a very interesting story," I interject. "Maybe we'll bore you with it some other time."

I glance at the house and smile when I spot Lacy. She's my ticket out of this. "Looks like your sister needs us," I say to Miles. "We should probably be going."

Miles turns his attention to Lacy and nods. "Thank you for stopping by, Rhett. I look forward to the Blue Shield Gala."

Rhett holds out his hand. "Actually, I also came here to discuss Shelby and his investigations." He gives Miles a slight nod and then motions to me. "Do you mind if we speak in private? I'm sure you can handle your sister."

"Of course. No problem."

I watch Miles walk into the house, my teeth gritted. I don't want to speak to this man about anything. He rubs me the wrong way. Everything about him. Even when I turn to face him, he still has that odd look. "What is it?" I snap. "I've got things to do."

Rhett, unfazed, says, "So, *Percy*—or should I call you *Pierce*?"

"Pierce is fine."

"So, you know I spoke with Miles at the hospital the other night, after talking to Shelby. Miles is very honest and up-front—it's a trait I like about him. You know what he said?"

I don't reply. The cold wind of dusk sweeps between us, and the orange of the sunset casts dark shadows across the dead lawn.

Rhett continues with "Miles said you both used to live in Noimore before moving here. Which is odd, considering what you told me at the police station. About how you've never been there before."

Again, I say nothing.

"And now I've come to hear you two met in Noimore. Oh, you know what else Miles said? He said you worked at a lumber mill. Do you know how many lumber mills are in Noimore, Pierce? Or how many are in the *county* of Noimore? You should take a guess. I mean, you worked in one, after all. I'm sure you'd know a little about it."

Hot rage mixes with icy dread throughout my system. But still, I remain stone silent.

Rhett takes a step closer to me, until we're only a few inches apart. In a hushed tone he says, "I'll give you a hint. It rhymes with *hero*. The last one closed eight years ago. Terrible economy these days, right? That must've been hard for you. Being unemployed for eight years."

"Is there a point to this?" I ask in the same hushed tone, though my voice betrays the surface of my anger.

"Oh, are you getting bored with me?" Rhett asks, his sarcasm adding fuel to my hate. "I haven't even told you about Shelby's report. You're an expert gunman according to him—but public record says that *Percy Adams* only ever got his hands on a gun a few months ago."

His green eyes stare into mine with a challenging aggression that gets me tense. I cross my arms, my hand resting over my handgun through my jacket.

"Tell me," he says, still somewhat sarcastic and amused. "Why lie? It's almost like you didn't think anyone would look into it."

"Maybe the police are incompetent," I reply. "And I don't trust them."

"A man like you wouldn't, would you?"

"What does it matter?" I say with a forced laugh. "Are there laws against faking a résumé? Otherwise we don't have any business, do we?"

"Not yet, anyway. But I have to ask one thing. Does Miles know? Does he know the real you, or this charade you're passing around?"

"Stay away from Miles," I growl through clenched teeth. "And unless you have something more than conjecture, *stay away from me as well.*"

Rhett keeps a hand on his belt, inches from his handgun, in a casual yet pragmatic stance. Is he hoping I'll attack him? Is that what he wants?

That *would* make things easy for him, wouldn't it? He wouldn't have to get evidence if I assaulted him and he "defended himself."

Maybe he's already tried to get evidence. He has quite a bit of knowledge about me—about the fake me, really—which tells me he's been looking into this. If he doesn't have anything to arrest me with but he suspects I'm some criminal in hiding, he might be here just to provoke a new crime.

Pretty fucking brazen. He must not consider me a threat—a *real* threat. He thinks he can waltz up and threaten my life without repercussions. He's got another thing coming.

Rhett takes a step back and exhales, his hand still resting close to his gun. "Miles is one of the best students I've ever had. I'd hate to see him dragged down by someone nowhere near his caliber."

His statement gives me pause. "I've seen the way you talk to him recently," I say. "I mean it when I say you need to back the fuck off."

"I'm an instructor at his academy. We'll see each other regularly, I'm afraid."

Is he saying this to get under my skin, or is he actually challenging me for Miles? I don't know, and I don't care. Either way, he's a piece of shit. If he wasn't a cop, I'd throw him off my property, but everything is a goddamn felony when used against anyone in blue. Instead I turn and head for the house—there's nothing left for us to say—leaving Rhett on the dead grass of our lawn.

Could he dig up something to arrest me? I doubt it. All his facts are wrong. Does that mean it's impossible? No. I'm sure if he snoops around long enough, I'll trip up and give him something to use against me. Which means I have to be on my guard until we leave this wretched city.

Rhett calls out, "I'm sure I'll see you again, Pierce. Sooner rather than later."

Perfect. Now I have to add *deal with Lieutenant Rhett Walker* to my ever-expanding to-do list.

CHAPTER SEVEN

I KNOCK on the neighbor's door. Nothing.

I knock louder. She has to be home. She's some old lady with no car and no discernable interests, not even cats. All old crones are up at eight in the morning. I glance at my phone. It's 8:15 a.m. She must be awake.

Or maybe she fell and died over the weekend. That would be inconvenient, but not the first time I've had to deal with an elderly corpse. I guess this time I can call the cops and have *them* handle it, however.

The door opens, snapping me from my morbid musings. The same sunbaked woman stands before me—a good foot shorter than I am, probably five two, if I had to give a guess—and she glares up at me with squinted eyes.

For a moment we're both silent. She doesn't say hello, and I sneer.

"Finally need help with that garden?" she asks, a slight smile on the corner of her mouth.

"No," I state. "I'm here on behalf of Shelby Private Investigations, a PI firm located in town. You're a witness in the case of *People vs. McMillian*, and I've come to get your statement."

She glances over her shoulder before shuffling out the door and closing it behind her. I lift an eyebrow, curious about the odd turn of events, but I don't say anything. It's not like this lady will try to shiv me or anything—or if she does, I'm confident I can handle myself.

"So you're a private dick?" she asks. "I wondered what you did for a living, but I guess this makes sense."

I hold back a laugh. Was she trying to make a joke? Maybe I underestimated the woman. "Look, uh—" I stare down at the file until I find her name. "—Patricia Timo, I need to get your statement in regards to McMillian's voluntary manslaughter."

"Would you mind keeping your voice down?" she asks in a calm manner. "And you can call me Grammy, or Ms. Timo, but not Patricia."

Tsk. Why do people do that? They should never tell anyone how to get under their skin—it's the fastest way to unhappiness outside of jumping into oncoming traffic.

"Listen, I need your statement. Why don't you tell me what happened, and I'll write it all down. Then you can go back to whatever the hell you were doing."

Ms. Timo opens her mouth to speak, but she catches her breath when a creak sounds from inside the house.

"Grammy?" I hear a voice ask, the feminine timbre muffled by the walls. "Grammy, where'd you go?"

Ms. Timo cracks open the front door and calls in, "I'm out here, sweetie. I'm speaking to our neighbor."

"That one with the terrible garden you're always talking about?"

"The very same."

The door swings in to its limit, and a young girl stares back at me. She and Ms. Timo are related—they have the same tan-olive skin, though the girl's is free from sun cracks, and their eyes are an odd shade of blue that looks closer to the gray of cement than anything found in a fashion magazine. Maybe she's eleven? Twelve? The same age as Lacy, I'd guess, given her small frame and awkward proportions.

The girl looks me over, her large eyes honing in on the manila file I have in my hands. "Are you a lawyer?" she asks. The girl walks outside and allows the door to shut behind her. "Is this about my mom and dad? Are they okay? Are they coming home soon?"

"Shannon," Ms. Timo says, a strain in her voice. "Why don't you wait inside and—"

"If it's about my mom and dad, I think I should get to know."

"This is a legal matter. Not for children. I'll let you know as soon as anything happens."

Shannon, the girl, straightens her bucket hat and throws her braided hair over her shoulder. "I understand legal things. I want to know what's going on."

"This is confidential," I snap. The girl flinches, like she didn't expect my anger, but I'm not interested in bullshit. I have other things on my plate, and listening to a grandma bicker with a kid isn't something I'm interested in.

Shannon backs up into the house without another word. After she shuts the door, I turn to Ms. Timo. "Well?" I drawl. "Can we get this over with?"

"Let's take a walk," Ms. Timo says, motioning to the cracked sidewalk.

I'm not in the mood, but I also don't have much fight in me today. I exhale and follow her away from her house, strolling down our ramshackle neighborhood with little interest for my surroundings. The old crone hobbles like she's got a bum ankle, and I alter my speed accordingly.

"I've noticed you have children in your house from time to time," she says, straight out of the blue.

"How observant."

"They seem nice."

"Heh. Apparently you're not *too* observant. One is fine, but the other should've been absorbed by a twin in the womb."

"I was hoping that my little Shannon would be able to visit and spend time with a girl her age."

"Look," I say, trying not let my anger take over my judgment. "I didn't stop by to play Suzy Homemaker. Just. Give me. The damn. Statement."

"She's following us," Ms. Timo states. She motions with a shift of her eyes, and I glance around, spotting the rustle of bushes one house down. How did I not notice it before? I know why, but I'm still frustrated. A lack of peripheral vision will do that to a man.

Ms. Timo lowers her voice and steps up closer to me, though her tone and pleasant disposition never change. "Shannon's father, my son, came home one night and found Shannon's mother in bed with another man. He called me after he calmed down, and I went over to the house. Shannon was staying with me, so I was the only one who got a good look at the aftermath."

I jot down a few notes, thankful she's speaking.

"Shannon doesn't know," Ms. Timo intones.

I hold back a sardonic laugh. "So you're hiding it from her?" I glance into the file and see who the victim is. Yup. McMillian killed his wife in the heat of passion. "Girl might be entitled to know her mother's dead."

Ms. Timo presses her lips together. "Keep your voice down."

I stare at the rustling bushes. She's much too far away to hear our conversation, but I indulge the old woman regardless. "What did you notice when you got to your son's house?"

"He was shaking. He had his gun on the table. It holds six rounds, but only one bullet was missing. I didn't get a good look at the bedroom. Some things you can't unsee."

"Did he say anything?"

"He kept saying he wished he could take it back. He shot once and instantly regretted it. I know he didn't mean it. He lost himself for one second. Just one."

Retelling the story obviously unnerves the old lady. She breathes with a choked-up rasp. But I've seen one too many corpses to get disturbed over a guy and his unfaithful wife.

"About what time did this all go down?" I ask, making sure to cover the last few details the attorney will want.

"Late at night. A little after ten."

"All right. Well, I'll walk over and talk to you if I need anything else. I suspect they won't take this to trial, but if they do, you'll be called to the stand."

"I've been homeschooling Shannon," she says after a deep breath, like she's ready to forget that whole conversation even happened. "But that means she isn't going outside much."

The girl, Shannon, shuffles closer and keeps to the shadows. Now that I know she's there, I can keep track of her movements, but she's rather quiet and talented at flitting from one early morning shadow to the next.

"You and your partner are homosexuals?" Ms. Timo asks.

I slowly pan my gaze over to hers. Did she just say *homosexuals* like we were on a 1930s radio show? "We fuck each other, if that's what you're asking."

Unfazed by my statement, she nods. "I want Shannon to have an example of a good relationship before… before I have to explain how one can go so wrong. Her parents argued nonstop. You and your partner seem good for each other. Not like how I was told homosexuals treated each other."

I snort and laugh. "Fun fact, true fact—*homosexuals* come in every flavor nonhomosexuals come in. Bad ones. Good ones. Crazy jealous ones who can't handle catching their partner in bed with another. Don't go romanticizing the first instance of something you see."

"What I want to ask is, can Shannon visit your little girl?"

"Ask Miles," I state. "It's his decision."

"He wears the pants in the relationship, I see."

I glower at the woman. "They're his siblings."

"Ah. Then I will ask him about it this evening."

"Fine." I nod to her and then turn on my heel, heading straight home. I really do have other things to deal with, and this witness statement ate way too much of my free time. Shannon hops from her hiding space once I'm a few houses away, and I catch sight of her speaking to her grandmother, a few twigs caught in her long braid.

I guess it's none of my business, but I would hate not having the facts straight. Shannon will have to go on not knowing about her father until her grandmother gets her act together.

"THAT'S NOT the proper form for lifting weights," Miles says, exasperation in his tone. "You're going to hurt your back like that. How many times do I have to tell you?"

I can't see what's going on in the back room, but I can picture it clear as day in my mind's eye. Jayden's gotta be fuckin' it up left and right. I'm sure he'll get it eventually—Miles knows his stuff, and Jayden has a track record of failing before turning it all around—but that doesn't mean it isn't funny in the meantime.

I tune them out and go back to my work.

With the TV on mute—and set to the news—I read over Shelby's reports. He seems to have every kidnapping record for the last twenty years, including confidential police records. I'm impressed and confused, but I suppose they'll come in handy. I was right about the uptick in crime in Noimore—especially kidnappings. People are going missing—which explains the police crackdown.

"So, uh, do you do anything for fun?" Shannon asks.

Lacy combs her long black hair with her fingers. "I run track and field. And I play the piano."

"Running and piano? Okay…. Do you have a piano here?"

"No. My brother doesn't have one."

"Right."

Silence settles over the kitchen. The two girls avoid staring at each other from opposite sides of the kitchen table, and I lament the fact that I agreed to watch over them while I worked.

It's not like I haven't watched kids before. Big Man Vice had me look after his three kids for years, but they had *things to do* and *toys to play with*. Shannon and Lacy sit around like lumps on a log, taking up space and air.

Shannon stares at me, her gaze unflinching. I rub at my forehead when I turn to her. "What is it?"

"Your eye is ugly."

Lacy's eyebrows lift, her straight-as-a-rod posture unbroken as she gives a disapproving frown.

"If you're gonna insult someone," I say, "at least be clever about it. Otherwise you're making enemies, and lookin' stupid while doin' it. A terrible combination."

"I wasn't insulting you. It's a fact."

"Don't you have any homework?" I ask with a long exhale.

Shannon rolls her eyes. "My grandma assigns me worksheets out of a textbook, but that's no fun."

"You haven't finished your homework for the day?" Lacy asks, aghast. She gets out of her chair and scoots it over to Shannon. "I'm going to be a professor one day. I'll help you." Her pomp and patronizing tone almost gets me laughing, but I hold back. Whatever keeps them busy, I suppose.

I stare at the television. The new deputy police chief of Noimore gives some sort of speech. Isn't he the one cracking down on crime? He's an intimidating guy. Skin so pale he looks like he's been dead for weeks—the red of his blood filters through and gives his balding head a pinkish sheen—and he's got muscles that threaten to rip the seams of his clothes and force all the veins out of his body.

Not a guy I would want to take a back-alley beating from, that's for sure.

Much to my surprise, I spot Rhett in the crowd of police officers standing around the podium. Apparently they're all getting awards for lowering the amount of crime around Lake Michigan. The numbers on the screen say muggings, robbery, burglary, and prostitution are all on the decline. Maybe they're not concerned with human trafficking. But why?

"This is all wrong," Lacy says, breaking my focus.

I slide my attention over to the girls. Shannon rolls her eyes. "It's dumb, anyway. Who cares?"

"You should try your hardest. This is terrible work."

"What do you know?"

"More than you."

"Hey," I bark, cutting them off before this turns into a prissy little passive-aggressive fight. "Let me see it." I hold out my hand, and

Shannon passes over the paper. The workbook assignment is juvenile at best and labeled "geometry." The directions say *name the shapes* with a bunch of multisided scribbles all down the middle. Under each one, Shannon wrote things like "Amy," "Bob," "Snoopy," and "Jamison."

Well, she did name them.

I chuckle, and Shannon gives me a slight smile. Then I glare at one of the shapes. "This really is a stupid assignment," I say. "What are these? These aren't circles and triangles. And isn't this one just a diamond?"

"It's a rhombus," Lacy says, matter-of-fact.

"How the fuck is that different from a diamond?"

"Well, a diamond is a rhombus. Any parallelogram with equal sides is, technically."

I laugh once and toss the paperwork back. "Yeah, that's useless. You can forget that right away."

"It won't be useless as an adult," Lacy pipes up, indignant.

Shannon snickers.

"Unless you live on the set of *Jeopardy!*, you'll use that knowledge exactly zero times as an adult. Trust me. I know."

Lacy crosses her arms. "Well, of course *you're* not using it. You're a criminal and a drug dealer. I meant when I become a proper adult."

The atmosphere of the kitchen gets tense as I sit up in my chair. Both girls go silent. I can't help but feel a cold rage in my system after hearing that. I have a goddamn lieutenant breathing down my neck— trying to find something that proves I'm who he thinks I am—and here I have some girl who's going around telling people that I'm a criminal?

"Who told you that?" I ask, attempting to keep my voice neutral, but I know I must sound like a murderer on the edge of sanity.

"Jayden," Lacy replies, her voice lower than before. "He told me to stay away from you. And that… and that you're not treating Miles right. That you force him to be with you."

I grind my teeth to stop myself from getting out of my chair and running that dumpster fire down. I hate the fact he knows who I once was. And he obviously can't keep his fat mouth shut about it.

"Is it true?" Shannon whispers, engrossed by the conversation and glancing between me and Lacy.

I force a laugh and rest back in my seat. "Of course not."

"That's what Jayden said," Lacy repeats.

"And you think Jayden is a credible source of information?"

"Well, yes. He's my brother."

"Jayden!" I shout, my anger fueling my volume.

"What?" he yells back.

"Tell me what a rhombus is!"

The quiet that follows is thick with confusion. Regardless, he eventually answers with "It's a tiny robot that vacuums your floors. Why?"

I give Lacy a smirk. "Your brother is so detached from reality that he doesn't even know what the fucking question is, let alone the right answer." With unfiltered sarcasm I continue, "He's definitely *my* source of information. Right alongside the *National Enquirer* and that drunken hobo I pass every morning on my way to work."

Shannon stifles a long line of laughs as she buries her head into the crook of her arm. Lacy's frown deepens, and with a sheepish tilt of her head, she hides most of her face behind her long black hair. I guess I should be thankful for Jayden's general incompetence.

I stand up and head for the back room. Lacy holds up a hand, and I stop.

"I'm sorry I called you a criminal," she says.

There isn't much I can say, so I leave without replying. A few short steps later and I'm with Jayden and Miles in the back room. We have a shitty workout bench, and Jayden lies back on it, propped up on his elbows. Miles stands nearby, fitting on the last of his academy uniform.

"You're leaving for class?" I ask him.

He nods. "Yeah. In a few minutes."

Maybe Miles is flaunting for me, but he examines his dark blue shirt and decides against it. He pulls it off, tosses it in the hamper, and walks over to the closet, his bare skin and taut muscles a sight for sore eyes. I see Jayden and Lacy have hung their clothes inside, but Miles still keeps all his weird academy clothing in the corner. Apparently he needs to wear nice shoes, specific pants, and a belt that carries all their practice weaponry.

Miles throws on a new shirt and then walks over to me, a slight smile on his face like he knew I watched him like a hawk. "I'll be back."

"Come home right after," I say. I don't want Rhett talking to him any longer than necessary.

"Right after?" Miles repeats, a mischievous look about him. "You gonna miss me?"

"Ugh," Jayden groans. "Don't do this."

"I'd prefer you be here," I say. Miles still takes it as a flirtation—rather than the jealousy it is—and nods. I watch him go, which leaves me and Jayden alone in the room.

The space is tiny. There's two twin-size beds that take up a good portion of the room, one dresser with a TV on top of it, and the cumbersome workout bench. No room for walking around, that's for sure. Despite that, I maneuver my way over to the bench and give Jayden a reverse nod—jutting my chin out in a quick gesture.

"Let's see how much you can lift," I say.

Jayden shivers at the sound of my coarse voice. "Uh, maybe some other time."

"Lie down," I command.

He visibly frets, tapping his fingers along the seat. After a long moment of internal debate, he leans back and scoots himself under the bar. Altogether, counting the weight of the bar itself, he has seventy pounds.

"Was your sister in here last?" I ask, motioning to the weights.

"Shut up," Jayden mutters. "I was in the hospital for a while. I got shot, remember? I'm working up to higher weights."

"Let's see you do a set of ten."

"Ten?"

"You heard me."

Jayden watches me with a frown, and he doesn't like it when I get behind the bench and stare down at him.

"I'm gonna spot you," I say.

"Right," he mutters.

He picks up the bar, and with a nervous jitter to him, he completes a single rep. I watch him, unblinking, and he avoids looking at me straight on.

"You know what you remind me of?" I ask him. "One of the pedestrians who walks out in front of traffic. You know the ones. They're not even in a crosswalk—they just walk out, like they don't give a fuck, because they know the drivers will stop."

Jayden gives me a perplexed stare as he continues with his reps. His breaths release in controlled exhales, but I don't care if he's doing his workout properly or not.

"You know why the drivers stop?" I continue. "Because they have a life, and they don't want to mess it up by killing some random fuckstick. They have things they want to get home to. People they want to see."

Around rep seven, Jayden starts to slow. It's kinda pathetic how weak he's gotten.

I offer him a half smile. "So, Jayden, when you go around flippantly telling people that I'm a criminal, that's the equivalent of walking right out into traffic."

Before he says anything, I grab the bar on the ninth rep. Jayden stares at me with wide eyes, his hands shaking. I press some of my weight down, and he fights against it, struggling to keep the bar off his body. I'm barely doing anything, and we both know that if I went all the way, this bar would be buried in his neck.

I lean in closer and continue, "And, if there ever comes a day that I don't have anything to live for—a day the cops come to take me, or a day that Miles gets in trouble for keeping my secret—you better believe I'm not gonna stop my car. Am I making any sense, Jayden?"

"Yeah, yeah," he murmurs. "Of course!"

I let up on the bar, and he pushes it back up onto the stand. From the kitchen I hear a round of giggles and laughter. Are the two girls getting along? I suspect so, though they weren't when I left.

Jayden sits up, sweat soaking his shirt and covering the bench.

"How many people have you told about me?" I ask, my voice hushed.

He shakes his head. "N-no one, really. Just my mom and her boyfriend."

"And Lacy."

"Yeah. And Lacy." Jayden turns around to face me. "You better not hurt her."

Or you'll do what? is what I want to ask, but I hold back my comment. I'm not going to threaten some eleven-year-old. It's not her fault she repeats what the people around her say. That's what kids do. Jayden, on the other hand, is fully aware of what he's doing.

I glare down at him, putting his words together in my head. "Is that why your mother doesn't care for me? Because of all your whispering?"

"It's not like it isn't true." He rubs at his neck and scoots away from me. "You're a psychopath."

"I don't force Miles to do anything."

Jayden stands and gives me a dirty sideways glance. It's fleeting, and he ducks away the moment I notice. "There's no way Miles is actually into a guy like you. I know you have something on him. Why else would he shack up with a murderous thug? He's better than that."

That's the first compliment I've heard from Jayden in reference to his brother. But his comment gets me thinking about Rhett. Is that how everyone sees this? That I'm holding Miles back?

Shannon and Lacy appear in the doorway, seemingly like they teleported, but I know I wasn't paying any attention. They smile and stare at me with bright expressions. They want something.

"What is it?" I ask.

"Can we go camping in the backyard?" Shannon asks. "My grandma has a tent we can use. I've done it before. I know how to set everything up. It's super fun too, and—"

"I don't care," I say, cutting her off. "Just stay close."

"Really?" Lacy says with a mild gasp. "You'll let us sleep outside? At night?"

"Whatever gets your rocks off."

Shannon and Lacy exchange delighted expressions before heading off. I suppose I could have given that more thought. Perhaps I should have, given Lacy's surprise. Maybe Lacy's prissy mother isn't into her perfect daughter getting dirty, but her prissy mother isn't here, is she?

"I'm gonna keep an eye on them all night," Jayden says to me, like it's some sort of halfhearted threat.

"You do that." Saves me the hassle.

CHAPTER EIGHT

"—AND THEN he had the audacity to threaten me on the front lawn," I say, unbuttoning my shirt and tossing it on the nightstand.

"Rhett did?" Miles asks.

"Who else have I been talking about?"

"I'm just surprised." Miles stands on the other side of our bed and mulls over the information. "Are you worried?"

"I don't know," I say, my tone terse. "He didn't have anything of substance, but he looked like he enjoyed the challenge of trying."

"If you think he's going to discover something, we should act. Leave, or hide any evidence you're afraid of him finding."

"It's too early to say." After a moment of remembering his smug face, I get heated all over again. "And I hate the way he looks at you. A piece of me thinks he wants to fuck with me just so he can have you to himself."

Miles laughs aloud as he walks over to our bedroom window. I glare, which only gets him laughing harder. "Are you serious?" he asks when I don't join in on his mirth. "Rhett isn't like that. He's my academy instructor. He's a stand-up and proper kinda guy. I don't even think he's into men."

I huff. "He's definitely into men."

With another chuckle, Miles pulls back the curtain and scopes out the backyard. The girls set up their tent right under our window—Miles's idea—so that, if anything happened, we would be close enough to deal with it. The only thing I hear is their squealing and laughing. The wall is thick enough to drown out speech, but not the shrill delight of preteen girls.

"Are you jealous?" he asks after he shuts the curtain.

"You're mine," I state as I rip off my belt and throw it to the floor. "And he knows it. That's the part that gets me pissed. He either thinks I'm not good enough, or he's so much better that he can take you from me."

"I seriously doubt he thinks like that. I'm telling you, he's a good guy. I thought you guys would be fast friends, to be honest. You're similar in a lot of ways."

"We're nothing alike," I growl.

With barely restrained rage, I yank off my slacks and boxers and get into the cool sheets of our bed. My breathing comes out in forced bursts—anger comes faster and faster these days—and I find myself craving a cigarette.

"Is there anything you want me to do?" Miles asks as he sheds his shirt.

"Stay away from him."

"I'll try."

"Tsk."

Shifting gears, Miles says, "Thank you for saying yes to Lacy's camping trip. She looks like she's having fun for once. My mom doesn't let her do things like this."

"Whatever. Thank the other girl—Shannon. It was her idea."

"Still. You approved. It meant a lot. I think Lacy even likes you a little now."

"Fantastic."

Miles finishes stripping and slides into bed next to me. He switches off the lamp, but the dim blue glow of our digital clock keeps the room more illuminated than I like. Miles says blue light helps put people at ease, or some shit like that, but I prefer the cold comfort of darkness. Reality is whatever you imagine it to be while wraps in shadows.

"Maybe you should consider getting colored contacts," Miles says. "If you're worried about people identifying you because of your eye."

"Fine," I snap as I roll onto my stomach and grip my pillow. I don't want to talk about this—I don't even want to imagine the police discovering my true identity.

Miles shifts across the bed and gets right up next to me. I feel his hot breath on my shoulder blade as he gently kisses my back. "No matter what happens," he whispers, "I got your back. You know that, right?"

I know he's trying to calm me down. I take a deep breath. "Yeah," I mutter.

He doesn't say anything else. Instead, Miles sits up and swings a leg over my back, straddling me. He proceeds to knead my spine with his knuckles, easing my tension, and I take in even breaths while he works.

"I want to know more about your past, Pierce," he whispers. "There's a lot you haven't told me."

"What is it you want to know?"

He thinks over his questions before asking, "Have you ever told someone you love them?"

"No."

"How many men have you been with?"

"Twenty."

"Twenty?" Miles repeats, surprise in voice.

"There a problem with that?" I ask, glancing back at him. The dim lighting highlights the edges of his body—the curves of muscle and the ends of his black locks. A slow burn of lust gets my blood flowing. I try not to think about it, so I focus on his questions, but the stiff mattress rubs me anytime I shift positions.

"Nothing wrong with that," Miles finally says. "I just didn't think it was that many." He continues massaging my back. "Have you ever been with any women?"

"Yes."

"How many?"

"Two."

"I take it… you didn't enjoy those that much?"

"I was young," I state. "It's what I thought I was supposed to do. They never matched up to my times with men, though. And after a while, even the thought of them suckin' me did nothing."

"Tell me about your first time. With a man."

I close my eyes and allow the heat from his body to burn away the last of my anger. My memories from two decades ago aren't that fresh, but a man doesn't forget a first-time sexual experience. I smirk. "It was with this guy named Desmond."

Miles stays quiet.

"He was an enforcer for Big Man Vice, and I was supposed to shadow him to learn the ropes. The guy was a horndog, though. We'd frequently hit all the local nightclubs while we worked. He was also into some darker shit—he liked power plays, really. Stuff where he did whatever he wanted, regardless of what his partner felt about the matter."

"How old were you?"

"Sixteen. Maybe seventeen."

"What happened? Specifically."

"He had been drinking most of the night," I murmur, picturing it all in my head like it happened yesterday. "We were out playing guard, so Desmond hadn't been to his usual stops. When we got back to his place, he started manhandling me pretty rough. I didn't know what was going on—he had never done anything like that to me before—but I quickly got the gist when he started taking off his clothes."

Miles goes back to silence, but I feel him getting hard through the sheets.

I continue, "I fought him every inch of the way, but he got me to the floor. Then he pressed his mouth to my ear and said, 'You can struggle or you can enjoy it, but either way, I'm fucking you tonight.'"

"Pierce," Miles murmurs. "I'm sorry."

I chortle. "Don't be. I enjoyed it."

"You did?" It practically takes him a handful of seconds to process the information. "Why? I thought you didn't like being the bottom? And, I mean, he forced you. You were a kid."

"I was already packin' a gun," I drawl. "The law wouldn't have treated me as a kid, that's for sure. And at first, it was all physiological. Because it hurt like fuck. But I'd play with myself at night thinking about it afterwards. It was dominant. He did whatever he wanted, and I had to obey."

Miles rubs my shoulders, and I can't help but notice how he grinds against the small of my back. "Still… it's hard to believe. That's not what you seem to want now."

"Heh," I mutter with a chuckle. "I've always been attracted to powerful men who know what they want and do what they want. I guess I like them so much I try to play the role myself."

Though I always end up the tool, like with Jeremy.

"Is that why everyone thought you had a thing for Big Man Vice?" Miles asks.

"I would've played bitch for him, yeah."

A moment of silence comes between us.

Before I say anything, Miles pulls off the sheets and slides down my body—so that his cock rests in the cleft of my ass. I tense and get up on my elbows. "*Miles,*" I growl.

He lies across my back and licks the shell of my ear. "I won't enter," he whispers as he thrusts against me, the raw friction of skin on skin getting his breathing heavy.

Reluctantly, I rest back down on the bed. He bucks with his hips, allowing the full length of his erection to rub hard against my ass. After a few rounds, he licks his hand and coats his cock with a mild amount of saliva. The natural lubricant makes his thrusting easier, and he picks up the pace.

Miles wraps his arms around my neck and chest, keeping me close. I can feel his heart beat against the back of my rib cage, and his hot breath warms the nape of my neck. His need for release is intoxicating. With every one of his thrusts I'm rubbed against the mattress, my own lust consuming most of my thoughts. He wants it bad, and I'm starting to hit my own limit.

I grind against the bed, enjoying the pressure. Each time I lift my ass a little higher, giving Miles more of an opportunity to get deep.

"Pierce," he rasps. "Please don't tempt me."

"Get under me, then," I command.

I go to get up, but Miles pushes me back down. He's strong—stronger than I thought he would be—and I get stiffer thinking this'll turn into a fight.

"Let me keep doing this," he pleads as he bites my ear. "I promise this is as far as it'll go."

Caving to his husky tone, I relax and allow him to continue. Miles slows his pace but rubs hard, a moan escaping him between long rounds. I enjoy the feel of him, especially the heat that radiates from his body. Sweat coats everything, sticking to the sheets and slicking up our skin.

Miles groans as he holds back his release. "Pierce. Tell me something else. Another time you… you were bottom."

It's hard to focus, and I mull over the request for an extended period of time, my own breathing coming out in pants. For most of my sexual experiences, I was the one in charge—it was a trust issue then, and I couldn't allow someone else control—but I trust Miles, so what is it now? I shake the thoughts from my head.

When was the last time I took it from a man?

"Jeremy fucked me damn near nightly," I intone.

I feel Miles tense up, but he keeps going, his breath reserved, like he's listening intently.

My mouth gets dry, and I force myself to swallow. My time with Jeremy was odd. Even my own memories feel like I'm watching someone else's life through their eyes—not feeling the sensations or even giving a damn about the circumstances. I didn't care about anything. I was broken.

Maybe I still am.

It's hard to talk about, but for whatever reason, I can for this moment.

"He liked makin' a big deal of it," I say. "Our sessions were never short, and sometimes he wanted an audience. He got off on having me say I wanted him, or making me beg. It was a spectacle. He loved the theatrics."

Miles tightens his hold around me. "You did all that?"

"I did whatever he wanted."

"Did you like it?" he whispers.

"No."

"Was it that bad?"

I close my eyes and picture an average encounter. Sure, Jeremy liked to be "dominant," but it was always off. Always insincere. Sadistic. Like he was afraid and overcompensating. Desmond wanted the pleasure and power—it was animalistic. Jeremy struggled with his own fetishes, like he both hated and adored them at the same time. It made his brand of dominance insufferable.

"He was rough," I say.

I hear Miles grit his teeth. "Rough?"

"Yeah."

"How rough?"

"He didn't like using lube. And on nights he wasn't in a good mood, he wanted me to bleed. It was his goal to get me to react. To get me to plead with him to stop. Sometimes he'd—"

"No more," Miles states, his tone curt. "I've heard enough."

He stops his grinding and grips me tighter, his nails digging into my skin. He's still hot, and his heart rate is through the roof. His precome coats my backside.

I spread my legs a bit. "Do it."

"What?" he asks.

"Fuck me."

"*Pierce*," he breathes, his voice on the verge of irritation. "That's not…."

"It's what you wanted, isn't it? Just get it over with."

Miles sits up, grabs my shoulder, and flips me over onto my back. I stare at him, the blue lighting enough only for silhouettes, but I feel how rigid he is—stiff and tense. He takes a few breaths before resting down on my chest, his mouth above mine.

"I'm sorry."

"For what?" I mutter.

He runs a hand through my hair and grazes his lips against mine. "That never should've happened. I should've been there. And… I don't want to hurt you. That's not what this is about."

"You're not gonna hurt me. Even if you did, I can handle it."

"I don't want you to think of me like Jeremy."

"You're nothing like Jeremy," I growl. Anger is all I feel as I get up on my elbows, shoving Miles away. "I thought about it, all right? I realized something—I let Jeremy have me any way he wanted, and I don't feel anything for the man. I *want* you. So why wouldn't I give you what you want?"

"You don't have to do this to keep me."

"Don't I?" I snap.

Miles pulls me close and presses his mouth against me, his tongue sliding across mine before I say anything. He gently pushes me back down and strokes my chest. I don't know what he's doing, but I enjoy the taste of him. Eventually I calm down and return to my lust-filled state. Miles brushes my disheveled hair from my face and breaks away.

"Pierce," he whispers.

I wait, but he never follows up his statement. Instead he reaches down between us and wraps his grip around my semihard erection. I suck in my breath, startled by the contact but not opposed to it. Miles presses himself against my length and proceeds to caress us both together. He's harder than I am—on the breaking point, really—but the heat from his crotch, combined with the precome, gets me back up to speed.

"Have you ever done this before?" he asks between heavy breaths.

"No."

Miles increases the pressure of his strokes, pumping with a steady rhythm. It's nice. It's not as pleasurable as alternative methods of fucking, but something about his intimate whisper keeps me in the mood for what he's doing.

His fingers slide along my length, and his pulse can be felt through his erection. I rest back, enjoying the sensations. Miles, on the other hand, must have been ready for some time. He digs his nails into my shoulder as he shudders, his seed coming out in two bursts and coating my chest.

He moans and shudders with each progressive stroke after his orgasm, like he's emptying the rest of his dick before stopping.

"You okay?" I ask.

Miles nods.

"Then you should get me a towel."

Always ready to comply, he jumps off and stumbles on unsteady legs. Once he's recovered, Miles walks to our dresser and pulls out a clean towel. He tosses it over, and I miss catching the thing. After some floundering in the dark, I get it and wipe my body clean of sweat and semen.

Miles crawls back into the bed. "What do you want?"

"Nothing," I state as I throw the towel to the floor. I'm already cold and back to my flaccid state. I'm sure I'll wake with a stiffy or have weird dreams, but I'm not in the mood.

"Pierce, you never have to be the bottom if that's not what you're into. I'm not going to force it."

"I know."

"Then forget I ever asked, all right?"

"How about this," I say as I roll onto my side and settle into the bed. "I'll play bitch for your birthday, and if I hate it, we'll go back to our old arrangement. Besides, I wouldn't want Jeremy to be the last man to have me, anyway."

Miles laughs. "You're gonna let me have sex with you as a birthday gift?"

"What? You don't want that?"

"No. No, I do."

"Good. Then what the hell are you complaining for?"

"This is it?" the attorney asks, his nostrils flaring. "This is everything?"

I give the guy a sideways glance. "Yeah. It's everything. Why? What's wrong with it? You want it typed out neater?"

"I want it to be complete! Have you not seen a witness statement? Ever?"

This guy's voice could deafen infants. It's piercing, and he yells like he needs the whole damn neighborhood to hear our conversation. When I don't answer, the attorney opens up his shiny black briefcase and hands over a sheet of paper. I take it and grit my teeth.

My witness statement is two short paragraphs explaining what Ms. Timo told me when I asked about her son's homicide. And that's about it. This other guy's witness statement is a novel unto itself, complete with the time the statement was taken and the signature of the individual in question. It also has a fancy PI firm letterhead at the top, making it look extra official.

Miles glances at the statement and then to mine, a neutral look on his face that betrays nothing. I stop myself from crumpling the paper as I hand it back.

"Your statement has zero value," the attorney continues. "I can't use this in court! This is completely unprofessional. I need you to go out and talk to the witness again. Do I make myself clear?"

"You'll get your statement," I state. "Keep your britches on."

The man flounces out of the lobby, slamming the glass door on his way out. I'm surprised it doesn't shatter, but it's not like the attorney has any muscle to him.

"Have you never taken a witness statement before?" Miles asks with a lifted eyebrow.

"No."

"Did Shelby leave you any examples?"

"I have a handbook and legal thing with all the local codes, laws, ordinances, and regulations."

I should probably read those.

Miles nods once. "Maybe you should take a look at that before you try to take another statement."

"Oh, *ya think*? Have any other insightful pieces of advice I already thought of?"

Miles chortles. "I wouldn't mind helping you study up on this subject."

"I don't need help studying up on anything," I say as I walk back to Shelby's office.

"There's no need to be ashamed of it."

I don't answer. What does he want me to say? I already feel like the *dunce cap kid* after getting yelled at by some asshole in a suit. I get it.

I'm not very good at paperwork. I've never done it in my life—not once. And I certainly don't want to flail around like an inept lump of jelly in front of Miles. I'll handle my own shit if it kills me.

We enter Shelby's office, and Miles lets out a long sigh. "Don't get like this."

"Like what?"

"Let me help you."

"I told you—I don't need your help."

"Okay…. As a favor to me, then. Let me help you."

I turn on my heel and find him staring at me with a level of determination he normally reserves for the extreme. His dark eyes are unambiguous. He wants to do this. I like the look, and it takes me a moment to remember what we're even fighting about.

"Fine," I mutter.

"Thank you."

"But no one else can know," I continue, curt.

Miles offers me a half smile. "Of course not."

I actively mocked Jayden for being incompetent—it's a little hypocritical, considering *I* have no education, *and* I'm much older, *and* I don't even have a grip on my own profession. It's starting to hit pathetic.

Shelby's bottom drawer still has some files I haven't examined, so I shake my head and walk over, intent on gathering them up. Before I stoop down, I spot a clean line through a patch of dust on a stack of files. I stop and glance around. There are hand marks on most of the files. And things have been moved around.

Davis is dead, and Shelby is in the hospital. Miles and I should be the only ones with access to this office.

"Hey," Miles whispers. "I think someone might have been here."

"Yeah," I reply. "I was thinkin' the same damn thing."

CHAPTER NINE

"Why?" Miles asks.

"I don't know."

"Did Shelby have something important in here?"

"I don't know."

"How well do you know Shelby?"

I give Miles a hard stare that says everything. I don't know Shelby at all. I worked with him because he didn't ask a lot of questions about my past. That's all I wanted. Now look what it's gotten me into....

Since I have no clue what someone was looking for, I go back to my own work. I pull out the rest of Shelby's files from the bottom file drawer and motion to the door. "Let's get out of here."

"You don't want to try to figure out what happened?"

"There aren't any cameras in here, and it's not like I knew what was here *before* someone snooped around. If something is missing, it's all a surprise to me. Do you have a better plan?"

"Maybe you should call Shelby. Tell him what happened."

That's a valid starting point. I pull out my phone and call the man. No answer.

With a long sigh, I type out a text message telling him I thought someone was in his office. I finish it up with: *This news to you?* I hope there's a logical explanation, because I'd hate to have to deal with yet another problem. I'm already trying to solve a human trafficking scheme, essentially—I don't have time for the *Mystery of the Dusty Office Caper*. I'm not a goddamn dime novel detective.

"All right," I say. "Let's go."

Miles and I leave the building after locking up, and head over to our junker. It creaks as we throw open the doors, but I ignore it as I take my seat in the front passenger position. Miles takes driver so that I can read through the files. As he pulls out of the parking lot, I kick open the glove compartment and pull out a spare cigarette and lighter.

After lighting myself a smoke, I lean back and start reading.

"Have you gone to the doctor's yet?" Miles asks.

"No."

"I think you should set up an appointment."

"I think you should stop bringing this up."

"You smoked for a really long time."

"And I drink a lot," I say, exhaling a line of smoke. "And my back hurts from time to time. We've all got problems. I'm nothing special."

Miles gets silent. I prefer it this way. I don't want to see a doctor. I can already hear his diagnosis. Too much smoking. Too many fights. Too much alcohol. You're set for an early grave.

I already know. Why bother wasting what little time I have with the process?

I engross myself in my reading in order to drown out reality. The macabre stories of kids going missing, teens found dead in basements, and boats filled with corpses are all distractions that remind me life is nothing but an unrelenting holocaust of dreams. So many stories of grisly death and heartache—it looks like Noimore has had a problem for three decades—but only recently has it hit epidemic levels.

But one file catches my eye.

Michael Shelby.

I flip through the pages and narrow my gaze. The file is old, the oldest one I have, and it has notes written all over it. Justin Shelby, age ten, no doubt Shelby's son, went missing. His body, found two years later, indicated he had been sexually abused before being dumped in the river. Injuries on the autopsy report reveal he'd been harmed for an extended period of time. Experts suspect longer than thirteen months.

I take a long drag on my cigarette.

Fuck me.

No wonder Shelby is obsessed with catching these guys.

"Pierce?" Miles asks, breaking my concentration. "Are you okay?"

"Yeah," I mutter as I exhale a line of smoke. "Why?"

"You look upset."

"Shelby's kid was kidnapped a long time ago."

Miles glances over at me with a frown before returning his attention to the road. "What happened?"

"He got tossed around between some guys and then thrown off a bridge into the Noimore River. He's been dead for about twenty years now."

Right around the same time Shelby said he got divorced. A perfect recipe for some old kook to go off the deep end.

I finish the file and realize that I've read everything Shelby gave me. But there's still no explanation as to why he knows where the kidnappers are or what their tentative schedule is. I flip over the paperwork and take another long drag on my cigarette.

"We're here," Miles announces.

The car comes to a stop, and I glance up. We're at some industrial district in Noimore—how long had I been reading?—but the early afternoon sun gives me reassurances. I doubt any guys will be wandering around at this time of the day. Thugs and shadows go together like peanut butter and jelly.

A trucker warehouse sits before us. The sign out front reads Under Construction. But there's no date for the estimated finish. There's a chain-link fence and a few pole-mounted cameras, but the rail yard had all of that and more. If these kidnappers are going to use this site for drop-off or pickup, they'll need to prep the area first.

"You think they'll use this spot?" Miles asks, keeping his voice low, for whatever reason.

"Yeah," I reply. "They used the trains to ship bodies when I first saw them. It doesn't surprise me that they'd use trucks too. They must be pickin' up people here in Noimore or the nearby area, maybe even Chicago, and takin' them elsewhere."

Miles leans back in his seat and sighs. "Why would anybody do this?"

"People love spendin' money," I mutter. "It's too bad injustice comes so cheap."

"So, do you think we should stake this place out until they show up?"

"We'll be waiting forever if we do that."

"I thought Shelby said they would be here any day? That's why he had you go instead of waiting until he was out of the hospital."

I open my mouth to offer a retort, but Miles holds up a hand to quiet me. I glare at him, confused by his gesture. His gaze is glued to something in the distance, and he grabs my shoulder in an attempt to get me to look in that direction. I squint and spot a car on the far side of the construction zone—a plain-looking white four-door car with tinted back windows.

"So?" I say. "They're likely construction workers."

Miles settles back down. "Maybe. But no one is here. No one is working."

I stare at all the cold equipment locked down by the portable office. There aren't any men in hard hats, nor does there seem to be any open gates around the fence, at least not on our side. But the white car must have gotten in somehow.

Miles and I watch in silence as two guys get out of the car and start walking around. It's hard to see them properly—especially when they walk behind stacks of wood or pipes—but they both head off in different directions, a purpose to their gait. One guy, large and sloppy about his weight, stops at the nearest camera pole and cuts the wire. The other guy does the same to a different camera.

"I don't think they're construction workers," Miles whispers.

One man turns in our direction. Miles and I both duck down into the car, and I feel my body get numb with adrenaline. I exhale a line of smoke and snuff the cigarette out in the car's ashtray.

"Do you have a pair of binoculars?" I ask.

Miles nods. He slithers back in his seat and reaches into the back, pulling up his academy school bag and withdrawing a handful of useful objects, including five pairs of zip-tie handcuffs. He hands over the binoculars, and I risk peeking over the dashboard.

The big guy with the gut, I don't recognize. The other guy—a gaunt motherfucker with a spray tan—I *do* remember seeing at the rail yard. He was the guy giving the orders, the one in charge of the situation when it got out of hand. He must be the one who handles shit. An enforcer, so to speak. The guy I used to be.

"These are the guys," I say, handing Miles back his binoculars. "The same ones. They're here to prep the place."

"So what're we going to do about it?"

"We'll get out of the car, skulk our way over to theirs, and then jump their asses."

Miles turns to me with a furrowed brow. "Why not call the cops?"

"They'll run when they hear the sirens. That's what they did last time. And even if the cops came quiet, it's not like these guys are gonna be here long. If we catch 'em, the cops can interrogate them."

"We can't go in and attack them," Miles states. "That's against the law. It would be trespassing, assault, and battery."

"Can't citizens arrest criminals? Ya know. Citizen's arrest?"

"They would've had to commit a felony—"

"Which they did," I interject. "Human trafficking."

"—and citizens making the arrest can only use *reasonable* force—"

"So we won't shoot them."

"—and the arresting citizen is liable for tortious injuries, like false imprisonment or wrongful death—"

"What're you trying to say?" I snap.

Miles exhales. "I'm trying to say that we can get in a shit ton of trouble if you're wrong about this. Plus, we don't have the kind of protection cops do. Again, we could both lose our careers before they even start if we get in trouble."

Goddamn. He really has been studying, hasn't he? He knows all those legal elements like the back of his hand.

"I'm certain that's the guy," I state. "And if we don't act fast, they're going to get away."

Miles meets my gaze with a hint of uncertainty.

"I got your back," I say with a smirk.

That's all he needed to hear, apparently—his determination overrides everything else. "Let's do this."

I open the car door as slowly as possible to avoid the creak. Miles does the same, and we keep ourselves low to the ground as we hustle over to the fence. Before I find a place to climb over, Miles hands me a set of the zip-tie handcuffs. I nod to him.

Once I'm out of sight of the kidnappers, I grab the fence and haul myself over. It's more difficult than it should be, and I end up gulping down air at an unsteady rate. When I land on the other side, I hold back coughs.

"You should see a doctor," Miles whispers to me after he effortlessly leaps the chain-link obstacle.

I wave away his comment and motion for us to continue.

The construction site is organized in a neat fashion, with all the lumber stacked together and separated out for the machines. It makes it easy to duck behind one stack and jump to the next without getting caught. The two thugs cutting cameras only have a handful to deal with. I see them finish their task by the time I reach the half-constructed building near their car.

"What're we going to do?" Miles asks as we kneel down behind a fabricated wall.

"You go for one guy, and I'll go for the other."

"Which one?"

"I got the thin one," I say. "You take the dude with the gut."

I assume the enforcer will be more difficult to deal with than the other one. I know I can handle myself, but I always worry with Miles. He's in good shape, but it's not like he's been in as many fights as I have.

To my surprise, both men head to different buildings rather than back to their car. The buildings are half-constructed office complexes— big, two stories, high ceilings—and it makes it easier for me and Miles to run up without them seeing. Miles heads to his building, and I head to mine. The moment I get close, the raspy voice of the enforcer draws my attention.

"Everything is set," he says.

I poke my head around the corner and stare inward. The floors aren't done. They're nothing but a cement foundation with steel beams stuck in as support. The enforcer wanders around, a cell phone pressed to his ear, and he stares at his feet while he walks.

"No," he says, curt. "Things are going to plan."

While he's distracted, I hustle into the building and duck behind a set of stairs that lead to the mezzanine floor. Now that I'm closer, I can hear the voice from the other side of the man's phone. His volume is set to the max, and I wonder if he has hearing problems. Guys who shoot a lot of guns sometimes get that.

"We've got another shipment's worth," he continues. "It's good stuff. Real good stuff."

"*How many more shipments are we going to make, Castor?*"

The enforcer, Castor, shrugs. "At the rate we're going, we'll have a few more within the month. Like I said, things are running smoothly. We got our drop-offs. We got our shipping. All we need now is—"

"*What about our loose end? Is he dead yet? We can't have guys betraying us.*"

"He's a hero right now. We don't want more media attention. We wait, and then we kill him."

"*Get rid of him before he starts more trouble.*"

I slide around the side of the stairs, the dusty air messing with my breathing. I coil in preparation for when this guy gets close, but my train of thought stops when I hear the distinct crack of gunfire.

Miles.

Castor snaps his attention to the door. "I'll call you back," he says. "I think we've been compromised."

He hangs up his phone, and I have to remind myself that I'm here for a purpose. Castor heads for the door, and I lunge at him. My shoulder connects with his back, and we both hit the ground, winded. I grab my gun and press it to his head, but he rolls to the side—faster and stronger than I anticipated—sending me to the floor.

Castor jumps to his feet. I fire, missing him, but his panicked dive for cover gives me long enough to stand. I rush after him and tackle the guy before he can get his own handgun up and ready. We struggle for a moment, and I wrench his weapon from his hand. Castor pulls back with a fist and cracks me hard across the face.

The next moment I'm on my back, my head pounding.

I get up, and that lunatic kicks me in the sternum like he's a goddamn soccer player. I stumble back and hit the stairs, unable to take in breath.

Castor runs for his handgun and I fire again, causing him to go for cover. With my strength returning in small amounts, I kick his handgun away and chase after him. Castor exits the building into the midafternoon light. He's running at full tilt—no way I'll catch him—and instead I fire at his legs, clipping his ankle and sending him to the dirt.

Before he can recover, I throw myself on top of the man and torque his arms around to his back. He thrashes about, the blood from his ankle splattering across the ground in light amounts. I use the zip-tie to keep his arms in place, but the man is thin like a boney coatrack. I fear he might be able to slip from the device.

The sound of a car peeling out across loose gravel draws my attention. A van—some dirty ice-cream truck thing—rolls through the construction site at a speed well beyond the posted limit. It heads straight for me, not but a hundred feet away, and my whole body tenses.

"Pierce!"

I jump up and shove Castor away from me, getting some extra momentum as I push him to safety. The tires of the van graze the tip of my shoes as I stumble back across the dirt, my heart pounding.

Gunfire rattles from the vehicle as a pair of lowlifes fire at me with fully automatic weapons. I scoot backward behind a stack of pipes and listen to the ricochet of bullets on metal.

Castor, handcuffed, snakes his way away. "Hey!" he barks. "Hey!" But his voice is drowned out by the roar of a car engine, the blasts of Uzis, and the general pandemonium of echoes across the construction yard.

As the van speeds off and begins to turn, I run over to Castor. Sure enough, the man is nimble and flexible. He jump ropes backward through his arms and gets his hands in front of him, though he can't seem to slip the handcuffs. I land a solid punch across his face, but he kicks me in the side with some roundhouse bullshit like he's a trained fucking fighter.

I'm ready to brawl, but he grabs my jacket and yanks me close. I struggle to get out of it, if only to shed the clothing he's holding, but Castor pushes me back just as I get my arms out, sending me to the ground as the van tears toward us.

Castor throws my jacket over me, temporarily blocking my sight, but panic fuels my flight as I leap up and away from the van's swerving. Bullets cut through the jacket at multiple points, and I wouldn't be surprised if I got hit, but my mind can't process pain at the moment. I rip the jacket off and chase after Castor as he limps away.

For the fourth time, I collide with him and we hit the ground, dirt filling my mouth. I spit, get up, and punch him in the side, my knuckles cracking down on ribs. Castor groans and goes still.

Sirens cut through the cacophony. I hold Castor down as I watch the van peel out of the construction site. Who called the cops? I shake my head. After all that gunfire, I wouldn't be surprised if the whole city called the cops.

Castor gets one good look at my arm—and my tattoo—and then stares up at me. I feel ice run through my veins when he gives me a look of recognition.

"You're with the Vice family?" he hisses. "*You fucking traitor. You've made a huge goddamn mistake.*"

CHAPTER TEN

I ROLL down my long sleeves and search for my gun. It's in the dirt, still loaded with a few bullets, and I scoop it up, ready to solve my latest problem. Miles jogs up to me from the other side of the construction site, a bruise over his right eye but otherwise unharmed. The sirens continue to shriek in the distance, closing in faster and faster.

"What's going on?" Miles asks.

I level the gun at Castor's head. "Nothing. I'm just correcting a mistake."

Miles grabs my arm and pushes it away, a look of incredulous disbelief written across his face. "You can't shoot him! This isn't street justice—we have to hand him over to the police!"

I pull Miles close. "He knows who I am," I growl. "He has to die."

"How? You two know each other from before?"

"My tattoo."

Castor, under my knee and thrashing about, spits at me, missing. "You're living on borrowed time, asshole! I don't know what you thought you would accomplish here, but going against us was the stupidest mistake you've—"

"Shut up," I state, cutting him off. I get it. They'll come after me. That's not news.

Sirens. They make my skin crawl. A shiver goes down my spine when I think about what Castor could say to them.

"We can't give him to the cops," I say. "Then they'll figure me out."

"We can't kill him," Miles replies. "We can't. Not when we have him subdued. It's straight-up murder at this point."

"If we let him go, he'll go straight to the Vice family with what he's seen."

We're running out of time. Every second adds a whole new layer of stress. What have I gotten us into? Fuck me. This is all my fault, and I need to pull it together. I pick up my ruined jacket and grit my teeth. Anything is better than inaction.

"Help me grab him," I command. "We'll decide this later."

"What do you mean, *later*?"

"When we aren't swarmed by the cops!"

Miles nods.

Castor, on the other hand, flails about. I take my gun and smash it across his face, and then repeat the action, blood and saliva splattering onto my knuckles. Miles grabs my arm, a look of panic and concern etched into his face. I stop. Castor isn't unconscious, but he's dazed to the point of stunned compliance. I grab him by his armpits and Miles takes his ankles.

Kidnapping a kidnapper. How ironic.

We get to the fence, and I know we'll never be able to carry a grown-ass man over the chain-link barrier. Miles knows it too, and drops Castor's feet in order to fling himself to the other side of the fence and jog to the car. Within seconds he's turned our vehicle around and speeds toward me. I drag Castor out of the way, just in time to see Miles smash a portion of the fence open enough for me to get through.

I open the trunk and unceremoniously heft Castor up into the thing. The smell of oil stings my nose, but I push it from my mind as I slam the hatch shut. After I get into the passenger seat, Miles peels away from the construction site, his eyes glued to the road. I grab another cigarette and light it up. Anything to relax.

"I can't believe what we've done," Miles mutters.

He speeds out of the area but forces himself to slow once he pulls out onto a busy road. The oppressive nature of Noimore is comforting—almost like the city is lulling us back into a world of crime—and I know that no one is going to bother us as long as we keep our heads down. Police vehicles speed by in the opposite direction, their sirens disrupting the peace.

"What happened?" I ask Miles, my mind going over our plan a hundred times in order to see what went wrong.

"I found my guy," he replies. "But when I jumped him, there were these *other* guys I hadn't even seen. I got away from them, well, after one guy tried to punch me and another tried to shoot me, but then they jumped in a van. When I got outside, you were already there and in a fight."

"So there were others?"

"Yeah. Two others."

"And your guy got away?"

"All three of them did! You saw the van."

Which means the cops will walk away empty-handed. I exhale a line of smoke and rub a hand down my face. "Listen, I'll take our guy to a spot I know, beat some information out of him, and then dump his corpse in the Noimore landfill." It's a pretty nice place to dump bodies. Sure, they find them occasionally, but never with any expediency.

"No," Miles says. "We can't kill him."

"Why not? He's a piece of shit. He shot Davis—he would have shot me—and he'll *definitely* go back to his scumbag ways if we let him go."

"We're on the side of the law now," Miles says with a tone of sardonic anger. "That's not what *cops* and *private detectives* do."

"Yeah, but this way I can work him over for information. That's what we want, right? Stopping these kidnappers will go ten times faster with some straight answers."

Miles grips the steering wheel like he's choking the damn thing. "We can't do that either."

"Why?"

"Illegally obtained information can't be used against someone," Miles states. "If we beat information out of this guy, we won't be able to use any of it to prove the guilt of the people we're trying to finger."

"Says who?"

"The federal government. Shelby didn't explain to you the fruit of the poisonous tree doctrine? It's a cornerstone of legal investigation."

Jesus Christ. Does he know everything about the law now? I take a long drag on my cigarette and exhale. "Fine. We can't kill him. We can't work him over for information. What do you want to do?"

"We should take him to the police station," Miles says. "We'll tell them that we arrested him and brought him straight there."

"I told you—we can't do that. If he tells the cops about me, we'll have *other* problems to deal with."

Miles gets quiet.

What other option is there? The only other thing is to let the guy go, and we can't do that either. He'll go straight to the Vice family, which might be worse than him going to the cops. Jeremy is unstable and *off* in the head. He'll do something—send enforcers to kill me, have someone bring me back, *something*—and I don't think I can deal with that.

So what choice do we have? Keep Castor in our trunk forever? That's tantamount to torture, and we won't even get any information out of it.

Miles comes to a four-way stop and stares at the street signs. One street leads deeper into the city, toward the central police station, and the opposite leads toward the freeways out of town. There's a honk from behind us, causing me to tense, and Miles turns the car toward Joliet. I exhale another line of smoke.

We still don't know what we're doing with this guy. We're just eating time.

"What if we drop him off anonymously?" Miles asks.

"I dunno. You tell me. Will the police take a person randomly gagged and bound on their front doorstep?"

"No," Miles murmurs.

"There you go."

I sigh. There isn't anyone in the police department I trust enough to leave this guy with. I know some officers who were on the Vice family payroll—and I would recognize them on sight—but they don't owe me any favors. If I went to them, they would go to Jeremy. Same problem, different chain of events.

We get onto the freeway and exit Noimore. No trouble. No hassle. I figured we'd be fine, but fate has a way of fucking with me. Still… the problem only gets worse the longer we go.

"I need to pick up Jayden and Lacy," Miles says.

"We should handle this first."

"I can't be late."

"Why? What does it matter? A few minutes won't kill them."

"I told them I'd be there," Miles states. "Okay? I know you don't care about them, but they mean a lot to me."

Yeah, I know. He went out of his way to save Jayden on more than one occasion. His siblings mean the world to him.

"Fine," I say. "Let's get them, drop them off at the house, ask our old neighbor lady to watch them, and then deal with this guy. One way or another."

Miles nods. "All right."

"—AND THEN we learned the basics of the quadratic formula," Lacy says, her voice blending together in my ears like one long uninterrupted sentence. Parts of my body feel like they're on fire, and listening to this isn't helping.

I forgot how fucking boring school was. Although if I had to do everything all over again, I might try to stick it out. But Lacy makes it seem like the secret circle of hell.

"You're learning about the quadratic formula in seventh grade?" Miles asks. "I'm surprised. I didn't learn about that until high school."

"It's a fancy prep school," Jayden interjects with a dismissive wave of his hand. "They keep telling us it's for college. Hell, some of the classes offer college credits. Lacy might have a degree by the time she graduates."

Lacy grabs the back of Miles's seat and sits forward. "Can Shannon come over today? I got a perfect score on my history exam."

"Of course," Miles replies.

A thump echoes throughout the cab of the car, and I know immediately that it's Castor in the trunk. Miles flips on the radio, no doubt understanding the situation as well, but it screeches with white noise like the piece of crap it is. He turns the radio off and pulls out his phone. He sets it to rock music—something with a buzz of bass—and then leaves it.

"Are you okay?" Jayden asks.

"Yes," Miles says, curt.

"Are you two fighting? You both have, like, bruises and stuff."

"We're fine."

Jayden leans in between the front two seats. He glances back and forth before smirking. "So, when you guys get a divorce, does that mean we won't be seeing Pierce any longer?"

"We aren't married," Miles states.

"So we definitely won't see Pierce any longer?"

"Jayden."

Miles's threatening tone gets his brother quiet. Jayden slinks back into his seat.

"Hey," Lacy says. "It's that police officer again. Who is he?"

I stare out the front windshield and grit my teeth. I knew fate wanted to fuck with me. Lieutenant Rhett Walker waits in front of our house like he's guarding the place, milling around the sidewalk next to his cruiser. The empty streets and sidewalks should have been a dead giveaway. Nobody wants to be out when there's a cop nearby.

Miles turns to me with a look of panic. I want to tell him *Hit Rhett with our car*, but I know that's not a real option. Well, not an option Miles would take.

"Park a few blocks away," I tell him as I remove my bullet-hole-ridden jacket and shoulder holster.

Miles nods.

I throw my equipment onto the floor of the car and make sure my sleeves are down to my wrists. I don't need any unnecessary questions.

We have a driveway, but Miles drives past and turns a corner, much to the confusion of his two siblings. Lacy stays quiet, but I don't think Jayden has it in him to keep his mouth shut.

"What're you doing?" Jayden asks. "What's going on?"

"Nothing," I tell him. "Get out of the car."

Everyone files out, and I walk around to the driver's side. I go for the keys, but Miles stops me. "We should all go up together," he says. "Rhett knows we're here now. Let's talk to him first."

I don't like this plan, but I'll go with it. I guess it's better than getting Rhett more suspicious than he already is by disappearing whenever he turns up.

We walk together around the corner and up the street. The uneven pavement threatens to trip me a few times, but I avoid stumbling thanks to the light of the descending sun. Lacy jumps over the cracks with grace but stops once we near Rhett. She gets odd and tense, like she doesn't trust him, and for a brief moment I like her a little more than before.

Rhett straightens himself when we get close, his dark hair windswept yet still styled—does he groom himself for the criminals, or was it prep for visiting us? I'd ask, but I don't think I could keep my condescension out of it.

"You parked pretty far away," Rhett comments. "Why?"

"So this fatass can burn some calories," I say as I motion to Jayden.

Jayden glares, his face a shade of red. "I'm not even that fat," he chokes out under his breath. "Why do you keep saying that?"

"Because you react."

"Jayden, Lacy," Miles says. "Go into the house, please."

His siblings walk away—Lacy more eager than Jayden—and I wait a few feet behind Miles, hoping this encounter will be over with quick. I doubt Rhett is here to arrest me, considering he hasn't done anything yet, but he may be here to question us. Why today, of all days?

Once the front door closes, Rhett crosses his arms over his chest and sighs. "I got a call today in conjunction with the group of human traffickers."

Miles and I remain silent.

Rhett continues, "Apparently there was a gunfight at a construction site in Noimore not but an hour ago. From all the reports we gathered, it looks like prep work was done on the place for our suspects to do their shipping, but everything was interrupted. An elderly gentleman in charge of the security says he saw two people in a *jalopy of a car* snooping around the area."

Silence settles between us. Everyone knows what Rhett's implied, but what does he think we'll say? It's not like we would out and out admit anything. Well, I wouldn't. A small piece of me thinks Miles might.

"What're you trying to say?" I ask, knowing full well what's going on. "We just got back from picking up some kids from school. We didn't have time to thwart some punks."

Rhett steps up closer to us and lowers his voice. "I know Shelby somehow has insider information on this whole thing. I know he's been using it too—like at the rail yard. Who else would be at the construction site when everything went down?"

"Well, it wasn't us."

"That's it? That's your only rebuttal?"

"It's all I need. You're barking up the wrong tree."

Rhett turns his attention to Miles. I also give him a sideways glance. Miles trusts Rhett for some reason, but I hope to God he doesn't spill anything he shouldn't. We have a man locked in our trunk, for fuck's sake. It doesn't look good for us, even if we explained the situation from beginning to end.

"You don't know anything about this?" Rhett asks.

Miles shakes his head. "No. I don't know what you're talking about."

I let out a short exhale, not even aware I had been holding my breath.

Again, quiet blankets the area. I get antsy thinking about Castor in the trunk, but I keep still. I don't want to look uncomfortable in the middle of a questioning—it would only encourage Rhett to continue.

"Miles," Rhett begins. He places his hands on his hips and stares at the cement sidewalk. "Listen. I still remember your first day in the academy. You introduced yourself and told your academy classmates a little about your past."

Miles nods but offers no commentary.

"You said you had people who depended on you. That you had a rough start in life, but you were back on track and ready to do what you had to, to make it right. Do you remember that? What you said?"

"Yeah," Miles says. "I remember."

Rhett sighs. "I didn't think much of it then, but after a few days as your instructor, I knew you were being sincere. Nobody works as hard as you. Nobody studies as much as you do. You're constantly improving—not just your physical body, but your knowledge base too. You have a drive. A passion. I see that you meant what you said and… I don't want to see you fail. I don't want to see you throw all your hard work away because of one stupid mistake. Do you understand?"

Miles tightens his hands into fists. His expression is unreadable, but I get tense and agitated by the speech.

When Miles doesn't say anything, Rhett continues, "I want to help you succeed, so I'm going to ask you—is there anything you want to tell me?"

For a moment, I fear Miles will talk. I cross my arms over my chest, gripping my arms in hope of relaxing, but it doesn't work. To my surprise, Miles steps up closer to Rhett and then throws his arms around him in a tight embrace.

Rhett, looking as stunned as I am, freezes up.

"Thank you," Miles says, keeping his hold. "It means a lot knowing that you're looking out for me. I didn't have that when I was younger. I didn't have anyone, really."

"Of c-course," Rhett stammers, his face flushed. He awkwardly returns the embrace as he gives me a quick guilty glance. I don't say anything, nor do I move or react. I don't want to cause a scene, but I'm on the verge of returning to the car to get my damn handgun.

Rhett takes a step back, breaking contact, and exhales. "Well, uh, all right. I have to go. I'll see you in class later tonight."

"Thank you again," Miles says. "I'll see you then."

Without another word, Rhett walks over to his police cruiser and hops in, his stiff gait betraying his flustered state. He must not be open to public affection, which I understand, but it's odd, considering the girls at his office seem to fling themselves at him. Or maybe he's so far in the closet he has a shoe rack up his ass.

The moment Rhett's gone, I turn to Miles. "What was that?"

"He stopped talking to us, didn't he?" Miles replies. "Now we can handle our other problem."

"You still think he doesn't want you?"

Miles's honeyed skin shifts to a shade of pink. "Um…. Well, I know he likes men. That much I'm sure of. It was very apparent."

I clench my teeth thinking about what that white-knight asshole must have been imagining while holding Miles. I swear I've never felt quite so *protective* of someone, but then again, I've never had a relationship like the one I have with Miles. I don't like the mood it gets me in, but I don't have time to think about that.

Miles walks up to me and runs his thumb along the bottom of my lip. "What happened?" he asks. The blood on his hand surprises me.

I touch my lip and feel the split. It must have been from the fighting in the construction site, exacerbated by my teeth grinding. "I'm fine," I say.

I'm surprised Rhett never mentioned our injuries.

"Let's talk inside while we take care of this."

I follow Miles into our house, still nervous about our problem, but it's better to talk in private. It's better to do everything in private, really. The public is unruly and bipolar—you never know what you'll get when you act out in front of them.

Miles takes me into our cramped bathroom, and I take note of the guest room's closed door. I figured Jayden would keep to himself, but I wonder if Lacy is still here or at the neighbor's. She shouldn't be gallivanting around.

Before I can say anything, Miles locks the door and gets a clean washcloth. He wipes away my blood, unbuttons my shirt, and then runs a hand along my side, his fingers tracing the grooves of my wifebeater undershirt. I'm a little confused but not opposed to his touch. Up until he presses against my bruised ribs.

"*Watch it*," I hiss as I grab his hand.

Miles stops and instead pushes me back against the counter. I rest against it as he pulls off my button-up shirt and unrolls a wad of gauze. "So what're we going to do? I don't see a good solution to this. Killing him is out of the question, so it's either let him go or take him to the police."

"I've killed a lot of guys before," I drawl. "No one will find out."

Miles ignores my comment and instead focuses his attention on my tattooed arm. I watch him as he runs his fingers over the mark. "You don't have to be this guy anymore," he says. "We can solve this a different way. And from now on, you'll be wearing bandages to cover this."

I lift an eyebrow at the command. He's never flat-out told me what to do before. I smirk. "Is that right?"

"Yes," he states unambiguously. "You've been too lax with this, your eye, your backstory—I know when you worked for Big Man Vice he would take care of things like that, but that's not what's going on anymore. We need to be careful."

"*I* need to be careful, you mean."

"No, I meant *we*. That's why I ordered you contact lenses, and you're going to wear this bandage."

"There's no point to wearing this bandage. I'll just keep my shirtsleeves down."

"You keep a knife in your sock?"

"Sometimes. Not always."

"Well, keep a knife here. Then it has a purpose."

I scoff. "I don't have one."

Miles reaches into his pants pocket and pulls out a pocket multitool knife. It's small, has a few fold-out blades, a bottle opener, and a thin pick, but it looks useful. He presses it against my arm and then wraps it with the gauze. "Here. Take this."

I pull my arm back. "I can take care of myself."

Miles retakes my arm and holds it close. "I don't want to lose you."

I want to say something, but I stop. Rhett's speech haunts my thoughts as I watch Miles finish wrapping my tattoo and the small multitool knife. If something happens—if I'm found out—Miles will be in jeopardy. His life. His goals. Everything. He has a bright future, and what do I have? By being careless I'm putting him at risk. I should've thought of this sooner.

"I'm gonna take that guy to the police," I mutter.

Miles meets my gaze with his own. "Why?"

"It's the only option."

"You said you were worried he would tell the police who you were."

"Most thugs aren't cooperative with the police. Besides, I think I can talk him into keeping his mouth shut." And by talk, I mean threaten. Guys like Castor understand promises of force and violence—and there will be a lot of that behind bars if we end up in the same facility.

Miles nods as he finishes his task. I can tell he's reluctant, and his pensive look bothers me. *I don't want to lose you either* is what I want to say, but I can't bring myself to do it. Tsk. Words are cheap. Instead of speaking, I lean forward and press my mouth against his, taking in the warmth of his breath and the taste of his tongue.

After a moment I pull away, surprised by the hot red spreading across Miles's face. We've kissed before. What's his problem?

"Pierce," he murmurs.

"Get ahold of yourself," I state.

Miles laughs once and smiles. "You don't normally initiate stuff like that."

I push away from the bathroom counter and slip back into my shirt. "I'm going to go take care of our problem," I say, ignoring his statement. "I'll be back shortly."

Miles doesn't stop me as I exit our house and take to the street. Our neighbors return to their porch lounging now that the cop is gone, and I nod to a few as I make my way past. I don't know them, and they don't know me, but a basic show of respect goes a long way. Besides, there's a good chance there are some unsavory types milling about. I wouldn't want to give them a reason to make me a target.

I get to my vehicle as the setting sun casts long shadows over the streets. A few eyes follow me, but I ignore them as I get into the driver's seat. After glancing around the cab—and making sure it's as I left it—I pull the vehicle out onto the street and head for the other side of town.

The dull drone of static from the radio gets my heart rate up as I swerve around traffic. There's a precinct on the edge of Noimore that will take Castor; I'm sure of it. The real problem is telling them how he came to be in my possession. I'm gonna have to bust up Castor until our stories match. There's a bridge I know where we can have some privacy, but I haven't been there in some time. I might have to scout out the place first.

I turn the car onto an on-ramp when the smell of oil burns my nose. Dread grips me as I glance up to the rearview mirror and spot the silhouette of Castor and his blade.

Fuck.

CHAPTER ELEVEN

I SLAM on the brakes at the edge of the freeway.

My seat belt digs into my chest and neck, but Castor doesn't have any such restraints. He flies past the front seat and hits the windshield, back first. The glass cracks and bends outward but doesn't actually shatter. My mind goes to my gun—it's on the floorboard of the passenger seat.

I don't even get a second to react before the car behind me swerves and clips my fender, sending the junker spinning into the first lane of traffic. I hold on to the steering wheel and hit the gas, but the engine sputters and locks up. The damn vehicle doesn't move.

Headlights and honking pull my attention to the road. Cars dart around, but the big rigs aren't as nimble. I unfasten my seat belt as fast as my hands will allow and slam open the door in an attempt to distance myself from oncoming traffic.

Castor, still conscious, kicks out the windshield and rolls off the hood, his legs wobbly but steady enough for him to walk. I go toward him but jump back when a motorcycle races by, inches from me. A truck grazes the side of my vehicle and sends it farther down the road and to the side, the scrape of metal and crunch of glass drowned out by the rush of speeding cars.

I take a step back and curse the twilight-darkness of the setting sun. Everything is so difficult to see, and it's not just my bum eye that's causing it!

While I move toward the on-ramp, Castor runs for the center divider.

Cars and trunks come to a stop before hitting my wrecked vehicle, but it's a little too late. Castor crosses the other four lanes on the opposite side, almost getting hit *twice* before jogging down the nearest on-ramp.

My ears ring, and I rub at the soreness of my tense muscles.

"Goddammit," I mutter.

Cars honk, the man that hit me asks for information—but I don't give a shit about any of that. Castor will go back to his buddies. He'll speak to the Vice family. They'll know I'm alive.

The realization drowns out all other sensations and emotions. This is the last thing I wanted to happen.

I PARK our new car in the driveway and relax back against the seat. It took all day yesterday to deal with the old POS and then to finalize a sale on some random used four-door Ford Taurus. I guess I should count myself lucky Castor didn't get out in our neighborhood, but that's a small consolation prize after everything that's happened. At least he doesn't know where we live.

He cut through the back of our old jalopy with a five-inch knife. I should have checked him, but we were in such a hurry to leave the construction site....

A small piece of me hopes he comes looking for me. Miles can't be upset with a self-defense killing. I run a hand along my holster. Until we solve this problem—or move—I'm not going anywhere without my gun.

I get out of the car and amble my way into the house. It's empty, which is odd, considering Miles didn't take either of his siblings to their prep school today. Squeals and laughter soon tell me everyone is in the backyard, however. I change into an easier set of attire, while keeping my jacket and gun, and then walk out back to do my daily gardening.

Anything to take my mind off the fact that Vice family goons could be looking for me.

Shannon and Lacy are seated at our lopsided picnic table. The table was there when we moved in—I certainly wouldn't have purchased something so pointless—but it seems to be a hit with the girls. They have a blanket draped over the top and a myriad of colorful crafting tools laid out before them.

Jayden sits on the cement porch with his nose buried in his smartphone. I like him better this way.

Miles, on the other hand, repairs our backyard fence. No doubt he's a little paranoid, but our place will be safer with secure boundaries. He's got nails, wood planks, and two new support posts. I don't think he knows what he's doing, however. He keeps glancing at some "how to" guide and hesitating on his placements. His portable radio plays soft, upbeat music, which has him bobbing along to the beat. I'm sure he'll do fine.

I walk over to my garden box and pull out my tools. No plants have sprouted. Have I done something wrong again? All I want is for *something* to go right.

"You're a little stubborn, aren't you?"

I glance up and find Ms. Timo standing in the opening to our fence, her squinted eyes locked on my garden. I sneer. "The book says the plants will grow eventually."

"So you believe whatever people tell you, so long as it's what you want to hear?"

"What do you want, old lady?" I snap.

"I want to help you," she says. Before I respond, she shuffles into the backyard and keeps her sunhat tilted forward. The afternoon sun, blocked occasionally by the clouds, warms up the backyard more than any August I've experienced before.

"Why?" I ask as she kneels on the opposite side of my garden box. "You want my terrible fresh produce?"

Ms. Timo laughs. "Hardly. I just want to participate in some gardening. Ever since the arthritis hit, I've had trouble holding the tools. I had to give it up."

"So you want to live vicariously through me."

"Isn't that what all grandmas want?"

I glance over my shoulder, making sure the others aren't paying any attention. Then I glance back. "I'll let you help—on one condition. You give me a better witness statement."

Ms. Timo's elderly face showcases her frown lines. I almost feel for her. Almost.

"I thought you got everything you needed?" she whispers.

"Yeah, well, apparently not. I'm also gonna need you to sign it."

"Can I write it down?"

"Yeah, fine," I state. "I need it soon."

"All right." Ms. Timo returns to her neutral expression as she pans her gray-blue eyes over my handiwork. "You're gonna need to dig this all up."

"What?" I ask, indignant. "Why?"

"The soil ain't ready for planting, like I told you. You're gonna need to dig this all up, and then you're gonna have to toss the dirt in with some detritus. Crumpled leaves and the like. And then you need to make deeper holes."

With a long exhale I get to work, ripping up all my effort and tossing it to the side in one massive pile. The task keeps my mind occupied, and for a moment, life is simple and easy. I like it. It feels right. And I never thought I'd be living in a house, in a suburb, working on a project with my neighbor while my significant other and his family enjoy the backyard. It's quaint and new—experiences I've never had before.

I get to my sole "Miles radish" and leave it be. Ms. Timo points to it.

"You need to pull that out too."

"No," I say. "I like that one."

"It's going to die."

"It hasn't yet."

"You're smothering it. The soil is bad. There's nowhere it can grow and no nutrients to get better."

"So?"

"So you should pull it out and plant it in a better garden box, or you should throw it away."

I touch the drooping leaves of the radish. It's lived so long through sheer tenacity. "I like it just the way it is."

Ms. Timo sighs. "I didn't peg you for someone blinded by sentimentality."

"Miles," Lacy calls out. "Is it okay for me to use a knife?"

I stop my conversation and turn to the girls. They've cleared a space to set up two small blocks of wood. What're they doing that requires a knife? Miles must think the same thing because he stops his hammering to stare at them with a furrowed brow.

"We're whittling," Shannon says as she throws her long braid over her shoulder. "My dad showed me how to do it. You take a knife and you cut *away* from your body until you make a shape. I made a bird once."

Although Miles seems uncertain, he eventually nods. "All right. Be careful."

Shannon claps once and then scoots closer to Lacy. "This is going to be awesome, you'll see. And once my mom and dad get back, I'm sure they can show us all sorts of cool tricks. My dad made a bear with a fish in its mouth. It's beautiful."

I turn back to Ms. Timo. "Remind me again—which one of us is blinded by sentimentality?"

"This is different," she replies. "Shannon is happy right now."

"Uh-huh."

Miles takes a moment to get a drink and mess with his radio. I watch as he splashes water over his face and his thick black hair, though I don't make any comments or draw attention to my staring. Ms. Timo notices, on the other hand.

"He's a good-lookin' boy," she comments.

I nod.

"He might be more comfortable working in all this heat if he weren't wearing a shirt."

I turn my attention back to her. She's staring just as hard as I was. "He's mine," I state. I guess it's only natural women would be interested in him. Still. Since when did lecherous old hags become a thing?

"Pish posh," Ms. Timo says. "Do you really think your handsome young friend would elope with a soggy old biscuit like myself? Let an old lady have her fun."

Heh. Her straightforward request strikes a chord with me. With a quick chuckle I concede her point. Miles hasn't expressed an interest in elderly women. Fine.

"Miles," I call out to him. "Give me your shirt. I need it."

He looks at me in confusion, but he complies with my demand regardless. He's always been willing to please—it's one of those traits I like about him—and he throws me his shirt without question. He sure does look good in the midafternoon sun. The grooves of his muscles are an appetizing sight.

I toss the shirt to the ground and go back to my gardening. Out of the corner of my eye I spot Miles staring, like he's bewildered by the transaction. After mulling it over, he returns to his work, flushed from embarrassment or sunlight, I don't know which.

Then he turns back around. "Uh, Ms. Timo? Would you be willing to watch Lacy and Jayden Friday night? It's my twenty-first birthday, and I expect Pierce and I will be out late."

Ms. Timo smiles and nods. "I would be happy to."

I can hear the two girls' excited whispers all the way from across the yard. I never had a sleepover as a child, but the way those two talk about it, I missed out on the most enriching experience of my life.

The news on the radio catches my interest the moment I hear words like "Noimore" and "crime rates."

"—the Noimore Police official statement is that the commotion within the New Grounds Construction Site was the result of gang infighting," the woman on the radio announces. "Deputy Chief Charleston further added that the quick response time was due, in part, to attentive citizens who contacted police after witnessing suspicious activity. Calling the police is—"

Miles switches the station to one with music.

"Was that you guys?" Jayden asks.

Everyone in the backyard stops what they're doing. After a moment, Miles returns to tapping his hammer against a half-buried nail. "What're you talking about?"

"Were you the guys who stopped that stuff in the construction yard? Wasn't that the day you were both messed up? That's why Pierce has all those bullet holes in his jacket."

I grit my teeth. Does that kid never learn? I swear he's secretly asking for me to beat his ass.

"Are you two detectives?" Shannon asks with a gasp. "I *knew* you must be working with the cops somehow!"

"I'm a student at a police academy," Miles replies, keeping his focus on his work. "And Pierce is a private investigator. We're not with the police, and we weren't at the construction site."

Shannon leaps away from the picnic table, leaving her whittling knife and woodblock with Lacy. In a few short bounds, she's by my side, her eyes wide and her energy visible in the way she shakes. "So you're the private detective on my parents' case, right? That's why you came to my house?"

"Look," I begin. "I'm not—"

"Are my mom and dad okay?" she asks. "When are they coming home?"

"Speak with your grandmother."

Ms. Timo regards me with the same deep frown as earlier. Shannon obviously doesn't like this answer. She throws her hands down in balled fists.

"I'm old enough to know," she yells.

I don't reply. Is it even my place to say? Seems like I should avoid getting involved at all costs. Ms. Timo must think the same damn thing because she clams up. Shannon switches her gaze from me to her grandmother, back to me.

"Tell me!"

"Your grandmother will tell you when she's damn good and ready," I snap, my voice louder than hers and no doubt carrying to the backyards of our surrounding neighbors.

Shannon gets misty-eyed. She turns and runs back to her house, never even bothering to confront her grandmother. Lacy gets off the table and chases after, but not before giving me a dirty look, like she's implying that this is somehow all my fault. What the hell did I do? It's Shannon's grandmother who can't handle the truth.

"I'll go talk with her," Ms. Timo says. "I'm sure she'll be fine."

"You gonna tell her everything?"

The old bag doesn't answer, which basically means *no*.

The moment me, Jayden, and Miles are alone in the backyard, Miles turns to his brother. "Hey. Don't ask us where we've been in front of Lacy. Got it?"

Jayden brings his phone back up, a weaselly little smirk etched into his face. "Heh. I knew it was you guys. I knew it."

"Got it?"

"Yeah. I'll keep it to myself."

"Good."

"YOU THINK they'll be okay?" Miles asks.

"Jayden and Lacy? Yeah. Of course."

It's not like Castor got a good look at Lacy or Jayden. Even if he was driving around our neighborhood, he wouldn't find anything he's looking for—not our car, not us. I know Miles worries, but it's not him or his siblings I'm concerned about.

Once Jeremy knows I'm alive, it'll be *me* he wants to deal with.

"How is the contact lens?"

I rub at my eye. "I'm blind, but I guess it does the trick."

"It's meant to cover an eye with cataract."

"Tsk. Perfect." I suppose, since a cataract will cloud the iris, the only way to hide it would be to blind someone, but it's weird to me that anyone would pick vanity over sight. Then again, I guess I don't have room to talk. I'm wearing it right now.

Oh, well. It's irritating and I dislike it, but I guess it's better than wearing sunglasses at all times. Miles keeps his gaze on the road as he drives deeper into Joliet. He clenches his jaw, however, and I know he isn't satisfied with the outcome.

"Maybe you should go through with a corrective surgery," he says.

"Tsk."

"Oh, uh, this is the place."

Miles parks the vehicle outside of some standard middle-class home. It's yellow, an odd color, but the same shade as all the other houses in both directions of the street, like they were all duplicated from the same photograph. I guess the designs of the houses are slightly different, but only slightly. It's pleasant enough, in a creepy way, and I hold back my commentary.

"This is Logan's house," Miles says.

"Logan?"

"He's a guy I go to the police academy with."

I groan. "*This* is where you wanted to go for your twenty-first birthday? To another suburb? Don't most kids your age want to get wasted?"

"I drink already," Miles says. "And getting wasted has never been my ideal way to pass the time."

"So what're we doing here?"

"They're having a barbecue. I figured I could introduce you to my academy friends."

Ah. Now it all makes sense. No wonder he didn't tell me where we were going beforehand. I've been avoiding his academy life like the plague—I don't trust cops. How many times do I have to tell him that?

"It'll be fun," he says.

I let out a long exhale. I've been to parties before, but I doubt this party will be anything like the mobster strip clubs and gambling houses I'm used to. Now *those* were insane parties. A good deal of drugs will make anything a form of entertainment, and there was enough sex to meet the definition of an orgy three times over.

What're we going to do here? Stand around and make small talk while we all slowly die of boredom? I guess that's the price I'll have to pay for a normal life.

"Fine," I say. "Let's get this over with."

I go to exit the car when Miles puts his hand on my leg. I stop and face him, but I have to turn my head all the way thanks to my blinded left eye. It's going to take some getting used to.

"We can go someplace else if you want to," he says. "We don't have to stay here if it'll upset you."

"It's your birthday. You decide what we do."

Miles smirks. "Well, we're already going to do what I want later tonight. I was hoping you wouldn't be in a foul mood up until then."

"Heh," I mutter. "Is that what you're worried about? Forget it. I'm not a *birthday* kinda guy."

"When is your birthday, by the way? You've never told me."

"It was last month. The eighteenth."

"Seriously?" Miles asks, a hint of anger in his tone. "And you didn't tell me?"

"I'm not into birthdays. I haven't celebrated mine since I was fifteen."

"So, you're thirty-seven now?"

"Yeah. What's it matter?"

Miles grips my pants leg. I get anxious when I'm not entirely sure what's going through his head. Is he upset? No man stops the march of time—I'm going to get older each year—and I'm not sure what he wants from me.

He takes a breath and lets out a strained exhale. "You should tell me these kinds of things. I want to know them."

"All right," I drawl. "I'll keep it in mind."

"Thank you."

We both exit the car and walk up to the solid wood door of Logan's house. The sounds of people emanate from the backyard, and I hear a steady beat of music playing from an overworked speaker. The door swings open before Miles can even knock, and the moment I see who it is, I once again get on edge.

I swear I can't escape Rhett's smug face.

CHAPTER TWELVE

"Miles," Rhett says. "It's good to see you again."

Miles smiles. "Rhett. I didn't know you'd be here."

"I didn't think I'd have time, but my schedule cleared up. Come on in. Logan is in the kitchen getting the rest of the food prepared."

The house is filled with the sweet and savory aromas only a chef can bring. I didn't think I was hungry, but now it's the only thing on my mind. The house itself is well-loved, with worn-in furniture, a million pictures covering the walls and end tables, and small toys for children tucked in the corners. The mismatched color scheme tells me the owners aren't rich—they pieced this place together when they had the funds to do so.

"Hello!" a man calls out from the kitchen. Before anyone can respond, he walks out into the living room wearing an apron that reads "Don't be afraid to take whisks."

I guess it fits, because the man is fairly hefty. He sports a handlebar mustache too, which is odd, but I've seen crazier things from druggies who think they're also hairdressers when the moon is full.

The man walks right up to me. I get nervous and tense—I don't know this asshole—but he either doesn't notice or doesn't care.

"I'm Logan," he says. "You must be a friend of Miles?"

"Yeah," I say.

"Logan," Miles interjects. "This is my boyfriend, Pierce."

Logan lifts his mini handlebar mustache eyebrows in surprise. "Oh, really! Bring it in, then! It's so good to finally meet you!"

I hold out my hand, but Logan pushes it aside.

"I'm a hugger," he declares as he wraps his arms around me in a tight embrace.

Gah—what is this fruit loop doing?—I remain stiff until he releases me, and then I take a step back and sneer. "Good to meet you." The man's embrace reminds me about the bruises left over from my fight and car accident. I should have brought some painkillers.

"There's a barbecue in the backyard," Logan says as he motions to the back door beyond the kitchen. "And I'm almost done with my home-style beans and bacon. Get out there and mingle! Everyone's been waitin' for you!"

"Thank you," Miles says.

He walks through the kitchen, and I go to follow, but Rhett holds me back. I give him a warning glance, but he maintains his hold.

"Miles," Rhett says. "We'll be out in a second."

Miles gives me a brief look before nodding. He walks to the backyard, and I hear a chorus of greetings. I guess I'm glad I missed out on that. I don't want to meet any more *huggers*.

I walk with Rhett to the front living room and wait for him to say something. He wouldn't try to provoke me in the middle of this party, would he? Seems low class for him, but I guess I don't know him that well.

He mulls over his own thoughts for a moment, and I'm forced to wait. The guy sure did dress up nice for the occasion—black slacks, a form-fitting button-up. He takes care of himself, that's for sure.

Rhett finally turns his full attention to me, a look of intensity most reserve for fighting. "Are you actually trying to dig up evidence against these traffickers?"

His question takes me by surprise. "Why?" I ask, not trusting his intentions.

"I need to know."

"What else would I be doing?" I ask, sarcasm in each syllable.

"Helping them."

I snort back a laugh. "You think I'm *helping them*?" I bet Castor wouldn't think I was helping him, that's for sure.

"You said you'd do whatever you were paid to do. And, given what I suspect about your past, I don't think it's outside the realm of possibility that you're aiding them."

I glance over my shoulder toward the kitchen. I doubt Logan can hear us, but I lower my voice anyway, hoping Rhett will take the hint. "Yeah, I do things for money. But I have standards." Even when I worked for the Vice family I wouldn't engage in scumbag behavior.

And Big Man Vice hated traffickers with a passion. We didn't do any of that shit.

"What about Shelby?"

"What about him?"

"I have reason to believe he's working with these traffickers. Lots of reasons, actually. Hard evidence."

"Bullshit."

Rhett narrows his eyes. "You know something?"

"I know Shelby's kid got murdered, and that's why the man has a vendetta the size of Illinois. I doubt he'd be helping his own kid's murderers do anything outside of finding a quick grave."

"His kid?"

"Yeah," I say. "His son got taken a few decades back. I don't know where you got your evidence, but it's questionable at best."

"It's legitimate," Rhett intones. "But maybe there's a reason for it all." He gives me a long stare before continuing. "What if I paid you to help me with this? To ask Shelby a few things and record them?"

"Can you do that?" I ask with a chuckle. "Pay me to cooperate?"

"I thought you didn't ask questions when money was involved?"

I cock an eyebrow. "How much?"

"Five hundred."

Tsk. Small-time. But I guess asking an old man about his sources isn't that risky either. "Sure," I say. "I'll talk to him."

"You have something to record him with?"

"Phones do everything these days."

Rhett reaches into his back pocket and pulls out his wallet. He plucks five hundred-dollar bills and hands the stack over. I offer him a one-sided smile and push the money back.

"You don't do this very often," I state with a hint of amusement. "Pay me after the job is done."

"Given your lengthy track record, I figured there was nothing to worry about."

I glare at the man. "I'm pretty sure the police don't have a track record for Percy Adams."

Rhett laughs and places his hands on his hips. "Look. I'm surprised you didn't skip town the moment I confronted you, I really am. But it's only a matter of time. Your new car, eye, and clothes aren't enough to hide what I already know about you. And men like you eventually slip up. Always."

"Making threats after we just struck a deal?" I ask. "You really don't do this very often, do you?"

"I'm trying to be frank. You seem like the kind of guy who appreciates facts over posturing. And I don't want you to get the impression that we're business buddies. This is a onetime occurrence."

"Fine. We done here?"

Rhett stares at the back door and then turns back to me, a pensive expression about him, like he's just thought of something interesting. "Actually, there's one other deal I'd like to strike with you."

"Oh? What's that?"

"What's your price to stay away from Miles?"

I ball my hands into fists and glower. "Fuck you." I turn to leave, but Rhett once again grabs my arm. I'm ready to throw a punch in his direction, but I grit my teeth and hold myself back as I turn to face him.

"You're gonna slip up," Rhett repeats, his voice low and threatening. "And I don't want to see Miles go down with you."

There's a burning tightness in my chest when he says all this— what I wouldn't give for a cigarette. I maintain my forced calm as I say, "Stay away from him."

I jerk my arm from his grasp and walk through the kitchen without truly seeing my surroundings. Once I'm outside, I allow myself to breathe again. I fucking hate Rhett. Nothing would make me happier than to send him over the side of a bridge.

Someone puts a hand on my shoulder, and I wheel around, ready to fight. Logan flinches back, startled.

"Sorry about that," he mutters. "I'm here to tell everyone the food is ready." He waves to the backyard. "Food is up, everyone! Come get it!"

There are at least thirty people at this get-together; a lot more than I thought would be here. They're all roughly the same age, I would guess in their midtwenties, but some, like Logan, are a little older, while others, like Miles, seem to be tweens. I give them all brief glances as they pass by and then make my way over to Miles. He's by the barbecue, chatting it up with the guy cooking, but he stops once I get close.

Miles taps the cook on the shoulder. "Lars, this is my boyfriend, Pierce."

I hate the word *boyfriend*. Every time he says it I curl my lip in disgust.

The cook turns around and gives me an odd glance. "Did you say *boyfriend*?" He quickly smiles and offers me his hand. "I, uh, didn't know you were seeing anyone. I'm Lars. Nice to meet you."

He's a small guy, practically a foot shorter than both Miles and I. With a quick nod I say, "Same here."

Lars gives me the once-over before returning his attention to the food. His brow is furrowed, like he's worried, and I wonder if I'm giving off some sort of aggressive aura. I try to relax, but it's easier said than done.

I pull out my cell phone and call Shelby.

Nothing.

I dial his number again.

Still no answer.

"You okay?" Miles asks me.

"Tell me," I drawl as I dial Shelby a third time, "is it legal for police officers to pay people to be a mole?"

"Uh, yeah. Kinda. They're called paid informants. I mean, not every officer is authorized to do that, but a police department could decide that—"

"That's all I needed to know."

Miles rubs at his neck. "What did Rhett want?"

"I'll tell you later."

When the third attempt doesn't go through, instead of dialing Shelby yet again, I decide to call the hospital. It's still within the visitation hours—the nurses should put a call through—and I wait impatiently through the ringing. When it clicks, I talk before the nurse can even get a word out.

"I need to speak to Michael Shelby."

"Who?" the nurse asks.

"Michael Shelby. In room—"

"Oh, I'm sorry," she says, cutting me off. "He was discharged several days ago."

"He's not there?" My mind goes blank for a moment, thinking back to when last I saw him. "Is he dead?"

"No, not that I'm aware of. He walked out of the hospital, spry as a fox."

I'm at a loss for words. Where is he? It's not like the nurse would know. "That's all I needed," I mutter before hanging up.

"I'm going to get us some food," Miles says. "I'll be right back."

I allow him to leave without commentary. Lars flips a few hamburgers and turns a couple hot dogs, glancing at me but never striking up a conversation. The smell of the barbecue reignites my hunger, and I focus on that rather than Shelby's disappearance. Before I mentally return to the party, I text Shelby and ask him to call.

"Hey!"

I look up and see a scrawny guy with a goatee standing before me. Lars gives him a quick nod, but the man never takes his eyes off me.

"It's nice that you have such a good relationship with your son," he says, elbowing my arm. "Not a lot of twenty-one-year-olds would take their father to their party."

Lars half spits in an attempt to stifle his laughter.

Tsk. And Miles wonders why I don't like socializing with his buddies. I roll my eyes and point to a cooler. "Hand me a beer."

The guy complies and tosses over some light brew bullshit that gets me frowning.

"I'm Julian," he says, "one of your son's classmates."

Lars's chuckles get louder.

"I'm not Miles's father," I drawl. "I'm his"—I still can't bring myself to say it—"significant other."

The statement rocks Julian. He stares at me with wide eyes and shifting eyebrows, caught between shock and confusion. I pop the top off my beer and take a swig. After the gears in his head rotate full circle, Julian cracks a smile.

"Really?" he asks. "Or are you pulling my leg?"

I don't answer.

"There's no way. Right? I mean, Miles looks like he should have a hot piece of ass at his side. Have you seen him? Any little Japanese lady would be happy to get with him, I think. Or Korean. Or whatever he said his mother was. Chinese? You would know."

Lars meets my gaze and mouths *I'm sorry*. He's red from empathic embarrassment, and I chortle to myself. Men like Julian don't bother me. Stupidity knows no restrictions, after all. I wonder how often Julian gets into fights over his unfiltered commentary. That would amuse me more than this inane conversation.

I take another swig of my disgusting beer. It's foul tasting and watered down. A shame.

"So," Julian continues, ignoring my lack of participation, "you are his father, right? That other part was a joke?"

I lift an eyebrow. "Did I stutter?"

That statement gets him quiet. Even Lars avoids looking at me. If this had happened while I worked for the Vice family, I might be worried. Some people get upset over simple bullshit or perceived insults, and when they're upset, they do all sorts of brazen things. Then you add guns and drugs to the mix, and there's a good chance people end up dead.

But this is a backyard barbecue. Any challenge to authority isn't going to end in a firefight.

"So," Julian once again continues, "you are his boyfriend? Like, he's gay? And you're gay for him? Because you don't look gay."

Lars pulls off a whole host of burgers and hot dogs as he says in a hushed tone, "Julian, *damn man,* drop it."

"I'm just curious."

I ignore their squabbling and pan my gaze over the crowd of people. Miles interacts with each individual as he walks back over to the barbecue. I hear a parade of *happy birthdays* and *you're finally all the way legal,* and Miles takes his time to acknowledge each one. He looks happy—and I know I shouldn't jeopardize that with my sour mood—so I take another swig of my beer and attempt to force a positive outlook on things.

As if the universe is conspiring against me, Rhett walks over and motions to a hot dog. He doesn't acknowledge my presence, which is for the best, but Julian takes it upon himself to correct everything.

"Hey, Rhett," Julian says. "Have you met Miles's boyfriend?" He leans in closer to the other man. "He isn't Miles's father."

"I've met Pierce," Rhett says. "He's a private detective here in town."

"Oh yeah? I guess it makes more sense now. Miles had to learn all his law from somewhere."

I hold back a laugh. Miles doesn't need me to teach him law—all I teach him is streetwise and gunplay—well, and "gunplay."

Rhett, now engaged in the conversation, turns his attention my way. "So, Pierce, why don't you tell us what school you went to for undergrad?"

"I didn't," I state, my tone curt.

"Oh yeah? Do you have any plans to attend? I know a good place if you're interested."

"No, thanks. If I'm interested, I'll find my own place."

Julian rubs at his copper-red goatee. "Rhett got his bachelor's degree at the top of his class, and he knows all kinds of things about the legal system. I bet whatever school he recommends is awesome."

Tsk. I guess some people are born to play the stooge in a relationship. Or maybe he wants to bootlick his instructor. Or, most likely, he's just a numbnut and doesn't understand the subtext to the conversation.

"Have you worked on any high-profile cases?" Rhett asks, driving us further into confrontation.

I throw back a mouthful of beer. "I haven't."

"Is that right? Well, how long have you been a PI?"

"I don't remember my start date."

"That long, huh? But no important cases. What did you do before you became a PI?"

Anger eats at my self-control. He knows I'm lying about my previous occupation. Does he want to correct me again, this time in front of everyone? Now I wish I *was* back in the Vice family compound. A firefight would handle this perfectly.

But, alas, we're in a goddamn backyard barbecue.

"I did some odd jobs," I reply after a strained moment. "That's when I met Miles. Life has been looking up since."

Rhett offers a quick smile. "That's good to hear."

Lars and Julian must finally pick up on our animosity, because they say nothing. When the silence persists, Rhett takes a bite of his hot dog and then regards Lars with a nod. "This is excellent," he says. "Best I've had outside of a baseball game."

"Of course you like it," I interject. "It's rather phallic."

From the look on his face—I wish I had been recording—he doesn't like me commenting on that *at all*. I can't help but chuckle. Lars and Julian slink away after exchanging knowing glances, leaving the barbecue unattended. I flip off the gas and grab a burger.

"What's wrong, Princess?" I ask Rhett. "You don't look so hot."

"Keep my personal life out of this," he commands, terse.

"What's that about your personal life? You want me to ask you a bunch of questions in front of other people like some sort of verbal dick-checking contest? I'll get right on that."

Miles walks up before Rhett utters another word. He has two plates of beans and chips. He hands me one, and I hand over the burger. The tension in the atmosphere doesn't wane. Miles flips his attention from me to Rhett, and back to me.

"Logan is a great cook," he says, picking the diplomatic route and ignoring the situation. "How do you like the food, Pierce?"

I take a bite of the beans. I wanted to snap back an answer, but the savory flavor of the food stops me dead in my tracks. You know what the Vice family parties lacked? Food like this. Sure, they got catering, but it lacked the magic. I don't even like baked beans—I got a scar once from opening a can of baked beans all wonky—but these are so good I might not eat anything else.

After a second mouthful, I nod. "I like it."

"Yeah, right? Logan has talent."

"Hm."

"So, how are you getting along with everyone? I saw you talking to Lars and Julian."

I finish up my fifth bite and snort. "Julian thought I was your father."

Miles half chokes on some of his beans. After he recovers, the hacking quickly turns to outright laughter. "Are you serious? Man, could you imagine if my father was actually here?"

"This party would devolve into an episode of *Cops*," I quip.

Miles and I share a round of chuckles. I guess good food really does help my spirits. Plus everything is a little better with Miles around. He's not the type of guy to get offended, even when the punch line is his own father.

Rhett glances between me and Miles, his expression neutral. "I take it your father isn't much in your life, Miles?"

"No," he replies. "But I've reconnected with my mother, and I have my brother and sister."

"What about your father?" Rhett asks me.

"Dead," I state. "Has been for some time."

"Sorry to hear that."

I shrug. It's hard to feel something when I never think of the man.

"Do you see your parents often?" Miles asks Rhett, no doubt being polite, but who really wants to talk about their old man and woman?

Rhett shakes his head. "No. They died a while back."

"DUI?" I ask.

Miles hits me in the ribs. "Pierce. We shouldn't talk about this."

"That's how my pops went. Killed himself in a car accident."

"Drive-by shooting, actually," Rhett intones. "We lived in a bad neighborhood and shared a duplex with a bunch of drug dealers, apparently."

Heh. That explains a lot. Guy really doesn't like crime, and I can see why.

"Sorry for your loss," Miles mutters.

I eat some more of my fancy beans and then lament the fact they're gone once I'm finished. I don't have much more to add to this conversation that wouldn't be callous or unnecessary. I'm not as hung up about death as most people seem to be. Who cares if my father wasted himself? I'm still drinking beer, aren't I? Or maybe I'm just a dumb fuck who hasn't learned his lesson.

My phone buzzes, and I pull it out to check the screen.

Shelby.

"I have to take this," I say to Miles. "I'll be right back."

He nods and then gives his attention to Rhett. I almost want to ignore the call and stop that from happening, but I really need to talk to Shelby. I walk a few paces away and then answer.

"Pierce?" I hear him say through the speaker.

"Yeah," I reply. "Where are you?"

"I'm in danger."

I hold my breath and wait. He says nothing. Finally, I mutter, "Okay. What're you doing about it?"

"Is anyone following you? Has anyone asked you to look for me?"

"Yeah. The cops."

"Are you helping them?"

"No."

"Then why did you call me?"

I let out a long exhale. "I need to talk to you about this case. I've discovered some weird stuff about it."

"Then meet me at Red Roof Inn," he says in a whispered voice. "Don't tell anyone, especially the cops."

"Right now?"

"Right now."

Fuck. I roll my eyes. "Fine," I say. "But this can't take long."

"Don't worry—it won't."

CHAPTER THIRTEEN

I PARK in front of the Red Roof Inn and stare at the generic cookie-cutter establishment. Better than Noimore, with its seedy businesses and shady practices, but it's still a lackluster hotel that reeks of mediocrity. I step out of my car and keep my new jacket zipped tight. I'm not a fan of this jacket—too stiff—but it's thick enough to hide a handgun.

My phone buzzes, and I glance at the screen. Miles sent me a message that reads: *if something happens, call me*. He didn't want me to go, I could see it in his eyes, but he didn't try to stop me. Probably for the best. I don't know how well I would have gotten along with his classmates anyway.

The parking lot has a few bums roaming around, but I ignore them as I walk into the lobby. To my surprise, Shelby is waiting for me, a long coat pulled tight across his large frame, the collar propped up.

He nods to me and then motions to the side door. I follow him out, and instead of going to a room, he takes me to the sidewalk and starts walking toward the outskirts of town. I get nervous—the farther from civilization, the more likely questionable things will happen—but I trust Shelby enough to give him the chance.

We pass an open field of grass lined by trees, and it's a pleasant evening sight. We continue a few blocks, into residential areas, and the quaint houses ease my anxiety. Shelby is silent, and he walks with stiff, locked legs, like he's hurting. Makes sense. He *should* be in the hospital. What little of his skin I see is paler than usual.

I wait.

Finally he says, "What have you found? Do you have any evidence yet?"

"It's been a week, old man. Sherlock Holmes wouldn't have this case solved."

"I don't have much time."

"You said you were in danger," I state, glancing over my shoulder and scanning the pleasant countryside. "What's going on? Who's on your trail? Why aren't you in the hospital?"

Shelby lowers his voice. "I've made a lot of enemies, Pierce. Davis didn't do me any favors when he got us caught. I'm running out of time."

"What's going on? Give it to me straight."

He stops. I follow suit. For a moment we regard each other. "Did the cops send you?" he asks.

"Yeah. A cop asked me to speak with you about your sources. He thinks you're helping the traffickers."

"And you're here for him?"

"Of course not. I don't trust cops. I came here because things aren't adding up. You said the cops are in on everything, but I don't see much evidence. They look busy picking up other criminal offenders. Or are you saying they're allowing it to happen?"

"That's not it."

He doesn't offer any more information. I step back, frustration eating my thoughts, but the coolness of the night relaxes me. I like the darkness. It's easier to think. Pulling my jacket close, I glance around for a second time. I can't see right with a blind eye. Anyone could be hiding in the shadows for all I know.

"The police pick up people to sell," Shelby states out of nowhere, drawing my attention back to him. "And then someone in the jails selects the right ones, and then someone else ships them out of the state for sale."

"What're you talking about?"

"Do I have to spell it out for you, Pierce? The police pick them up. Prostitutes. Druggies. And then someone in the jails sets them up. They're discharged straight into the human traffickers' hands, before they reach the street again, and then they're shipped out of town, ready for sale."

I piece all of Shelby's words together. "So who's packing them and who's shipping them?"

"I don't know," Shelby says through a forceful cough. "Some older organization has a hold on the jails. It's been around for decades, but it was chased out of Chicago and Noimore until just recently. They came back, and they're operating in full force now that they have shippers willing to run bodies for them."

I hold my breath as my thoughts drift. Those prostitutes from Noimore, Kimmy and Nash, told us all about Jeremy's new shipping operation. But when did that start?

"How long have they been back in operation?" I ask. "This older organization."

"Six months, I'd say."

The exact time Jeremy got out of custody and started his new business. I doubt that's coincidence. I exhale and shake my head. "Do you know anything about the Vice family?" I didn't think they would be involved, but Castor's recognition of my tattoo and his comment about "betraying him" makes me think they definitely are.

Shelby grabs my arm and holds me close. He seems a little unstable, maybe desperate, and I feel the shake of his body through his grip. "What do you know about the Vice family mob?" he asks.

"I think they might be the ones doing all the shipping."

This wouldn't have happened if Big Man Vice was still in charge. He never would have engaged in human trafficking. It went against his principles. But then again, Jeremy isn't his father. He barely knows how to run a proper syndicate.

"That would make sense," Shelby whispers. "The police. The Vice family. And whoever is in charge of the jails. All three of them. An evil trifecta."

Who runs the jails? With the police on their side and the Vice family mob doing their shipping, they hold all the aces. Whoever they are, they sure as fuck aren't going to like a couple of private investigators snooping around their business. Is that who's after Shelby?

"How do you know all this?" I ask.

Shelby releases his grip on me and sighs. "I worked for them before all this nonsense went down at the railway. For the deputy chief of police in Noimore. Deputy Chief Charleston. He's got his men helping at every turn—under the guise of making the streets safe, of course."

"You actually helped them?" I balk. How could he? After what happened to his son?

"Don't look at me like that," he snaps. "*What was I supposed to do?* I'm one man. I needed all the advantages I could get. Working with them allowed me to save a few kids—and to learn a lot of their secrets—but it's not enough. I have to bring them all down, you understand me? Even if I turned in the officers I have info on, the traffickers will find others.

And even if I help bring down the last of the Vice mob, the traffickers will find other means of transport."

That's a fucking slippery slope. I can't believe he turned into one of them in order to learn all about their secrets. And he doesn't even know who *exactly* is behind it all. No wonder he wants to catch them in the act—at the point they deliver the bodies to the Vice family.

"Why are you telling me all this now?" I ask. "Why didn't you tell me this earlier?"

"I didn't know it would get this bad. I didn't think I'd be on the run. And I didn't know for sure the Vice family was involved. My plan was to catch them and expose the whole thing, but now that I've been shot and they know I'm after them, the cops are going to kill me. I don't think they know you're onto them as well. I think they think you're just a lowly trainee."

"I am just a lowly trainee."

"Don't lie to me. You know more than you're letting on, and despite what the news speculates, I know it was you at the construction site. You know this life. You know what these guys are capable of. I need you to keep investigating. We can do this together."

I get tense and shake my head. No. No, this is too much. I didn't become a private investigator because I thought the world needed saving and this was how I was going to do it. No—I did this because it's the only job outside of flipping burgers that I might be good at. It's getting way too risky, and I don't want to reengage with the Vice family, not when they'll know I'm "back from the grave."

"Forget it," I state. "I'm not going any further. I'm out."

"What?" Shelby asks. "Don't forget our deal. I'm signing off on your training."

"Not anymore. I'll do it the long way."

"Are you planning on turning me over to the cops? Is that it?"

"Of course not. You can do whatever kooky plan you want, and I'm not gonna get in your way. But I don't have to stick my neck out for you either."

Shelby grunts and curses under his breath.

My first thoughts go to Miles. That's the real reason I need to stop this. Rhett is right. I can't risk Miles's future because of this. Signing off on three years' worth of experience isn't worth jeopardizing everything Miles has been working toward. I should pull out now, find some other

PI to work with, and pretend this never happened. Maybe if I stay away from Noimore, Jeremy and his goons will never find me.

It's for the best.

When Shelby has nothing else to say, I turn back toward the hotel. "I'm going," I state as I begin the short trot back to my car.

"Pierce."

I stop and wait.

"If something should happen to me…." Shelby's voice quavers. I don't glance back at him, but I can hear that he's straining to speak straight. "Can you deliver what little evidence I've gathered to the proper authorities?"

I say nothing as I mull over his comment. It'll make me a lot of enemies.

He continues, his voice raw with emotion, "I don't want to fail my boy, ya know? I've struggled so long, trying to get those men to pay…. At least, if I fail now, I want to take that eternal rest knowing some justice will be served. Knowing I can look my son in the eyes and say I never forgot him."

His earnest pleading eats at me. "Fine," I say. "If something happens— and *only* if something happens—I'll turn over your evidence."

"Thank you, Pierce. I have it in my car."

"You have it with you?" I ask, glancing over my shoulder. That's a risk I didn't think he would take.

"I got your text about people breaking into my office. It was the cops, I know it. Nothing is safe there anymore. They're looking for all the evidence I've gathered on them."

Fuck me. The cops are the ones breaking into Shelby's office? And the ones out to kill him? How do you fight people like that? Who do you even call to report it? I really don't want those kinds of enemies, but I guess I have no choice.

With a heavy sigh, I continue on my way. Hopefully I won't have to do anything with this information.

I UNLOCK the front door and enter the void of our dark living room. It's quiet. Although that's a pleasant change, I get nervous. Our house hasn't been this quiet in a while. Where are Jayden and Lacy? I shake my head. Right. They're with the neighbor. Everything is still within the realm of normal.

How long are his siblings going to be with us? Miles agreed to whole fucking month, which means at some level Jayden's mother needed thirty whole days to recover from his presence. Pretty quick. It takes me a moment to remember that they're here for the whole fucking month. Miles's mother and her boy toy are on some vacation, and Miles volunteered to care for his siblings during that time. I didn't object, but sometimes I wish I had.

But for now, I'm alone.

The realization gets me pensive, and I hate when I overthink things. I take Shelby's paperwork—a whole file of pictures, DVDs, records, and bank statements that connect key police officers to the human traffickers—and walk to my closet. Before I hide the information away, I open up the records and search for the one officer I'd love to see on the list.

Just my luck. Lieutenant Rhett Walker isn't on the list of dirty cops. He's clean.

With a sigh, I reach my closet door. There's a storage space in the floor, where I keep my other files, but I remove those, throw them on my nightstand, and tuck Shelby's information inside instead. This is better than with him? He must really be desperate.

My phone buzzes. Miles sent me a message that reads: *you don't need to pick me up, I got a ride home.* I text back, telling him I'm here already, and my throat gets tight. Something about his birthday gift has me feeling uneasy. Why? I don't know. It's stupid to feel so anxious and uncertain, but I suppose I've never worried about the long-term ramifications of sexual compatibility. Before Miles, when I got tired of a guy, or if he wanted something I wasn't willing to give, I would find a new one to fuck and think nothing of it.

And I never thought—never—what if the other guy isn't satisfied?

Jesus Christ, is that what I'm worried about? Whether or not Miles will….

I enter the bathroom and turn on the shower as I try to clear my thoughts. With awkward motions I remove my contact and rip off the bandages on my arm, careful about the multitool underneath. I huff and step into the cold water. I've got to prep if I'm going to play bitch—at least, if I'm going to do it right.

I lean against the shower stall wall and curse at myself. What's my problem? I hate the tight feeling in my chest. I never felt this way with Jeremy. Hell, I didn't feel anything at all with Jeremy. I don't know if I'd prefer that or not.

Without any haste in my actions, I clean myself. The water goes from cold, to hot, to warm, to cold again before I exit the stall. I dry myself off and hesitate when dressing—what's the point?—but opt for slacks and a wifebeater.

Refreshed and ready, I amble out to the kitchen and light up one of my last two cigarettes I have stashed away. The burn of the smoke eases my doubt. I exhale, take a seat at the table, and switch on the television, though I don't give it my full attention. I just want the noise and dim lighting.

A pair of hands slides over my shoulders and down my chest. Adrenaline rushes through my veins, getting my muscles stiff and ready for a fight, but I relax the second I realize it's Miles. He wraps his arms around me as he brings his mouth to bear on my neck.

"When did you get in?" I ask, tilting my head to the side to allow Miles more access to my flesh.

"While you were in the shower," he replies in a slow and husky tone. His tongue laps against my skin as he gently bites down.

I switch off the television and take a long drag on my cigarette. "You have fun?"

"Yeah. But all I could think about was getting home to you."

"Heh."

He chuckles while he drags his mouth up my ear. The warmth of his body and breath get my heart rate up. "*Pierce*," he whispers, gruff and forceful. "You can struggle or you can enjoy it, but either way, I'm fucking you tonight."

Heat sluices through me the moment Miles finishes his statement.

I stand, flick my cigarette into the sink, and then turn around to face him. The gloom is thick without the brightness of the television, but I don't give a shit. There's enough light to see what I want.

I grab Miles and slam him onto his back on the kitchen table, nearly shattering the thing. He gasps in surprise when I get between his legs and pin his arms above his head. With powerful need, I lean down and bite the base of his neck, enjoying the taste of him as I rip open his pants, breaking the button in the process.

He's hard—fully ready to go and straining his boxers—and tilts his head back with a soft moan. I laugh as I open his button-up shirt. "That's it?" I ask. "That's all you got?"

Miles snaps his attention to me, his brow furrowed. "What do you mean?"

"I know you enjoy taking it, but I thought you'd try a little harder to play top, especially after all your pleading."

He stares at me for a short moment while I pull up his undershirt. I like feeling his hot skin, and I can't stop myself from running my free hand down his body.

Miles gets rigid under my touch. "I thought this was your way of saying you changed your mind. That you'd rather not be—"

"You came in here talkin' like you were gonna force me," I interject with a smirk. "But by your lack of fight, I'd say *this* is what you secretly wanted all along." I get in close and run my teeth along his jawline. "If you want me to be rough, all you had to do was ask."

"Is that what this is?" he says between low and husky breaths. "One of us is going to force the other?"

"I'd say one of us already did."

I go to pull down his pants, but Miles brings his foot up, plants it on my hip, and then shoves. I stagger back a few feet as he slides off the table and straightens his clothes. The quiet shadows of our house drown in humid tension, and my skin's already dappled with sweat.

It's a good thing his siblings aren't here. I doubt this'll end quiet.

CHAPTER FOURTEEN

MILES LUNGES, much to my surprise—I didn't think he'd be *this* quick to force—and we stumble into the living room. I twist and slam him into the nearest wall, rocking the end table by the front door. He grabs the collar of my shirt and shoves me onto the couch, but I move aside when he comes close and knock him to the cushions.

The legs of the couch scratch the wood floor as the piece of furniture slides around with the force of our struggle. I attempt to get up as Miles wraps an arm around my neck and pulls back. We knock over the couch and hit the floor, which loosens Miles's grip, and I spin around enough to wrench myself free.

I get to my feet and shove Miles while he tries to stand, sending him back into the kitchen on all fours. I get up behind him and torque his arm around, forcing it up along his spine. He half cries out, but he stifles the noise. I grab a fistful of his hair and yank his head back.

"Admit this is what you wanted all along," I growl. "It's obvious you're not even trying."

Miles answers with a single dark chuckle. He jumps from his knees to his feet in one swift motion, pushing me back as he stands. I keep hold of his arm, but he's strong enough to shove me backward into the kitchen cabinets, the metal handle of one digging straight into my shoulder blade.

My momentary flare of agony is enough for him to free his arm, spin around, and grab mine. He throws me into the table through a sheer show of force, and I realize how fucking strong he's gotten over the past few months. The far leg of the table snaps after I hit, causing the thing to wobble and crash, but that doesn't stop Miles from descending upon me.

I try to stand, but the persistent ache I feel through the adrenaline rush is enough to hinder me. The fight at the construction site and the car accident both have taken their toll, preventing me from getting to my feet before Miles grabs my upper arm and manhandles me against the wall, shoving me face-first into the wallpaper.

He twists my right arm back and around in a similar move to the one I had him in, but he doesn't ease up or even take it lightly. The pain is enough to force me to whimper through clenched teeth.

"That's it?" Miles asks, mocking my tone from earlier. "That's all you got?"

I attempt to break away, but Miles's hold prevents me from getting far. Instead of keeping me pinned to the wall, he pulls me back and forces to me to the ground on my stomach. I gulp down air as Miles grabs my other arm and traps it on my lower back. Panic grips me the moment I feel the plastic zip-tie cuffs fasten around my wrists.

"Miles," I hiss. He kept a pair of cuffs on him? Has he been worried we'll run into someone on the streets? And when did I say he could—

I catch my breath as Miles runs a hand over my ass and between my legs. He stops on the bulge of my slacks, kneading me through the fabric. "You seem pretty excited, Pierce," he says between heavy breaths. "Eager?"

I close my eyes and grind my teeth. My heart beats hard, and I can't seem to quell the heat and tension in my body.

Miles stands and drags me up with him. I jerk my elbow from his grip, and he shoves me back against the wall, twisting both my arms up into excruciating positions. I let out a yell but bite back any further sounds when he doesn't continue.

"I'll fuck you on the kitchen floor if I have to," Miles mutters under his breath. "But I'd rather do this in our room. What's it going be, Pierce?"

I force myself to relax and allow Miles to push me down the hall and into our room. Despite the darkness, he shoves me onto the bed and follows close behind, never really taking his hands off me. With an urgency that betrays his lust, he undoes my slacks and tears them off. Before I can react, he pushes me face-first into the mattress and drags my hips back until I'm propped up on my knees.

Again, he runs a hand over my ass and straight around to my cock, this time stroking me with force. I'm hard and leaking precome—almost moaning with each caress—and I spread my legs to give him better access.

Miles leans over and rummages through our nightstand until I hear the click of the lube bottle we keep there. He coats my backside for only a second before forcing in a probing finger. I bite the sheets and breathe deep, the pain and pleasure of the sensation all too familiar.

Miles fumbles with his pants while he eases a single digit in and out of me, but that doesn't last long. He pulls his hand away and slides his erection along the cleft of my ass, moaning aloud from the release it brings him.

With the haste of an amateur, he aligns himself and then thrusts halfway in, desperate for satisfaction. I groan into the sheets, the sudden burning agony enough to remind me why it's important to take it slow. I don't object, though, and instead hold back my pained cries.

Shaking and panting, Miles hooks his fingers around my hips and pulls me back onto him. I relax a bit, alleviating some of the stress to my body. Miles must take it as a sign of encouragement, however, as he pulls back and thrusts again, his force and urgency building. The moment he gets fully flush in me, he growls in contentment, like the pleasure is overwhelming.

I can feel every inch of him as he rocks back and forth, the heat from his body spreading to mine until I can barely think. When I struggle to move my arms, I'm reminded of the handcuffs—that I'm restrained—and it adds a whole new level of intensity to the moment. He's going to fuck me no matter what, and there's not much I can do to stop him.

After only a few pumps, Miles loses what little control he had and digs his nails into my flesh as he thrusts hard. His harsh moans become louder the closer he gets, and I enjoy the animalistic way he forces me back onto him with each motion. The pain and pleasure both build in my gut, threatening to become agony, but not before Miles swells and reaches his breaking point.

He tenses and leans forward as he fills me with his seed. I can hear the strangled groan of gratification escape his clenched jaw when relief comes in waves.

For a moment, Miles doesn't move. Before I say anything, he leans down and reaches a hand around to play with my throbbing cock. I need release more than I realized—the moment he skates his fingers over me, I shudder.

"Admit you wanted this," he commands, his tone gruff and low.

His statement alone gets me a little closer to the edge. He takes his hand away, though, and I cave under my lust. "I wanted this," I breathe.

Miles rewards my compliance with a couple forceful strokes of his hand. It's all I need. I seize up and grit my teeth as I empty myself onto the sheets of our bed. My hot breath comes out in huffs as waves of sweet pleasure wash over my body. Miles—still in me—makes a few odd noises as I convulse around him.

I collapse onto the bed and exhale, drained. Miles withdraws and rolls over, hitting the mattress on his back.

Without the numbing effect of passion, my body reminds me that I'm still recovering. Sore in more places than one, I lie motionless. Miles curls up next to me.

"Are you okay?" he whispers.

"Yeah," I grunt. "Happy birthday."

He laughs into my shoulder. And then he gets quiet. "You're not… angry with me?"

"No."

"Would you want to do this again?"

I remain silent as I mull over his question. Finally I say, "Uncuff me."

It's dark, except for the blue glow of our digital clock, and Miles struggles to undo the zip-tie cuffs for longer than he should. Once they're off, I relax and roll over. I should probably shower, but I can't muster the energy to do so.

"We can do this again," I state.

"And you want to? I'm not making you do something you'd hate?"

"Of course not." I grab a pillow and place it under my head. "But I don't want it to be the standard." I don't know if I—or our house—could take it.

"That's fine. More than fine, really. I like it when you're the one on top."

Miles curls up next to me again. I allow the coolness of the night to take away the last of my heat before pulling up the blankets. With my other arm, I hold Miles close. The tranquil serenity is a welcome change of pace.

"What did Shelby want?" Miles asks.

"Fuck 'im," I reply. "I'm not part of his investigation any longer."

"What? Why?"

"Shelby's known all along that the cops are the ones picking up vagabonds and throwing them in jail—only to have some other organization pack them up for sale. And, to make matters worse, the Vice family mob are the guys responsible for the shipping. It's too much to handle as a little PI firm. Plus, I don't want to lead the Vice family back here. I want to avoid them at all costs."

Miles gets up on his elbows. "The cops are throwing low-level criminals to the traffickers for sale?"

"Yeah."

"What about Roslyn?"

I turn and give Miles a sideways glance. "Who the fuck is Roslyn?"

He chuckles. "The girl that Kimmy asked us to look for. The one who went to jail, remember?"

Oh, yeah. Kimmy's hooker friend. I had almost forgotten we said we'd speak to her in the jail. But what does it matter now? "It's no longer my concern."

Miles kisses my shoulder. "Is that what you really think?"

I give him another odd glance. "What's that supposed to mean?"

"I mean, what's the harm of going to the jail and asking to speak to her? Maybe we can save her from being packed up like the rest."

His statement is true, and I let out a long exhale. "The more we dig around this, the more likely we'll see someone coming to look for me."

"Is that the only thing you're worried about?"

"I'm worried about *you*. There's no reason for you to get mixed into all this. I'll go to the jail myself, if need be."

Miles shakes his head. "No. We should go together."

"Remember how you kept saying we could get thrown out of our respective careers for getting caught in questionable activities? Take your own damn advice."

"I said that to dissuade you from acting rash," Miles states, his tone heated, "not because I didn't agree with our objective. I think we should help that girl. I think we should continue investigating."

Miles is a better person than I am. He gives a lot for other people, and maybe I should take his example, but I'm always afraid of the worst. Especially now that I have something I'd hate to lose.

"We'll go to the jailhouse," I drawl. "But we aren't going to any more of Shelby's drop sites. We're not going to risk that much."

"All right. That's a fair compromise."

Miles pulls me closer and presses his mouth against mine. Normally it's a quick thing, but tonight he takes his time, running his tongue against my lip and deeper along my own. He tastes of excitement and salt. It's a good feeling, and I close my eyes to enjoy it.

When he breaks away, I almost pull him back.

"Thank you," he whispers.

"Don't."

"It's not just for the birthday thing. I feel like… you always have my interests at heart, Pierce."

"I've got your back."

He half laughs as he grazes my jawline with his fingers. "And I yours."

THE KNOCKING on the front door jars me awake.

I sit up, glance around the room, and stare at the wall for thirty seconds like a useless lump of jelly. Another round of knocking gets me to my feet. What time is it? The digital clock says 10:00 a.m., but it's a lying sack of shit. There's no way it's ten in the goddamn morning.

Miles is sound asleep on the bed, his head covered in a pile of blankets. How can he sleep like that?

Another round of knocking.

I huff and rub at my face, well aware I'm not decent. My wifebeater is crusty with dried bodily fluid, and I remind myself I should shower. Since I don't have time, I rip it off, toss it to the floor, and then pull on a pair of sweatpants. My body is sore, but I push through the stiffness of my muscles. Groggy and barely functioning, I shamble out to the living room and answer the front door.

Ms. Timo, Jayden, Shannon, and Lacy stand before me, their shocked and wide-eyed faces greeting me rather than words.

"What happened?" Shannon asks, breaking the daze over the group.

I give myself the once-over and chuckle. Without a shirt it's plain as day to see the many scars, bruises, and scrapes I carry all over my body. Especially after my recent fights. And last night.

"I was in a car accident," I drone. "That's why we have a new car."

"Oh, right," Shannon mutters, her eyes fixated on some of my oldest scars. Those aren't from a car accident, that's for sure.

Lacy also stares, but her eyes are set more on my tattoo. I'd cover it, but I'm not worried about the other three knowing what it means. Instead of drawing attention to the thing, I ignore Lacy's interest.

"I need to go to the grocery store," Ms. Timo says, a chipper tone to her voice. "I was hoping you could take back the children. Will that be okay? I don't mean to impose."

Unlike the others, who regard me with a shocked curiosity, like they've never truly seen me before, Ms. Timo stares and grows a slight shade of pink. The lecherous old woman gets me smiling. At least she knows what she likes.

"Get in," I tell the kids as I step aside. They all comply with my command. I nod to Ms. Timo. "Thanks for watching them."

"Any time."

I shut the door and turn around to find all three of the kids more surprised than when I answered the door. Jayden gives me an incredulous stare, like I've done him some personal wrong.

"What happened here?" he asks.

Both Shannon and Lacy wait for an answer.

I pan my gaze over the kitchen and living room, taking in the flipped-over couch, broken table, and open kitchen cabinets. The place looks like a hurricane rocked the inside.

"A robber broke in," I say, part of me not even realizing the contents of my speech as I fabricate a quick lie. I doubt Miles wants me telling the kids about our sexual escapades.

"Really?" Lacy asks with a gasp. "What happened?"

I shrug and answer in a disinterested tone, "I kicked his ass. End of story."

Shannon plays with her long braid. "Was he a big guy?"

"Sure. Yeah. A few inches taller than me. A real bruiser."

"Did he show up to kill you?" Jayden asks.

I almost want to throttle the guy. He can't piece this together? He's seventeen, for fuck's sake. I'm lying to spare the girls an early conversation about lust and overzealous aggression, not him.

With a roll of my eyes I reply, "No, he was a robber. He came to rob things. I stopped him. It's all good. Go back to doing whatever you were doing."

"So you can fight guys?" Shannon asks, her enthusiasm growing with each moment. "You look like you fought a lot of guys! Have you arrested a ton of people too?"

Lacy swishes her hair and turns away. "I think you should put on a shirt. It's too late in the day to be dressed like you are."

Well, then, the prissy princess has spoken. I hold back all sarcastic commentary as I step past them and head to the bathroom. I hear the shower running and know Miles is up and awake.

While I search my closet for suitable clothing that won't offend Lacy, I spot Jayden hovering around the door to my room. I stop what I'm doing and glower at the kid, irritated he would darken my mood with his presence.

"Hey," he mutters. "Someone really *didn't* come to kill you, right? We're still safe here?"

Eh. Why am I always dealing with this simpleton? "No one broke in last night," I reply, curt. "Your brother and I got out of hand *celebrating*."

It takes the rusty cogs of his mind a minute to comprehend what I've told him. "Are you serious?" Jayden finally says. "All this was from you guys…?"

"Yeah. Now get out of my face."

Miles exits the bathroom, a towel around his waist, and gives his brother an odd look. "Jayden? Is everything okay?"

Even I can see the marks from last night, and I have a bum eye. Miles has a few bruises, his neck still sports the rawness of my bite, and he moves as though he's sore. Jayden takes it all in like he's watching a horror movie—he recoils and frowns.

"Why do you let him do this?" Jayden asks, almost at his normal volume. "Are you sick in the head or something?"

Miles sighs. "It's none of your business. We're perfectly fine."

"You kept telling me I had to get my life together, but you're doing all this? It's a little hypocritical."

"Don't talk to me about being *hypocritical*, Jayden," Miles snaps. "I said everything is fine, and I mean it."

The definitive, almost harsh tone gets Jayden to shut up. He offers Miles a single nod before walking down the hallway, leaving me alone with his brother. There's a piece of me that doesn't like the fact Jayden thinks our relationship is violent and abusive, but another piece of me doesn't want to explain it all either. Why won't he believe his brother?

"When are we going to the jailhouse?" Miles asks.

"As soon as Ms. Timo gets back from the grocery store."

CHAPTER FIFTEEN

THE NOIMORE City Adult Detention Facility is the municipality's primary jailhouse. The tan cement building—two stories in height—has the air of government bureaucracy. It looks like a place where taxpayer money comes to die. Big. Bloated. Overly fancy landscaping. I'm not a fan.

Then again, as a former career criminal, I may be biased.

Miles saunters up next to me after exiting our car. He glances around the deluxe parking lot, takes note of the many police cars, and then cocks an eyebrow. "You really think people are kidnapped from here and sold in human markets?"

"Seems like the perfect place to do it," I drawl.

"There are so many officers."

"Yeah, but they're not a fan of criminals. Have you seen how overcrowded these places are? I'm sure the jailors love the fact people are disappearing. And the people are already conveniently rounded up into one location."

Miles and I walk up to the front doors of the building and enter the cold lobby. Plastic chairs attached to the floor fill the waiting area, and two slobs mill around the vending machine, no doubt ready to ask people for money. I walk up to the front desk and nod to the lady sitting behind the counter.

"I'm Percy Adams, with the Michael Shelby Private Investigator Agency," I state as I flash my trainee badge. "I'm here to see…." I turn to Miles.

He holds up his phone and reads, "Roslyn Applegate."

The correction officer types into her computer. I lean over and catch a glimpse of the screen. It's a list of inmates a mile long, all sorted in alphabetical order. The lady scans the "A" section and then does so a second time.

"Roslyn Applegate was discharged a month ago," the officer replies. "She's no longer here."

"Do you know who visited her last?" I ask. "Or who came to pick her up when she was discharged?"

"That kind of information is confidential."

"All right, give us a second. We might need to speak to someone else."

The lady regards me with a disinterested nod, and I walk back toward the front door with Miles in tow. I stop and turn to him, mindful to keep my voice low.

"I need to look at her computer," I say.

Miles crosses his arms over his chest. "Why?"

"All the information about the inmates is there. I need to look at the visitor list."

"Don't you remember what I said about illegally gathered information?"

"We aren't looking to take this to court, are we? We're here to save a girl from the cops. Now isn't the time to be worried about criminal procedure."

Miles gets pink in the face and looks away. "R-right. You're right. We're not here as investigators." He rubs at his chin and stares at the front door of the building, his gaze unfocused but his eyes alight with deep thought. Finally he continues with "I'll cause a distraction. You mess with the computer."

"All right."

I don't ask him his plan—I'm sure he's smart enough to concoct something without my help—but I do worry about him. I'd hate to have to bail him out of jail for disorderly conduct or some shit.

Miles walks over to the vending machine and engages the two loitering schmoes in conversation. People wait at the jailhouse all the time. Boyfriends. Girlfriends. Gang buddies. Family members. All sorts of people have nothing better to do than wait for someone to be discharged. I suppose it's for the best—I bet the people with loved ones waiting aren't the target of our human traffickers.

I bide my time, glancing through my phone. I know these things play games, but all I can find is solitaire.

One angry grunt later and my attention is back on Miles. The two men by the vending machine are in some sort of scuffle. They grab at each other's shirts in an attempt to fight, though it's clear they're both incompetent. I've seen schoolyard children with better grace and moxie than these two fools.

The woman behind the counter stands and shouts, "Hey! Stop that!"

The two men ignore her. One punches the other—a weak strike to the chest—and then they grapple close and attempt to go to the ground. I chuckle at the sight.

Things get real when they hit the floor, however. One man gets on top of the other and starts punching down, adding gravity to his blows and aiming for the face. The corrections officer gets out of her chair, pulls her Taser, and then rushes over to the vending machines.

Ah. I see my chance and take it. While she's distracted, I move over to the counter and click through her computer, searching the list at a fast pace. Instead of taking my time to read the information, I open the camera on my phone and take a picture. Once I have Applegate's file, I glance over my shoulder.

They're still busy.

I go to the next inmate, and then the next, taking pictures of their visitation history and status. I'm sure taking a picture of a computer screen doesn't make for a fantastic photo, but I don't need to win any awards—all I need is to read the damn information.

I stop when I hit the "M" section of the list, my gaze honing in on one name in particular.

McMillian.

Shannon's father.

I back away from the computer and stare at my phone as the corrections officer finally puts an end to the fighting by physically breaking it up. Miles jumps to my side, not involved in the conflict, and smiles to me.

"What was that all about?" I whisper.

"I paid them to fight," Miles replies with a nervous laugh. "Not the cleverest plan, but it worked."

I chortle to myself and shrug. "Better than nothing, I guess."

"Yeah, but at the rate we're spending money, we're definitely going to need jobs after this."

A small piece of me laughs. We still have plenty of money. My money, really. I can take a bit of solace knowing that I provide for Miles in some way. And by "provide," I apparently mean so he can pay two men to fight each other as a form of distraction.

The two men are thrown from the jailhouse, and I watch them go with a smile. They don't look disgruntled or irritated, and I'm sure that confuses the corrections officer, but that doesn't matter now. I return to the counter.

"You okay?" I ask her.

The corrections officer nods as she tucks away her Taser. She seems like a tough broad, and when she gives me an *I can handle myself* look, I believe her.

"I need to speak to McMillian," I say. "Is he still here, or was he discharged as well?"

She takes a seat and types at her computer. "Yeah," she replies. "He's here. One moment." Using the radio mounted to her shirt, she calls up for McMillian and then motions me back to the personnel door.

Normally visitors have to walk through a metal detector, but cops, detectives, PIs, and attorneys get to walk in without the hassle. It's nice, because I don't want to part with any of my weapons, but I'm acutely aware that anyone else we meet will also have their tools.

"He'll be in room 2B," the officer says. "Walk straight down the hall until you reach it."

Miles and I are buzzed in through the electronic door and enter a massive hallway devoid of windows. The cheerless gray walls, stagnant air, and narrow space add together to create an anxiety-inducing atmosphere. I hate this place. I've only been here for thirty seconds, and all I can think about is leaving.

"What's wrong?" Miles mutters under his breath as we walk down the hall.

"Nothing," I reply, my gaze locked onto the corrections officers who walk past.

"Why are we talking to this guy? That wasn't part of the plan."

"I'm already regretting it, but I wanted to speak with him."

"Who is he?"

"Shannon's father."

The information gets Miles quiet. For the rest of the walk, neither of us says a word.

Room 2B is nothing special. It's a heavy metal door with a small viewing window, exactly the same as the twenty doors we passed in order to get to it. A corrections officer opens the door as Miles and I get near, and he motions us in with a jerk of his head.

I enter to find a single circular table and four flimsy plastic chairs in an otherwise drab room. Sitting in one chair, in the farthest corner, is some sad sack with heavy rings under his eyes, wearing the jail uniform—tan scrubs. He sits with a pronounced slouch and doesn't bother to straighten himself when I draw near.

There's a one-way mirror on the opposite side of the room, but I ignore it. I doubt anyone is going to spy on this riveting conversation between a PI and some asshole who shot his wife.

Once the door shuts, I clear my throat.

"McMillian?" I ask.

The man nods. He has Shannon's unruly brown hair, but his is drenched in a week's worth of unwashed natural oil.

"I'm a private investigator with the Michael Shelby Private Investigator Agency."

He glances up, a hint of confusion in his features. "I spoke to my attorney," he mutters. "I'm going to plead guilty. What're you even investigating?"

"I just need to ask you a few questions."

Again, he nods. Not much fight in the guy as he returns to his slouch, his attention square on the table in front of him.

"Anyone come to visit you in here lately?" I ask.

"Visit me?" McMillian narrows his eyes. "Yeah."

"Who?"

"My attorney. Some family. Why?"

Although I should probably focus all my efforts on figuring out these traffickers, I've become curious. "Have you seen your daughter?"

"Shannon?" No change in his voice. He's just as melancholy as when I entered. "No."

"You planning on telling her what happened?"

He shrugs. "I hadn't thought about it."

I give Miles a sideways glance. He returns the look with one of bewilderment. I guess Miles hasn't had to deal with many people who are on the verge of suicidal, but they always have similar tells. Not thinking about the future is one of them.

"Don't be a complete piece of shit," I say. "At least think about *her* before you do anything else you'll regret."

McMillian jerks his gaze up to meet mine, a flare of hate and life that wasn't present before. Miles steps in front of me and interjects with

"What Pierce is trying to say is—Shannon asks about you all the time! Maybe you should talk to her."

"What're you saying?" McMillian snaps. "You spoke with Shannon?"

"Yes," Miles continues, cutting me off before I can say anything. "She asked if you were okay and when she'll be able to see you again."

"She said that?" McMillian whispers, his face twisted as he looks away from me and returns to staring at the table.

"Maybe you could call her. I think she wants to hear from you more than anything else."

"I… don't know what I would say."

"Say you've been thinking about her. Say that you want to be a good father."

"No kid wants to hear from their jailbird father."

"I did," Miles states, an earnest conviction in his voice. It takes me by surprise. His father—what little I saw of him—is garbage.

When McMillian remains quiet, Miles continues, "My dad went to jail a few times when I was younger. I wanted to hear from him. I wanted to think he thought of me from time to time. Even if he was in jail."

Eh. Kids. They're like a dog that loves their abusive owners no matter what. I guess kids eventually grow up into resentful adults, unlike animals, but still. It's sad sometimes to see loving devotion poured onto someone who doesn't deserve it. Miles's father sure as fuck didn't deserve a kid who wanted to hear from him.

"All right," McMillian mutters. "I'll call when I get the chance."

Miles relaxes a bit and nods. "I think that's for the best."

For the first time since we entered the room, McMillian straightens his posture and holds his head up, like he finally has something to look forward to. I nudge Miles. There's nothing left for us here, and I don't even know what questions I could ask to point us in a new direction. I doubt McMillian is on the target list for people to sell, and it's not like he's getting out anytime soon.

"Thanks for your time," I say to the guy as I exit the room. The corrections officer enters after to take McMillian back to his cell.

"So Roslyn isn't here and we don't know who took her?" Miles asks as we make the long walk back to the lobby.

"We have information to sift through," I say. "And that's what we'll do."

"SO ANY of these attorneys could be the connection we're looking for?" Miles asks.

I took twenty-three pictures, which seems like a small number when I think about it, but when printed out and spread across our bed, it makes for a huge mess. Miles examines each list of visitors on all the inmates I managed to get info on.

There are a lot of visitors. More than I thought anyone in jail would receive.

A lot of attorneys. A lot of detectives. A lot of PIs.

Someone here isn't an innocent party. How are we supposed to narrow it down? I can see now why Shelby had a hard time.

"Maybe a law firm is behind it," I drawl.

"Well, there are way too many law firms represented here...." Miles pushes a few papers around. "Do you think we'll find Roslyn?"

"Not if she disappeared a month ago."

"Really?"

"That's a long time to not hear from somebody."

Miles gets quiet. I don't know why he keeps thinking about her, but it's obvious to me he's been worried about the girl since we spoke to Kimmy and Nash in Noimore. Then again, he's a good guy. Good guys concern themselves with the safety of others.

"Can you check on Jayden, Lacy, and Shannon?" Miles asks, his gaze fixed to the pictures. "They should be heading to bed soon."

I glance over at the clock. 10:00 p.m. Fuck. That's later than I thought.

With a strong exhale, I exit our bedroom and wander to the guest room. Jayden sits, alone, on one of the twin beds. He's watching something on a little tablet, and I leave him be. He's almost a grown-ass adult—he can make his own decisions.

Lacy and Shannon, on the other hand, are glued at the hip and practically living in that tent outside. I suppose I would too, if I were a preteen girl forced to share a room with Jayden. Hell, I might do it now, as a grown man.

I slide open the back door and catch the girls talking.

"—and then that's when I scuffed up my knee," Shannon says.

"I broke my arm once," Lacy replies. "When I fell off the monkey bars at school."

"Hey, do you like going to school? Is it fun? I haven't been in over a year. I miss it."

"Of course. I have friends, and clubs, and excellent teachers."

"Must be nice."

"Why aren't you in school?" Lacy asks.

I walk up to the tent—my socks making little noise across the cement of the patio—and neither girl stops their conversation. Do they even know I'm here? I doubt it.

Shannon sighs. "My grandmother can't drive me."

"You could take the bus."

"She thinks the other kids will bully me because my parents are in jail."

The silence that follows stills my voice. A piece of me wants to know how Lacy will respond. She's so prim and proper—I wouldn't be surprised to hear her mock the other girl right now.

"If I tell you something, will you keep it a secret?" Lacy murmurs, so quiet I almost miss it.

"Yeah, of course."

"My father went to jail. More than once." There's a pause, but Lacy continues, "Some people made fun of me for it, but not much. If you want, we could pretend to be cousins, and I'll tell people your parents are fine. They don't have to know. It's none of their business anyway."

"Really? But…." Shannon fixes her breathing and clears her throat. "But you don't think I'm a bad person?"

"Never. It's not your fault they went to jail."

I step away from the tent, confused and uncertain. That's not where I thought that conversation would go. Instead of revealing my presence, I return to the house and shut the back door. I don't mind if the girls stay up. It sounds like they should keep talking.

And for the second time in one day, I'm reminded of Miles's terrible father. I'm surprised Lacy brought it up, especially when she sounded embarrassed by the fact. Perhaps she's more like Miles than I thought—maybe I give her too much of a hard time. I respect her more for helping Shannon cope.

I enter the bedroom to find Miles poring over the pictures. He's written out his own list and keeps referring to it as he works. He doesn't even acknowledge my presence as I amble over to the opposite side of the bed.

"Shannon thinks she's a bad person because her parents are in jail," I say aloud, confident the girls outside can't hear me if I use a normal tone. "That's an odd thought."

"Not so odd," Miles answers in an absentminded manner.

"Why do you say that? She's not the one sitting behind bars."

"Maybe it's genetic."

"What's that supposed to mean?"

"I mean, the apple never falls far from the tree, right?"

I force out a single laugh. "You don't think that."

Miles stops what he's doing and gives me his full attention. For a moment he says nothing, and I stare into his dark eyes to see a world of emotion I didn't know I was touching upon.

"You honestly think you're like your father?" I ask him, trying to hold back the sarcastic laugh. Miles is ten times the man anyone in his family is. How could he possibly doubt? If anyone should be doubting, it should be me—the one with a hard record.

"I don't know," Miles mutters, breaking eye contact with me and staring at the floor. "But sometimes I think I'm… I don't know. I mean, even after everything you told me about Jeremy, I still…. Well, I enjoyed it, but that's the part that worries me. I felt like I hurt you, at some level, and I liked it. Maybe that's the piece of me I got from my father, ya know?"

What is he even talking about? Is he referring to the other night, on his birthday? He's worried that he's treating me like Jeremy and that playing the top is somehow him enjoying hurting others? What kind of bullshit logic is this?

"You're nothing like your father," I state. "Don't worry about it."

"I don't think it's that easy."

I wave away the comment. "Well *I* think it is that easy," I say, my voice heated. "So if you have to listen to someone, listen to me. I've seen a lot of evil men in my time. You're not one of them. End of story. No need to doubt."

Miles returns his gaze to mine with a one-sided smile. "You sound confident."

"Who're you gonna believe? Your own self-doubting demons, or a guy who knows sadists when he sees them?"

Miles chuckles. "All right. Next time I'll come to you when I start doubting."

"Tsk."

"But I think I found something. Take a look."

I walk around the bed and stand next to him. He's compiled a list of all the people who visited each inmate. Two names are circled, but he's crossed one of them out. Miles points to the remaining name—Jorge Rosario.

"An attorney?" I ask.

"No. I looked him up. He works for Worldwide Decurion. They're a criminal analysis firm."

"What the fuck is that?"

"An organization that collects crime statistics and data. They go into jails, prisons, police stations, sheriff's offices, courtrooms—all manner of criminal sites—and gather up information. How many crimes were committed, what races the victims were, where the crimes took place. Stuff like that."

I give Miles a questioning glance. "You think a number-crunching business is behind this?"

He shrugs. "This guy visited everyone, and it's not out of the ordinary for him to do so. Even Roslyn. If he's there to ask questions—like about the families and financial status of the inmates—it seems like he would be figuring out everything he needed to know about his potential victim."

Miles throws down his list. "Besides, weren't you the one who said they go after people with no one to come looking for them? Seems to me they would be the group to figure that out."

"So we should look up information on Worldwide Decurion?" I ask.

"I think that's our best bet."

But do I even want to do that? We're too late to save Roslyn. What's the point?

"Let's keep going with this," Miles says. He must know exactly what I'm thinking, because there's an edge to his voice, like he really wants to continue. "There's no harm in looking up public information. And maybe we can tell Rhett about it at the Blue Shield Gala."

Eh. I forgot about that stupid gala. And I'm not keen on the idea of talking to Rhett, but he wasn't on Shelby's list of crooked cops, so I guess it'll be safe.

I roll my eyes. "Fine. But we're not going anywhere to investigate. Got it?"

"Yeah, of course. We'll research everything from the safety of our own home."

CHAPTER SIXTEEN

"Aren't you worried about your vegetables?" Shannon asks, staring out the glass of the back door and pointing to my garden box. The rain hammers down on it relentlessly.

I straighten my tie and shrug. "If the damn plants can't handle a little water, maybe they don't deserve to live."

"That's mean."

"I didn't plant vegetables to coddle them."

Shannon places both her hands on the glass and gaze glued to the darkness of the storm. "No wonder all your gardens die. You're callous."

Yeah, just what I needed—to be judged by a prepubescent girl.

Miles walks out of the back with Jayden and Lacy in tow. I take a moment to stare as he finishes buttoning his shirt. I've always liked him in a suit, but it doesn't fit quite right anymore, thanks to Miles's improved physique. The thing is too tight, but not so taut that he can't wear it. As long as he stands relaxed, it hugs his body just right.

"You guys aren't going to leave us overnight again, are you?" Jayden asks, the whine in his tone an overload of insufferable. "I'm not a fan of old-lady smell."

"Hey," Shannon snaps. "Grammy doesn't smell that bad."

"It's not like you're denying she smells, though."

Lacy raises a hand and quiets both her friend and brother. "It's rude to talk about people like that. Ms. Timo is nice to let us stay with her, so we should at least be thankful."

Miles fastens a black tie around his neck. "Thank you, Lacy. I appreciate that."

She holds her head up and nods, self-congratulatory in her smug smile. Still—she's the only one with an understanding of the situation. Jayden's comprehension of the universe seems limited to his own self-absorbed bubble. I've known psychopaths with a firmer grip on reality.

"She has terrible food," Jayden mutters once Miles is in the kitchen.

I turn to Lacy and motion her over. She walks up, her lips pursed and her brow furrowed. I'd guess she's confused, but I think it borders on irritation. "Here," I say, handing her a hundred from my wallet. "Save Ms. Timo the hassle and get whatever you kids want."

She takes the bill with both hands. "You want me to handle it?"

"You're the one I trust the most to get the job done."

The one sentence transforms Lacy's whole demeanor. She snaps her gaze to mine, her eyes wide. "Really?" My unabashed approval must go to her head, because she pockets the cash and swishes her long black hair over her shoulder with a flick of her hand. "Well, I am the responsible one. I'll make sure it's done, and I'll keep the receipts."

I turn away and smirk, content in my decision. I really did misjudge Lacy. She's a little more stiff and stern than Miles, but they're definitely related. They want to do right by the people around them, which is a quality I've only recently come to know. Most guys I've associated with wanted to *get the job done* or *get as much as possible without much effort*, damn the consequences. I'd say Jayden fits into that boat. I'd say *I* fit into that boat.

Sometimes I wonder why Miles and I get along as well as we do.

"So," Jayden says, panning his gaze from my shoes to my head. "Now that you're a jobless bum, I take it you're Miles's trophy wife? I don't think he's going to impress anyone with *you* by his side."

I stop myself from punching the guy, but my muscles tense from frustration. Then again, there's a terrible seed of truth to the words that haunts me. It chills my anger.

Lacy rolls her eyes with dramatic flair. "Why are you always so rude, Jayden?"

"I think you look nice tonight," Shannon says to me. "Your eye isn't even gross-looking."

Before I can respond to any of them, Miles pulls on his dark gray blazer and motions to the front door. "Ready?" he says to me.

I nod and grab my own jacket off the kitchen table, lamenting the fact I don't have my shoulder holster or handgun. We head to the front door, and the kids follow us out. The rain and wind greet us with open arms, forcing Lacy, Shannon, and Jayden to rush across the yard to Ms. Timo's without a second's delay. Miles and I jog over to the car.

"Can you drive?" he asks.

I take the driver's seat and slam the door once I'm situated. Miles tosses me the keys as he takes his seat. We're both half-soaked from the brief moment it took us to reach the vehicle. I don't care, but it ruins any sophistication I once had.

It isn't late, but the clouds and chill make it feel like the midnight hour. I drive through the suburban streets and deeper into Joliet, taking the back roads to avoid the hesitant motorists who can't handle the weather. The Blue Shield Gala is in Noimore, a fair distance away, but I'm certain I'll make it there in time.

With the radio silent, I allow my thoughts to wander, directionless. For whatever reason, I think of my useless garden. Well, not the garden, but the tenacious radish. I'm half tempted to call Ms. Timo and ask her to look after the thing.

But then I remember I'm thinking about a radish and how fucking stupid it is to be worried about it. I'm at a weird point in my life. I don't like it.

I don't want to think of my failings.

I glance over at Miles. He's buried in the glow of his phone and reading like a madman.

"Talk to me," I demand.

Miles tears himself away from his device and stares at me for a long moment. "Uh, well, Worldwide Decurion was founded in the 1950s. They do criminal analysis work for over fifty different countries."

Ah. That's what he's been reading. That's what he's been reading for the past week, actually. He can't stop himself from looking into this, even after I told him I've lost my drive. Ever since I spoke with Shelby.

"Their headquarters for this region wasn't in operation for the last twenty years," Miles continues, regardless of my lack of participation. "They only recently opened it back up, and it seems they're focused on major metropolitan areas with high crime rates, like Chicago and Noimore."

"Hm."

Miles laughs, and in a voice that betrays his barely restrained enthusiasm, says, "Which makes sense, if you think about it. If their goal is to sell low-level criminals off to body purchasers, these kinds of cities have an abundance of them. *And* there aren't many criminal advocacy groups, meaning most people aren't concerned with their disappearance—a lot of people even celebrate it—and fellow criminals are less likely to turn to the police for help, given their history."

"You sound excited about this."

"I think they *have* to be the middleman we're looking for. I'm certain of it."

"Speculation isn't evidence."

"Yeah, but given what they do, they most likely give reports to their men on the streets. Ya know, files about the victims they're supposed to pick up. I know Shelby told you he wanted physical proof of the people doing the drop-offs, but I think the real evidence is in the paperwork, so to speak. Maybe all we need to find is a guy willing to talk and show us everything."

"We're not doing any of that," I state.

Miles rubs at his neck. "Why not?"

"I told you. It's not worth the risk. We're just two guys. That's not enough."

"Shelby thought one guy could get enough evidence to attract the attention of the authorities. I think he had the right idea. We don't have to personally kill everyone in a criminal syndicate."

"I'm not a PI, and you're not a PI," I snap, gripping the steering wheel hard enough to strain my knuckles. "You're in a police academy. Focus on that."

"Pierce?" he asks, his tone one of confusion. "What's wrong?"

What does he mean, *what's wrong*? It's obvious we can't handle this—not while staying inside the law and doing everything else we need to do in life. Shelby gave up everything, basically, and he's being hunted by the cops, fearing death around every corner. Miles doesn't need that kind of life. And it's my fault he's even getting near it.

"We shouldn't be dealing with this," I say.

"But people are in danger and—"

"I don't care," I interject. "All right? Fucking drop it. I'm not in the mood."

The silence grows sour. Miles remains quiet, however, and returns to his phone.

Perhaps this is for the best. I don't want to discuss this, and I don't have anything substantial to replace it with. What am I even going to do in the future? Shelby was the only one who took me on as a PI. Maybe I'll just have to wait until we move out of this wretched area.

"Hey," Miles says, drawing my attention back to him. "I've been meaning to ask you to lighten up on Jayden."

"Why?"

"You're harsh on him. Does he really need that?"

"He held a gun to my head," I intone, "and threw a couple cheap shots to my face when I was tied down. I'd say we aren't yet even."

"That was a while ago," Miles replies with a single nervous laugh.

"It's been less than a year."

"Well, he was also high, and not himself. He wouldn't do that now."

"Tell me, does *being high* work as a defense in the courts?" I ask, my unrestrained sarcasm thick on every syllable. In my best mock-Jayden performance, I continue, "*I'm sorry, Your Honor. I didn't know what I was doing because I was high as fuck. Don't be mad at me, be mad at wasted-me!*"

"Your aggression isn't helping him, though. He's still a kid."

"Is this my punishment for not talking about Worldwide Decurion? A discussion on how I should behave around Jayden?"

"I want him to get better," Miles says with a hint of anger. "You're not helping. Can you at least try? It would mean a lot to me."

His terse tone says more than his words. I bite back the remainder of my comments and force an exhale. God, I want a cigarette. Why did I have to smoke them all? Hopefully they'll have drinks at this event. Anything to dull reality.

Again, the cab of our vehicle returns to silence. The soft beat of rain and the occasional passing car become a blanket of white noise that eases me back into my thoughts. This is supposed to be some sort of special event for law enforcement officials—one where Miles earned admittance through sheer study and hard work, an honor, really—yet here I am, destroying his mood with my mere presence.

I'm such a jackass.

Disgusted with my own attitude, I attempt to blank my mind and focus solely on driving. I swerve at the last minute when I spot a pothole, causing Miles to give me a sideways glance, but it's not my fault half my vision is obstructed with a contact lens. It seems that no matter what I narrow my attention on, I don't have a grasp on myself.

Time flies when my thoughts are a void. Before I know it, I'm at the border of Noimore, staring at the miserable city from the outskirts. It doesn't take long to cross the threshold.

The streets of Noimore, busy and bustling at all times in the evening, become impossible to pass once we near the Grand Noimore

Waterfront Hotel. The spotlights, shining despite the rain, move back and forth, attracting attention for the world to see. Banners hung on the street posts read: A SALUTE TO ILLINOIS'S FINEST.

Technically, I could have some valet chump park our car, but I dislike the idea of handing over my keys to anyone who isn't in my direct circle of associates. Instead I turn down a narrow road, looking for a spot to park that isn't taken.

"We're going to walk through the rain?" Miles asks.

I can't believe it's still raining. Then again, it gets wet this time of year. "You want me to drop you off? I'll find a place to park."

"Sure."

I turn the car back around, navigate the unruly traffic, and allow Miles to exit at the front door. It feels right, somehow, to let him go in without me. I'm out of place here.

Before I allow my depression to catch me like quicksand, I instead admire the elegant decorations and lighting hung around the entrance of the hotel. The place is a palace—grandiose without crossing over to gaudy—styled with white, gold, and silver. The pillars that frame the double doors even have the state flag unfurled and hanging with tassels. The storm attempts to tarnish the view, but the magnificence is grand enough to withstand some water and bluster.

I park a few streets down, in the parking lot of a Denny's, and lock the vehicle before starting my trek. The water is unforgiving, and I'm soaked by the time I reach the first crosswalk. When I step down into the street, I half plunge into a puddle, soaking one shoe and sock. I exhale and continue on my way, too lost in detachment to care.

By the time I reach the hotel, I'm cold and have my hands buried in my pockets. I walk up the steps to the doors, and a man in a bellhop uniform jumps into my path. He straightens his little square cap and gives me the once-over. Then he sneers.

"Sir, the hotel is hosting a private event," he says. "There's another entrance on the far side, and—"

"I'm here for the gala," I say, practically growling.

"Oh, I'm sorry. It's very exclusive. Only those with a ticket can attend. We don't sell them here."

I reach into my jacket and withdraw the small slip of paper Miles gave me. It's an event ticket—four hundred dollars a pop, apparently— and I hand it to the overzealous bellhop.

"Now get out of my way." I push the scrawny guy off to the side as I enter the building. The light and warmth of the lobby hits me full force once the door closes. It's glorious, but at the same time, I'm reminded how much I stand out.

There are hundreds of people in attendance, each one fancier than the last. Elegant gowns, tuxedos, expensive suits, some in officer's uniforms—and I'm wearing fifty pounds of water, plus a wrinkled suit. My hair, clinging to my face, dries at a slow pace. Droplets of water hit my shoes at regular intervals.

I walk forward, a squish and squeak to my step, and I grit my teeth. There's no way to avoid everyone while I search for Miles, but I do keep to the wall to minimize my presence. Champagne is passed around, glasses are clinked together, and conversation fills the air. It's a nicer affair than I imagined, nicer than anything I've ever attended. No gun-toting thugs, no quick hits of meth and coke—a celebration grand without the dark taint that lingered over every party Big Man Vice ever threw.

Miles isn't far. I spot him within a group, men and women engaging him in pleasantries. I walk past a myriad of round tables covered in white cloth and duck behind a few pillars that act as support. I don't want to walk up to him while he's talking—no doubt he'll introduce me as his boyfriend or some shit—so instead I wait nearby, hovering around the limited shadows and slicking back my hair with a free hand.

"All your instructors speak highly of you," a woman in a red evening gown says, her hand on Miles's shoulder. "The moment you said your name, I knew who you were."

"That's flattering," Miles replies as he swirls his glass of champagne.

A man joins the conversation with "Top of your class is nothing to sneer at. Have you spoken to any of the lieutenants? Most of those guys were top of their class. It shows you're dedicated. Captains like that." His bulky frame screams *police officer*, and I wouldn't be surprised to hear he's part of a Special Forces unit.

Another man joins in, this one older than the last and rather portly. "I know three individuals who became chief of police. Each one excelled academically. You're on the right path, my boy. If you keep this up, earn a few degrees, you could be enjoying a similar future."

"Th-thank you," Miles says, his hand on the back of his neck. "I don't know what I'll be doing exactly, but I appreciate the kind words."

"Don't you ever limit yourself. That's the problem a lot of young people face. They think they need to put their careers on hold for other aspects of life. Get your career underway first, and then start a family. That's a real piece of advice."

The bulky guy adds several *yeah, yeah*s to the statement before saying, "Most of these career cops have family members already on the force when they start, so it's easy for them to stay focused and know what to do. Guys like us—with no family in law enforcement—we gotta work extra hard to stay on track. It's worth it, though. And rewarding."

Miles nods. "I'm looking forward to it. A few of my instructors say they can get me a job as soon as I graduate."

"Most definitely. Every department wants the best of the best. Top of the class students are the cream of the crop, so to speak."

The older man with the gut rubs at his lower back. "Excuse me," he says with a grunt. "I need to use the restroom." He walks away, one leg stiff.

I stare down at my soaked outfit. I'm not presentable in the least bit. I follow the other gentlemen to the restroom, intent on drying off physically, if need be, and catch him standing at the middle sink, washing his face.

I grab a few paper towels and take the sink next to him, drying my hair and brushing off my jacket.

"How's it goin'?" I ask.

The bathroom, while occupied with a few individuals, is quiet enough for private conversation. It's also large enough for forty people, which helps too.

"Very well," the man replies, splashing water across his cheeks.

"I heard what you said back there," I say, cutting to the chase. "Did you say all those things just to puff the kid up?"

The man smiles. "Who, Miles? Oh, no. I meant it. The last chief of police for Rockford is a close friend of mine. He was top of his class in the police academy, earned a bachelor's degree while working as a beat cop, got a master's degree—on the dean's list, to boot—and became a captain ten years into his career, at the age of thirty. His advance knew no bounds. Three years later he was chief of police and held that title for close to two decades."

"Isn't that position rather political?" I ask as I faux wash my hands.

"It can get political in some cities, yes. But Miles is a polite and good-humored young man. That often wins over more people than you think."

Oh, I know.

"Interesting," I say. "Thanks for the chat."

I exit the bathroom while the guy responds. I don't hear a thing, but I don't care either.

Miles's success doesn't surprise me. I knew he was a smart kid the first night I spent any time with him. Maybe I didn't understand how far his cleverness extended, since his meteoric strides have caught me off guard. Everyone wants to bat their eyes and compliment him—which means they think he's going to be somebody one day. Somebody important.

When I return, he's still engaged in conversation, but with fewer people. I take my place at his side, interrupting all discussion with my presence.

Miles turns and looks me over. "Pierce? How far away did you park? You're soaked."

"It wasn't far," I state.

The woman in a red dress holds out a hand. "I'm Sergeant Cabana. Nice to meet you."

I shake her hand. It's a sturdy thing—and I appreciate that—but she's still a cop. I say nothing.

"Pierce and I are dating," Miles says, making up for my lack of communication.

"Oh," Sergeant Cabana replies, her voice betraying some displeasure brought about by the information. "Well, you two might want to find your seats and get settled, then. It was nice speaking to you."

"Yes. It was nice speaking with you too."

She turns and walks off, leaving Miles and me "alone" in a sea of people. Miles takes my arm and then jerks away his hand, his gaze locked on to my clothes as he wipes his palm off on his slacks.

"Did you fall into the swimming pool before you got here?" he quips.

"It was the rain," I say.

Miles waits for further explanation. I don't offer it.

"Our seats are over here," he eventually says as he motions to a table. "We're going to eat, and then they're going to hand out awards and give a few speeches."

"How long does this go?"

"It's scheduled to go to midnight."

"Hm."

"Is that okay?"

"It's fine."

I walk over with Miles and take my seat at the table. We have assigned seating, with names at every chair. I'm "Miles's Guest." A few others have taken their place as well, and all three of them regard Miles with wide eyes and smiles.

"There he is!" the first man says, his voice loud and distinct. "First in our class!"

"Hello, Barry," Miles says. "No need to shout."

"Everyone should know, though. It was tough fought. More than two hundred people in the academy this year too. That's more than the last five years in a row."

"Yeah, but still. It's no big deal."

Barry laughs and then turns back to his conversation with the other two people at our table. I don't have any need or desire to chat with anyone else, so I ignore their prattling and give my full attention to Miles.

"There were more than two hundred other students?" I ask. For some reason I thought there would be twenty or thirty, at the most. *Two hundred*? That makes his accomplishment much more significant.

"Yeah," Miles says. "It's a large academy. They run once a year, but they have three different sessions. Morning classes, afternoon classes, and night classes. All the students are counted together in the same class."

"You never told me that."

"I didn't think you wanted to hear about it."

I don't reply. I never asked him because I didn't much care for the institution. But there are tons of people here, and everyone knows his name. Even if *I* didn't think it was a worthwhile achievement, obviously they did.

"I want to find Rhett," Miles says, glancing around. "I want to tell him about the Worldwide Decurion stuff." He leans in closer to me and lowers his voice, his hot breath on my neck. "Do you think any of those crooked police officers are here?"

"I'm sure they are," I drawl.

"Who are they? Do you remember?"

"No. I only glanced through the files to see if Rhett was one of them." There were other names, and maybe I could remember them if I tried, but I don't have enough *giving a damn* to care.

"We should know those names by heart. If you let me see the files, I can make a list."

"Sure. Whatever."

Miles narrows his eyes and places a hand on my knee. "Hey."

I lock my gaze to his.

"Remember how I said I wanted to know more about you?" he asks, his voice still a whisper. "I want you to talk to me. What's wrong? You've been weird for a while now. Getting angry, getting depressed. But it's worse tonight. Why?"

"I'm out of my element here."

It's not a lie. It seems to placate Miles. He leans away, his face marred by concern. He turns to Barry.

"Hey, do you know where Rhett is?"

Barry glances over his shoulder. "Oh, uh, he's not going to be here tonight. He's got some sort of special assignment he's working on. There was a homicide and everything."

"Really? I didn't know that."

"Yeah. It's a shame. He wanted to be here to cheer us on."

"I had things to discuss with him, but I guess it'll have to wait."

At least one thing has gone my way tonight.

Miles keeps his hand on my leg as he and Barry engage in further conversation that I'm deaf to. The glitz and glamour of our surroundings don't mirror my thoughts. Everything is bright from here to the stage, to the front door, to the second floor of balcony seating—but my mind stews in a dark place.

It took me six months to find a job, and two months—maybe three, who's keeping track?—to lose it. Miles, on the other hand, jumped into an academy after not being in school for a couple years and pushed himself to become top of his class. He's got a career lined up, and I'm spinning my tires in the mud. I'm not who I used to be.

And the real truth is… my association with him is a hazard. What if, in ten years, when he's a hotshot captain, someone finds out about my past? What will Miles do then? He'll throw away everything he's worked for in order to help me. That's what he does. He has a genuine altruistic streak that isn't healthy.

The fact of the matter is, when we first met, he needed me. He needed help and advice and guidance, and I was there to give it to him.

Now he doesn't need me at all. I didn't help him become top of his class. I'm not going to be a benefit when he advances in his career. If anything, I need *him*. He's the only thing I have and the only reason I even keep trying.

I don't have a purpose.

The realization hits me harder than I ever thought it would.

Even my investigation under Shelby isn't something I can pursue. I don't want it to harm Miles, which means fucking with major criminal organizations is out of the question.

What am I even doing here? A real man would pick himself up and make a decision. They wouldn't wallow in whatever I'm sinking into. Am I here for Miles? For myself? What am I going to do moving forward?

Or… maybe I should call it quits. Move on. I've had a good run.

And maybe it would be better for Miles, which, if I'm honest, really is the only reason I do anything anymore.

CHAPTER SEVENTEEN

I DOWN my seventh glass of champagne and enjoy the buzz that courses through my system.

The warmth of the hotel dries my clothing, but I know I look like nine miles of bad road. Wrinkled clothes. Disheveled hair. Vague, disinterested posture. I'm well fucking aware.

Miles keeps his hand on my leg whenever possible, however, even during our three-course meal. I don't know what he's thinking. I imagined he would be upset—this probably isn't the impression he wanted me to give his peers—but he never mentions it.

The others at the table make their displeasure known. They regard me with brief glances and offhanded remarks, never actually speaking to me. That's fine. I don't give a shit about them either. I'd rather be anywhere else than here.

People tink glasses, and some toasts are made. I'm sure it's the height of civility, but I don't listen. All these speeches praising the police force are nothing more than a glorified circle-jerk. Might as well skip the words and go straight to suckin' each other's cocks—at least that would be more entertaining.

Miles listens.

Of course he does. He's polite and attentive, and someday he'll need to give his own speech.

A woman walks by our table and places a hand on Miles's shoulder. He turns to her, and she motions toward the stage before walking off to tap someone else on the shoulder. Miles leans in closer to me and squeezes my knee.

"I need to go up on stage," he murmurs.

"Why?" I ask.

"They're honoring the top students from the three largest academies in the area. I'm not going to talk. They just want us to be up there when they say a few words."

I shrug.

"Don't leave," he says, and I hear an odd weakness to his voice. I glance over, and he looks at me with a furrowed brow.

"I might step out to get some fresh air," I say. "But I won't leave."

Miles hesitates a moment before standing and then leaving alongside his classmate, Barry. The moment he disappears into the sea of people and tables, I stand and amble my way to the nearest door. I really do need to get some fresh air. All this champagne has gone to my head.

I step out into a covered patio area, admiring the blue glow from the Olympic regulation-sized swimming pool they have for their guests. The sprinkle of water over the surface causes the inner light to shimmer. It's pleasant enough, and I lean onto the patio railing in order to clear my thoughts.

I'm alone. Who would want to stand around on the patio in the middle of a storm? Occasionally the rain sweeps sideways with the wind, dotting my sleeves.

The door opens and closes. Someone's on the patio with me, but I don't turn around to see who.

"You weren't hard to find."

Rhett's voice is unmistakable, despite the howl of wind and the patter of rain.

I exhale and keep my attention on the blue of the pool. "I thought you wouldn't be here tonight. Something about a homicide."

"Michael Shelby is dead."

The statement catches me by surprise. I stare at the water, unseeing, and for a moment, I wonder if Rhett was the one to do him in.

No. Not him. He isn't one of the guys working with Worldwide Decurion or the Vice mob. He's straightlaced. Like Miles.

"Where was he?" I ask.

"Staying with a friend. He was shot in their living room by a man named Donny McCoy. I picked up Donny not but two hours ago. He told me *a man with a messed-up eye* hired him for the hit."

I don't move, not while I process the information.

Donny McCoy? I let out a single laugh and smirk. Oh, I see where this is going. Donny is an old fling of mine—a man deep in the Vice family's pocket. I sure as hell didn't hire him to kill Shelby, which means he was told to say something like that after he intentionally got caught.

Castor must have reported back about me, and maybe this is Jeremy's attempt to get me in his grasp. If some of the cops are in league with him, it'll be easy to find me in jail, where I'll be behind bars and he'll have all the power. Pretty clever. I underestimate Jeremy far too often.

Rhett walks over to me and stops a foot away. "Why'd you do it?" he asks. "Does Shelby know all about your shady past? Is that what's going on?"

"Shelby had a lot of info on dirty cops," I say. "But he didn't know anything about me."

"Dirty cops? What's that supposed to mean?"

"Exactly what it sounds like. The guy was paranoid at the end. Knew cops were out for him. They had to silence him, which is what they did, but I guess they want to bring me down too."

Makes sense. Maybe Castor spoke about my attempt to bring him in to the police. Maybe they're onto my investigation and want me to stop. Permanently.

"You expect me to believe you had nothing to do with this?" Rhett asks, amusement in his voice.

"No," I say. "I expect you're happy to bring me in, no matter how tenuous the connection."

"This Donny character seems to know you. I'm willing to bet he can identify you in all sorts of crimes."

"I bet he can."

Rhett chuckles. "I knew you were a thug, but I didn't think you'd be this blasé about it."

Eh. Rhett caught me on the right night. It was bound to happen eventually. I've been too lax, and now I've got a hardline decision to make. It's better that this happened sooner rather than later. I've already made up my mind in terms of Miles—there's nothing left I can do for him besides bow out and let him continue, unburdened by my past. Me getting arrested will force the issue. I can't mess up anything for him later.

But I told Miles I wouldn't leave the event, though it looks like I don't have much of a choice. I stand up straight, face Rhett, and hold out my arms. "Let's get this over with," I mutter.

Rhett, dressed in a bulletproof vest and tactical gear, takes a step back and places a hand on his sidearm. I roll my eyes, turn around, and get my arms behind my back.

Odd he came alone to apprehend me. I figured cops brought backup to showdowns like this, but what do I know? Maybe he has a buddy with a sniper rifle in the next building over. Or maybe he's always been brazen and figures I'm no threat.

Rhett grabs my arm and jerks me close. I glare, and he returns the gesture. "Let's not make a scene," he says. "For Miles's sake. He doesn't need any sort of negative reputation starting his career."

"Am I being cooperative, or am I being cooperative?" I ask, sardonic.

"Stay close. I have a transport team ready to take you in."

He leads me away from the patio and back into the main room.

The speakers are still giving speeches—all about the great achievements of the students and the police officers who came before— but we leave the banquet hall in favor of a much narrower corridor. Rhett, attentive as ever, keeps one eye on me the whole time.

My thoughts linger on Jeremy, however, not so much escape. What's going to happen when I get back in that man's company? I doubt he'll be forgiving. I watched the man shoot his own father because he wasn't given enough power within the syndicate fast enough. That's not the type of person to be reasonable.

Maybe I should struggle to get Rhett's gun. Not because I want to fight my way out of custody, but because *suicide by cop* is still technically an option. An option I won't have once Jeremy comes to collect me.

"A word of advice," Rhett says as we travel down the long, empty corridor. "Don't make up bullshit about dirty cops to take the heat off yourself. Judges prefer straight-up honesty."

"Then me and judges have a lot in common."

"Don't start. You've already said too much."

"Shelby really wanted to catch his kid's killers. He gave me all his hard evidence on the cops. He said I should turn it in if he died. I guess there's going to be a shitstorm in your department."

Rhett pulls me to a stop. "You have proof?" he asks, curt. "Physical proof?"

"Yeah."

"Where?"

"My house." I offer him a one-sided smile. "You wanna take a detour on the way to the slammer, Princess? I don't give a fuck. Either we'll get it, or Miles will turn it in tomorrow after he hears what's happened."

"Miles knows where it is?" Rhett mulls over the bit of information before pushing me back into a walk. "I'll get it with him later tonight."

The statement sends a twinge of rage through my system, like he's insinuating he's going to do something else, but I hold it back, a little shocked at how fast I went from not feeling anything to full-blown anger.

Rhett stops at a metal door and pushes me through. The chill of the parking garage greets me with a powerful whoosh of air rushing to get inside the hotel. Rhett keeps ahold of my arm as he steps out with me. Standing around an armored police van, dressed for an insurgency, are thirteen special-response unit officers, one of which stands six inches taller than the rest.

"Deputy Chief Charleston," Rhett says, his voice betraying his shock. "I… didn't think you'd be here. How did you even—"

"Thompson called me," the larger man interjects, the grate of his voice deep and baritone.

He steps forward, and I have to tilt my head back to take him all in. I recognize him, the deputy chief of police from Noimore, from all the news interviews and reports on television. The camera doesn't capture his full imposing presence, however. I'm no drug expert, but he doesn't take steroids—he eats them. His muscles strain against his skin, threatening to burst out if the guy flexes too hard.

"Why didn't you take the team to apprehend this man?" Deputy Chief Charleston asks. "If he double-crossed and murdered Shelby, he's dangerous."

"I've worked with this PI in the past. I knew I could handle him," Rhett responds, relaxing a bit as though in the company of friends rather than the shark tank we're actually in. The other twelve guys fan out a bit, some with their rifles hanging on straps over their shoulder. They could heft them at any time and waste us; it wouldn't take much effort.

I didn't look at the name on the police list, but I do remember Shelby mentioning Deputy Chief Charleston, the ringleader for the police force when it came to this human trafficking business. And if Thompson called the deputy chief over when Rhett came to get me—me, the PI trainee who helped Shelby, the man who has info on corrupt cops—I'm willing to bet I know what's happening here.

I'm not gonna make it to a jail cell.

"I'll take it from here," Deputy Chief Charleston says, confirming all my suspicions. "I'm head of the task force investigation, after all. I want to be the one handling this."

"Of course."

Rhett grabs my arms and forces them behind my back. I don't struggle as he handcuffs me, nor do I protest when he pats me down and takes my keys and cell phone. Once he's finished, he escorts me the ten feet over to the deputy chief.

I know a lowlife when I see one, but Deputy Chief Charleston doesn't appreciate the way I stare. He scowls and then smiles.

"Pieces of shit like you don't deserve the comfort our prison system offers inmates," he says, slow and menacing. "If it were up to me, we'd have a fast lane to the electric chair."

I don't reply.

There's nothing to say, really. I could attempt to call out his hypocrisy, but he might actually believe *I'm* the scum and *he's* the hero. Getting a criminal off the streets—no matter the means, be it criminal itself—could be his end goal. Which, I guess, he's succeeding at.

Not to mention we're on his turf, not mine, and he's packing all the heat. I'm gonna keep my fucking mouth shut. It's the smart move.

"There's one other thing," Rhett says, obviously not in the same boat as me when it comes to keeping quiet. "Pierce mentioned that Shelby had some information regarding dirty cops."

Oh, Jesus Christ.

I swear the parking garage gets three degrees chillier the moment Rhett finishes his sentence. Each and every one of the special-response guys gets tense, and they exchange knowing glances. Rhett isn't in on their operation. That much I'm certain.

And if they were willing to kill Shelby to keep him quiet….

Rhett never should've admitted he knew.

"Is that true?" Deputy Chief Charleston asks me. "You tried to disparage my fine brothers and sisters in uniform?"

What am I going to say? Yes? No? Either way, I'm fucked. I grit my teeth and stare.

Without warning, and much faster than I expected, Deputy Chief Charleston punches me in my undefended gut. His muscles aren't for show—I swear I feel organs burst—and I lose my breath as I hit my knees and then fall forward, my forehead hitting his polished boot. Hot, blinding agony rips through my body.

"Charleston!" Rhett barks. "What're you—"

The deputy chief chortles, eliciting similar responses from his men. "He was resisting arrest."

"No, he wasn't! He's been nothing but cooperative! It's abuse of your authority to strike a man in custody!"

Rhett kneels down and places a hand on my back. I attempt to stand but end up vomiting a mouthful of blood and what little dinner I ate with Miles. If I had been prepared, maybe the bone-shattering blow wouldn't have been so bad. I'm in no condition to fight now, however.

"Leave that filth alone," Deputy Chief Charleston drawls. "He's a criminal with the audacity to say we're just like him. That's as slimy as they come. Don't be the chump he manipulates for pity."

"He said he has proof," Rhett says as he stands. "Physical proof. I don't think he would make up claims like that for misdirection and pity. And Shelby worked with several police departments during his tenure. I think we should take this seriously and investigate."

I want to turn to the man and plead with him to stop talking, but I'm too busy attempting to take in air. I wish I could use my arms. I remain curled in on myself, blood soaking into my hair as I slide away from the deputy chief.

Deputy Chief Charleston offers a grunt of disapproval. "Rhett, you've been helpful in this investigation, but we're in Noimore—my jurisdiction. I'll handle everything from here. Forget you even talked to this scum."

"Well, Joliet is *my* jurisdiction," Rhett says, firm in his stance and confidence. "And that's where Shelby had his office. You can take Pierce and question him, but I'm going to investigate his claim. We should know if someone in our ranks is using their post for personal gain. *Especially* if it involves human trafficking."

Deputy Chief Charleston doesn't answer.

"And to be frank," Rhett continues, "it disturbs me how quick you were to manhandle someone in custody. You're the deputy chief of police. The officers of Noimore look to you for guidance. I have half a mind to report you."

I got to give it to Rhett… he has some testicles. He's naïve as fuck, but at least he's no coward. Even through the agony and dull ache, I half smile at his bravado and confidence.

To my surprise, Deputy Chief Charleston laughs. "Ya know, Rhett? You're right. Maybe I'm just overworked and takin' it out on the little guys. Tell ya what. You take this scumbag over to the station, and I'll speak to Chief Huang on the subject. Maybe she'll have a plan to utilize some of the detectives within Internal Affairs."

Rhett takes in a deep breath and then exhales. "All right. I'll take him in and get you the report as soon as possible."

"Good man."

Rhett takes one of my arms and helps me to my feet, but I struggle the entire way, nauseated. Despite that, I see the officer coming up behind Rhett, his Taser at the ready, and I cough when I attempt to speak. Rhett must sense something is up, because he turns on his heel, ready to engage. He grabs the other officer and twists his forearm. When Rhett goes to pull his gun, three other officers fire cartridge Tasers, two of which strike Rhett on the exposed skin of his neck, dropping him hard.

The other men of the special-response unit leap on Rhett the moment he's down. They remove his weapons, belt, radio, and bulletproof vest before handcuffing him. When Rhett thrashes and fights, they plant knuckles onto his face—a few one-two combinations to the cabbage and the guy is more cooperative.

When the police thugs gather around me, I remain as passive as I've been this whole meeting. I don't need another strike to the gut to know I'm at a disadvantage. They don't rough me up, but they do jerk me around like they're hoping I step out of line.

"Take these two to Castor," Deputy Chief Charleston commands. "He'll handle the rest."

"Even Rhett?" one officer asks.

Poor, stupid officer. Did he not learn his lesson?

Deputy Chief Charleston wheels on him, the veins of his body pulsing with restrained rage for the world to see. "Do you want to go with him to make sure he's okay?" he growls through thick clenched teeth. "Otherwise, you forget you ever saw Rhett here, do you understand me?

You're all to write reports that Rhett went rogue on this. That he went to apprehend this piece of shit and never came back. Got it?"

The officers nod. No further questions.

They lead me over to the armored police van, and there's a piece of me that wishes I hadn't left the gala. Even if I meant to leave Miles, this isn't my preferred method of doing so. Anything would be better than getting a bloody beating at the hands of corrupt cops and their stooges.

CHAPTER EIGHTEEN

"YOU DON'T have to do this," Rhett says, his back to the corner of the van, his arms handcuffed and restrained to the reinforced steel siding. "Anderson, Thompson… you both have wives and kids. What would they say if they saw you—"

"Shut up!" one officer barks. He stands, moves a short distance down the van, and pulls his gun. "Don't you mention my family again."

"Calm down, Anderson," another officer says. "Just ignore him. This'll all be over soon."

Rhett sits up as straight as he can, his expression neutral. "Whatever you've done, it can be mitigated if you turn yourself in and stop this. It only gets worse the longer you go."

Anderson rushes over, grabs Rhett by his black police shirt, and jerks him close. "This didn't have to happen! It's *your* fault we have to do this! If you had let it go—if you weren't such a fucking Boy Scout— we all could've gone on our merry way!"

"I didn't force you to do this," Rhett states. "You could've just done your job."

There's a quiet moment where nothing happens before Anderson completely loses his shit. He punches Rhett with the gun in his hand, allowing the weight of the weapon to add to the strike. After the second go, he switches to using the handgun as a blunt club, bashing in part of Rhett's ear and splattering blood across the floor.

Two officers jump up to stop Anderson's attack. I move out of their way, pressing myself up against the side of the van and holding my breath. I don't think they're aware of my presence as they scramble to control the situation.

Once Anderson is corralled, the van gets thick with silence. The officers stay near the front cab, while Rhett and I are left to the shadows of the back. Each bump on the road is felt through the cold steel of the vehicle, but I don't complain. And neither does Rhett. I guess he's given up on trying to persuade them to turn themselves in. Probably for the best. I doubt he can hear anything with his messed-up ear.

It doesn't take long before the van comes to a halt. Three of the officers hop out and open the back doors. With uncaring force they pull me and Rhett out by our arms and drag us across a small dirt lot.

The smell of the river is unmistakable. I glance around and spot the Grand Noimore Waterfront Hotel in the distance, across the water—the bright lights cutting through the gloom of the dwindling storm. The drizzle of rain isn't so much a bother, but it hinders my already poor eyesight. Besides the hotel, I don't recognize much.

A group of gangbangers stands nearby, ready to greet us. They saunter over, guns on display, and nod to the police officers with cordial but hesitant mannerisms.

Castor, the enforcer, steps forward and takes the lead. He's so thin and tall, when he smiles he looks like a skeleton.

"Charleston got me up to speed," he says. "We'll handle it from here."

Anderson pushes me forward. "You gotta get whatever information they have. And call us afterward with the drop-off details. We'll be the team that picks everything up."

"I said, *Charleston got me up to speed*. You pigs don't need to tell me twice." Castor motions to his six buddies to take me and Rhett. Again, I don't struggle, but Rhett doesn't take my lead. The hired guns wrestle with him a bit before planting the barrel of a firearm in his spine and pushing him along.

Castor speaks with the officers a bit longer. I don't hear a word, not through the dying storm, and I instead focus on our destination. A boathouse—a large one, by the looks of things—with covered docks for personal vessels. I don't like that we're getting close to the river, but then again, I wouldn't mind getting out of the rain.

"They might as well rename this the River Styx," I say to the thug holding my arm with a vise grip. "What with all the dead bodies they throw in."

Four out of the six men chuckle, and the guy manhandling me replies with a grin, "You're the funny one, then?"

"I'm just more relaxed now that I'm not in the company of cops."

"Yeah, you don't look like one of 'em, that's for sure."

We enter the boathouse. It's dry, for the most part, but water laps up onto the docks with the occasional wave. The boat doors are closed, keeping the place mostly shut off from the outside, if you don't count the water. The men shove me and Rhett to the back end of the dock and force us to kneel up against the wall.

I know why—it'll be harder to run out the front door if we have to pass each motherfucker from here to the door—and my quick glance around the room tells me there isn't much hope. There are some boxes, human-sized boxes, and a few metal crates, but not many tools, and no extra guns.

"This Vice family owned?" I ask as the thugs take a step back.

"That's right," the one says. "You know them?"

"Once. Yeah."

"Then you should know we're not gonna be the ones beating the information out of you. Jeremy Vice hired himself a real professional surgeon." The guy chortles. "You sure you don't want to tell us what you know right now? I'll make sure you get out of here if you do."

I let out a single laugh and smile. Maybe if that were an actual offer, I would take it. But Castor is in charge, not this random asshole. The enforcers aren't obligated to keep the word of their lackeys.

"I'll wait for the surgeon," I drawl. "I already have an appointment, after all."

"Gonna be a smartass, huh? Suit yourself."

The guys don't wander far. They stop halfway down the dock and shove a few boxes around until they have a makeshift sitting area. One man withdraws a deck of cards, but I don't see any drinks.

They're professionals. Hired help rather than kids off the street. I know from the rail yard that they're also ruthless, if need be. They aren't going to get high or fuck around while on the job. They're going to sit and watch me and Rhett get tortured before dumping our bodies in a plausible location. They'll probably even make it look like we killed each other. And it's not like the deputy chief will want to investigate too hard.

Rhett relaxes back against the wall and exhales. "They're calling in a surgeon?" he asks under his breath.

"A man who specializes in torturing fools," I reply. "He's gonna get us to talk."

"By cutting into us?"

"Maybe. Most guys break after having their fingernails ripped off, but you're fairly stubborn. They might get to the part where they start slicing things up that aren't too important."

Rhett is quiet for a moment before continuing, "You're rather calm."

"Heh. I should be more like you—that way we can both get our asses kicked."

"This isn't a game," Rhett growls between clenched teeth. "Have you given up on life? Is that what this is? You reek like a man dead inside."

I glance over at him and stare. "You're real good at makin' enemies."

"You're not worried about Miles?" Rhett turns away, glaring at the wood between us. "I knew you were just using him, but this is cold."

"You think they'll go after Miles? Why?"

"You live together, don't you? Where do you think they'll go once they're done with us?"

Fuck me. Somehow, even in my fall, I'm dragging Miles along for the ride. But what am I going to do? It's not like I've had many opportunities to turn the tables. And Rhett is anything but an asset.

The roar of a boat motor gets everyone's attention. Castor enters the boathouse and slams his fist on the boat door opener, causing the garage-door-style shutter to lift up, slowly and surely.

A center console boat slips in—the type of open hull boat with the steering console in the middle—and the grumble of the powerful motor fills the atmosphere as it drives down the dock at a steady pace. Castor and his men get up and ready to greet the guy who came to torture us, but I guess this is as good an opportunity as any.

I press my shoulder up to Rhett and run my bandaged forearm down his. "Do you know how to undo cuffs if you had a knife?"

"Yeah," Rhett replies.

"I have one under the bandages. Pull it out and get this done."

The thing is wrapped pretty tight around my arm, but it doesn't take Rhett long to rip it up enough to pry the multitool out. I can't see a goddamn thing, but I feel him shift around until he has a good angle with the lock. I guess cops know their way around handcuffs—he unclicks it and releases me before the boat has come to a complete stop. Once the engine cuts out, the place gets quiet once again.

I take the multitool from Rhett, remove my blazer, and get to my feet in a crouching position. While the surgeon disembarks, I shuffle behind a pile of boxes and grab a metal crate. Rhett remains still and doesn't glance over at me. Smart move. At least he won't inadvertently give away my position.

I throw the metal crate into the water, careful to keep my body concealed by the boxes. The loud splash echoes within the enclosed space, drawing the attention of the thugs.

"The fuck?" one shouts.

"One of them's gone!"

"Goddamn it," Castor yells out, his voice barely intelligible through his thick rage. "You two! Get in the water! You three, follow me! We're searching the shore! You stay with the boat!"

The four thugs exit the boathouse in a hurry, leaving the rest uncertain, but they follow through with commands.

Two men run down to the end of the dock, passing me without seeing. The first one rips off his jacket and jumps in, gun and all. The second one hangs back, delaying the dunk into ice water, and that's all I need.

I lunge for the guy—not to punch him out, but to grab for his firearm—and I yank it from his hand while I push him over. The guy tries to grab me, and for a second he teeters, but I fire his .45, and the kick sends him sailing into the river with a cascade of blood as his herald. The guy in the water gasps up a mouthful, and I fire twice into the drink, catching him both times, based on the crimson that floats to the surface.

The boat guard fires at me, and I duck behind the boxes. He takes cover behind the boat, but I don't have time to play around. When he crouches down, I jump over the boxes, leaping down to the dock and dashing toward the surgeon. He's unarmed and turns to run, but I grab the older man by his thin, wrinkly throat and hold him against me. I like him better as a meat shield.

The boat guard fires wildly, clipping both me and the surgeon across the calf. I fire back, generous with the bullets, shattering part of the hull, but also the guy's skull in the process.

I shove the surgeon forward and rush over to the dead boat guard. My leg gives out right as I reach my destination. I hadn't realized I had been holding my breath, nor did I notice how fucked-up my calf is. Blood soaks my sock and shoe, and my leg trembles when I attempt to stand.

Three guys burst back into the boathouse. I fire twice, and they leap behind boxes, but my magazine is empty. I drop the clip and scramble for another, searching the corpse I'm half standing on. The surgeon grabs for my gun. I punch the guy in his side, and the old man whimpers out a cry. I guess he hasn't been in a fight for a while.

Bullets whiz by as I reload my gun. More and more of the boat's hull disappears, and I fire above it, not even bothering to aim; all I want is for them to keep their distance. I push the surgeon out into the open, and the men shoot at him, filling his old body full of lead. I stand and fire while they kill their own, catching two off guard before I have crouch back into cover.

The last guy runs forward and leaps over the damaged hull. I didn't see it coming, and he stomps down with his boot to my shoulder, torqueing it good. We both fire, the guns close and my ears screaming with an incessant ring that won't go away.

The guy falls, coughing up blood. I fire again, in the head, blowing brains across the planks of the dock. I want to gasp and catch my breath, but Castor enters the boathouse fresh and ready to go. Covered in sweat and blood, I hunker down on the other side of the boat, keeping the vehicle between me and him.

I hear nothing. The ringing kills all nuance.

Not knowing where he is frightens me more than all the other guys combined. I glance over my shoulder, and then to the bow of the ship, switching my gaze back and forth with panicked motions. My shoulder throbs with a steady ache. Moving my neck becomes a terrible ordeal.

Silence.

Where is he? Do I risk looking over the boat? He could be at the door, holding his firearm at the ready, prepared to shoot me like some sort of sick whack-a-mole game.

I attempt to scoot around, but I stagger and hit the edge of the dock, nearly falling into the river. I'm in no condition to run or jump. I could play a round of quick draw, but everything else will be in Castor's favor. I have to spot him first.

"He's getting into the boat!" Rhett yells.

I don't dwell on the statement. I pull down on the edge of the boat and heft myself over the ledge, allowing the rocking to aid me. Castor fires and stumbles, but he isn't looking at me—he shoots at Rhett, no doubt having forgotten the other man existed until he opened his mouth. I lift my gun to fire, but Castor whips around, catching my arm.

Again, the boat rocks with our movements. When he steps forward, I reach for his gun arm, and we become locked in an odd dance to disarm each other. The man trips me with ease, but I maintain my hold and we both hit the deck of the ship, tumbling around the sodden grip carpeting.

I knee him in the gut and he drops his handgun, but he stomps down into my bruised midsection, weakening me.

We roll again, and Castor pulls a knife—a seven-inch black carbon steel blade that looks sharp enough to slice a piece of hair down the middle. Unable to fire my gun, I drop it in favor of controlling Castor's arm. He gets on top of me, his skill at grappling far exceeding my own. With gravity on his side, he thrusts down, attempting to slice open my neck. I hold him back with both arms, but it's a struggle given my shoulder.

He presses harder and harder, his intense gaze so focused on mine it's hard not to stare back, and I know he wants me dead. I'll lose if I keep this up.

I spit in his face, right across the eyes. When Castor flinches, I kick up with the rock of the boat and get on top of him, reversing our positions. Grabbing the hilt of his blade over his hand, I push down, angling the thing to cut him. He thrashes up, his elbow clipping the left side of my face, and the contact lens in my eye jams back past the eyelid, cutting something along the way.

Bloody tears weep from my injured eye, but I double down, knowing I *have* to get him here or else I'll lose later.

Pressing my full weight on the blade, I drive it down on his throat, slow and steady. His skin and muscles offer little resistance against the edge of the blade, and the moment I cut through, blood gushes over the handle, getting everything slick. Despite me cutting into him—despite hearing him choke on his own fucking blood—he continues to fight me, his struggle becoming ever more intense.

Castor lifts up and elbows me again, my eye socket bruised and my eyebrow cut open. Why won't this fucker just die? I pump down with my body, like I'm giving CPR, and plunge the knife deeper. The next ten seconds play out as though neither of us moves, but the strain is real. Finally his strength fails, and I feel the life leave him as the cold sets in.

I stand, leaving the knife, and stumble back, shaken. I've fought lots of thugs before, but no encounter was quite so fervent. I pick up my gun and limp to the side of the boat. I disembark with the grace of a drunkard, half falling into a stack of boxes.

I chuckle to myself. Nothing lifts my spirits like fighting to the death and coming out on top. I'm a goddamn animal—that's eight men dead. Well, I didn't kill the surgeon, but still. Eight motherfuckers thought they could do me in. I didn't run as Big Man Vice's top enforcer because of my good looks, and I guess they all learned that lesson the hard way.

Rhett goes to stand, though it's awkward given his arms are trapped behind his back. I point my handgun at him. He freezes midway, his eyes narrowing with realization. He gets back down on his knees as I hobble over.

He regards me with a look of uncertainty. I continue until I'm a foot away, my gun half-cocked but not pointing straight at him. I have all the power, and he knows it, but the man has a spine of steel. He glares up at me, one eye black and blue, with dried blood stuck to the side of face and neck.

Rhett doesn't quaver or shake when I bring the handgun up. The intensity in his gaze tells me he's ready for anything, even death.

He's been a thorn in my side since we met, and he wants to lock me up for the rest of my life. It would be easy—so easy—to shoot him here and have the Worldwide Decurion people take the blame. No one would know. There aren't any witnesses, and I could make my getaway before anyone tracked me down. Simple stuff.

But….

I exhale and lower my gun.

"You don't want to die here, I take it?" I ask him, more amusing thoughts crossing my mind now that I've decided I won't kill him. No reason I can't fuck with him.

Rhett hesitates for a moment. "What're you saying?"

I smirk. "Well, you like men, don't ya? That'll make what comes next real easy for you."

His resolve flickers for a moment as my words settle over him. He regains himself and shifts his gaze to the floor, glaring at the wood planks that creak with the water.

"Don't get shy, Princess. All I'm asking is for a run of your pretty mouth. That's fair, right? Your life's worth that much, at least?"

"You're a sick bastard," he forces out, no longer able to meet my gaze.

I can practically see his internal struggle, and I get an inordinate amount of pleasure in watching the turmoil play out. I have to stifle my laughter lest I sound like a cartoony villain—but I fucking love it. His face gets red from what I imagine is both indignant rage and hot shame.

Heh. He's considering it. The conflicted look of a man ready to break down and suck cock gets me in the mood. Hell, the whole fucking situation has me rock-hard, who I am kidding? Even the pain that permeates my body can't diminish the feeling.

"There isn't any other way?" Rhett asks, like he's hoping he can talk his way out of this situation.

"Maybe I just like fucking arrogant pricks."

"So that's your game? You want to watch me swallow my pride?"

"I wanna watch you swallow a lot more than that."

He closes his eyes and clenches his jaw.

I'm such an asshole.

After a long, tense moment, Rhett goes to answer, but I press the barrel of the gun to his forehead. He quiets himself and finally looks up at me, confusion written across his face.

"I know you were secretly looking forward to it," I drawl, "but you don't get to suck anything tonight."

His expression turns to livid anger in the blink of an eye.

"Let's make a deal," I say. "I let you go, and you don't tell anyone about my past. I didn't hire Donny to kill Shelby—I'm sure you know that by now—and we can both go on our separate ways. Fair, right? Better than the alternative."

I pull back the hammer of the handgun until it clicks into place.

For another long moment, Rhett is silent.

CHAPTER NINETEEN

"Fuck you," Rhett growls.

"Don't be like that," I say with a laugh. "Your pride is wounded, but that doesn't mean you can't think straight."

"There's nothing left to think about. You've heard my answer."

I press the gun hard against his forehead. He doesn't flinch.

"Why?" I ask. "Is turning me in really worth dying for? At least tell me you're gonna take the deal and then turn me in after. What's the point of taking a stand? No one is here to reward you for being heroic."

Rhett shakes his head, his entire body tense. "You think men like Anderson and Thompson started killing their fellow officers one day out of the blue? No. I'm sure they made minor deals with criminals and their fellow cops, bending the rules here and there until it became a full-blown problem they had to cover no matter the cost. Now look at them. They can't turn back—they're the worst kind of criminal. I'm not going to make a deal with you, asshole. I'm going to do my job, and I'm going to do it right."

"That won't happen if you're dead, genius."

"Men like you will never understand. When I die, there won't be any regrets."

Ugh. Rhett is the definition of self-righteous. I'm sure it's his holier-than-thou attitude that blinded him to the questionable activities of his coworkers.

I lower my gun.

Even if I hate him for who he is, he's a better man than me. He doesn't deserve to die. And I guess he called my bluff.

"Get up," I command. "We should get out of here."

He waits for a moment, his expression shifting back to one of confusion. "Just because you're not shooting me doesn't mean I'm letting you go."

"Yeah, I got that," I snap.

He doesn't respond.

"Stop bitching, already. Arrest me once we're not in the heart of Vice family territory."

He gets to his feet. I stumble over to the thugs' makeshift table. All of Rhett's gear sits off to the side, ready to be planted on his body once he died. I pick it up and toss it toward him, but my aim is terrible. The gear hits a pile of boxes halfway over and clunks onto the dock, the stuff spilling everywhere. Rhett gives me a sardonic *are you serious?* kind of glance.

I point to my eye—the one sealed shut and weeping blood. "I've got problems."

I can still feel the contact lens wedged deep into my eyelid. Everything hurts, but that bothers me most of all.

"Can you at least get the keys to the handcuffs?" Rhett asks.

With a heavy sigh, I walk over to his gear and fish out the keys. He turns around, and I unlock the damn handcuffs. He stretches for a moment, rotating his arms, and then turns back around to face me.

"You handled yourself well with a gun," he states. "Despite your problems."

"Yeah, by using way more bullets than necessary. Kids on the street call it *spray-n-pray.*" I check the clip of my gun. I've got two inside and one in the barrel. Not the best ratio of kills to ammunition.

The rumble of an engine causes me and Rhett to stiffen. I listen to the skid across dirt and the familiar sound of doors slamming before I turn my attention back to Rhett.

"Castor must've called for backup," I mutter. That's what I would've done—clever fucking bastard. He's still trying to kill me, even after he's dead.

Rhett slips on his bulletproof vest, and I hand him my gun. He looks at it, then to me, and then back to the handgun. "Giving up your only weapon?"

"We've already established my shortcomings. Handle these guys, or else we're both dying here."

I duck behind a pile of boxes and take a seat. My body feels heavy, like I won't be able to stand again, and I'm placing all my chips in the basket of Rhett's gunplay. The door to the boathouse opens, and I glance around the edge, despite the pain in my neck and shoulder. Three guys. That's more than I would have sent for, but I guess Castor wanted to be thorough.

Perhaps the element of surprise is still on our side. I return to cover and hold my breath.

Boots on wood echo throughout the area, and I suspect the thugs are searching the joint. I'm not sure what Rhett's up to—he could have left me to these goons, for all I know—and I close my one good eye to revel in the comfort of darkness.

"Look at all this blood," I hear a guy mutter.

"Stay focused," another growls.

"This is Lieutenant Rhett Walker with the Joliet City PD," Rhett shouts. "Lay down your weapons and get down on the ground, or I'll be forced to shoot."

Oh, for fuck's sake. We *did* have the element of surprise.

"The cops are here?" the first guy says, his voice shaken. "Man, I knew this was a bad idea!"

The same buddy replies with a grunt. "I swear to God, Lopez, if you put your gun down, I'll shoot you myself."

"The cops are supposed to be helpin' us. I didn't want to fight no cops."

"*Lopez.*"

I hear the thunk of metal on wood. I'm surprised one of them wanted out so bad he's willing to throw down his weapon. I've known a few guys who got cold feet on missions. Didn't turn out well for them, though.

I flinch at the sound of two gunshots. That's it. Two. There's a crash and another gunshot, but afterward all I hear is silence. Although I'm concerned about the outcome, I'm more concerned about my messed-up calf. I bring my leg closer and remove the last of the bandages covering my tattoo. With careful movements I wrap my injury, trying not to focus on the visible muscle that glistens thanks to the missing chunk of skin.

"Get down on the floor," Rhett yells.

I breathe easy. At least, whatever happened, Rhett came out on top.

Once I'm done with my leg, I attempt to stand. It doesn't work, and I struggle against the boxes. I give up and wait. When Rhett rounds the corner of the pile, I stare up at him with my one eye. He gives me the once-over, and I know I look like shit.

"Just give me a hand," I mutter.

"Maybe I should do a cute bit where I hold a gun to your head until you do what I say," he quips.

"I'd like you a little more if you did."

Rhett lets out a single laugh and smirks. I laugh too, if only because I didn't think he would appreciate that joke. He offers his hand and I take it. I get to my feet, and it's hard to stay standing, but I manage.

I spot one of the thugs facedown on the dock with his hands on top of his head. The other two are dead in a pool of their bodily fluids, each with a hole through the back of their skulls.

"Two shots was all it took you?" I ask Rhett.

"Kids on the street call it *going to the gun range and practicing*."

What a smartass. I had eight guys to deal with—he's still playing in the baby leagues.

Rhett walks over and takes a cell phone out of a guy's pants pocket. He dials something quick and then holds the phone close to his mouth.

"Hello?" he says into the speaker. "There's been an emergency at the Noimore docks. Officer down. Ten bodies. One in custody."

Before anything else is said, he ends the call and throws the device back on the corpse. He rummages around the other pockets as I watch, half amused.

"I've fondled plenty of things in my day," I drawl, "but dead bodies aren't one of them."

Rhett snorts but otherwise doesn't reply. Instead he pulls a key ring from the sad sack on the floor and turns toward the boathouse door. He motions for me to follow. I limp after him, leaving my blazer and knife. Without the rush of a life-or-death fight, things slow down. I want to lie down and sleep. It's all I think about until we reach the little four-door sedan parked in the dirt lot.

He unlocks the vehicle, and I slide into the front passenger's seat, comforted by the soft fabric of the chair. After sitting in a metal van, fucking around on a dock, and tussling on a shitty boat, I'm ready for some luxury.

Rhett starts the thing up and peels out of the parking lot, speeding away as if he's avoiding someone. I get my seat belt on, but not without struggle. My shoulder aches with each movement, and I tilt the seat back in order to rest. He blasts the heater to fight the cold. Within seconds I'm sweating, and I roll up my sleeves and press my skin against the coolness of the window.

"You have a cigarette?" I ask.

"No," he replies, curt.

I kick one foot up on the dashboard and relax. Rhett shakes his head.

"Sit normally. It's dangerous to position yourself like that."

I kick the other foot up and hook my ankles. "Life's short. I don't give a fuck."

He takes a hard turn onto the street, and I have to grip the door to keep in my seat. I give him a glare. "You tryin' to make this dangerous?"

"We don't have time to mess around."

It's a manual shift vehicle—I haven't seen one of those in two decades—and he shifts the thing like he knows what he's doing. I admire the fact he can drive, but I can't bring myself to compliment the man. I've already dug a pit of hatred for him… climbing out now would be tiresome.

I close my eye and focus on breathing even. Soon I'll be in a jail cell, and I'm sure they'll have some drugs for me. Rhett takes another hard turn, and I jerk my gaze over to him.

"What're you doing?" I demand.

"Beating Charleston to the punch," he mutters.

"What're you trying to beat him to?"

"Your house."

"You think he's going there to get the evidence?"

"There's no doubt in my mind."

Eh. Even at the rate we're going, it'll take at least thirty minutes to get to Joliet. I relax back in my seat and exhale. At least I might see Miles again before I go to the slammer. Though, the more I think about it, the more I don't want to see him at all. He's not the type of guy who would leave me to my fate in a jail cell. He's the type of guy who would visit three times a week and write daily.

And if Rhett exposes the crooked cops with Shelby's evidence, Jeremy won't have an easy avenue to reach me, which means I'll be locked up for some time, no doubt.

We reach the back roads of Noimore, and Rhett speeds along the dark lanes with tunnel-vision focus. He must know his way through the city—he avoids all the major cop spots. When we get halfway to our destination, he relaxes a bit, but not enough to take either of his hands from the steering wheel.

"Hey," I say to him, breaking the silent tension that had settled between us. "Do cops ever have a say on which prison convicts are housed in?"

"No," Rhett states. "There's a prison designation board that determines your facility based on your security rating, criminal record, area code of residence, and availability. Sometimes a judge can make a recommendation on your behalf, but that's rare."

I mull over the information and offer no further commentary.

"Why?" he asks. "You have friends you want to reconnect with?"

"I wanna be placed as far away from Miles as possible."

He squints at the road and tightens his grip on the steering wheel. "Why?"

I turn to Rhett, half-tempted to tell him everything on my mind, but I hold myself back. After another round of uncertainty, I decide to speak, though I look away, unwilling or unable to stare at him directly, I don't know.

"He won't leave his siblings, and I'd rather him not visit. He's got…. Well, he's got better things to do with his time. Maybe once things are all said and done, you can… you can be the one who helps him move on. If he has someone, it'll make things easier."

"You want me to be the one who helps him move on?" He chuckles. "What're you implying, Pierce?"

"You know damn well what I'm implying!" I slam my feet on the floor of the car and sit up straight, riled with anger and frustration. I bite back all my crude remarks and grit my teeth. *I* was the one to suggest this. Why does it hurt so much to think about?

"I know you want him," I force out. "You two are similar in, well, many regards. I know he wouldn't be unhappy. That's what I care about, all right? Did I make myself perfectly fucking clear?"

Rhett doesn't answer. We sit in the sweltering cab, no radio, and say nothing. I know he's not comfortable with himself—not with the way he seems to hate me talking about his sexual proclivities—but I don't know what else to say to him. I think I've made my point; all I can do now is hope Miles doesn't do anything crazy.

I turn off the heater. Fuck that heater.

"Why are you so deep in the closet?" I ask, unabashed. I need to know.

"I'm not," he snaps. "I just like to keep my personal life private. Is that so much to ask for? Privacy?"

Nothing wrong with privacy. I love my privacy. Still, I wouldn't deny the fact I like men. Then again, I guess Rhett never has. He simply avoids the conversation, which isn't a bad way to handle it if he wants to keep things private. Maybe Miles was right. Maybe I *do* have more in common with Rhett than I realized.

"Humor me," Rhett says, drawing me out of my musings. "Hypothetically speaking, let's say you are who I think you are. Some gangster lowlife. Now let's pretend you *didn't* hire a hitman to kill Shelby. Why would someone claim that you had?"

"Hypothetically speaking?" I ask.

"Yeah. Pretend. We're pretending that's reality."

"Then I would tell you that no one leaves a gang without consequences. And that some of my old hypothetical associates would be displeased with my current occupation and consider it traitorous. I don't think we need to imagine what happens to traitors, right? I'd bet they'd go to great lengths to make sure I was hypothetically taken out of the picture."

"Some guy would be willing to go to prison to bring you in?"

"You'd be surprised at how far certain influences go. It's always nice to have a middleman in prison—lots of gangbangers there need goods to push. Think of it more like a sideways promotion."

"Is our prison system really that bad?" Rhett asks, half to himself and half to me.

I chuckle. "It holds individuals well enough. Organizations are a different matter."

There's a piece of me that wonders why Rhett didn't straight up ask me, but I don't press him for the details. If he wants to ask me odd, roundabout questions, I'm not going to stop him.

"Why are you and Miles together?" he asks, continuing his parade of bizarre inquiries. "And I'm not asking about how you met or why you're together now. I mean, why stay together at all? He's not like you."

"I ask myself the same damn question," I murmur as I stare out the window. The rain comes and goes, like the clouds can't make up their minds. "But I think Miles feels he owes me. I helped him get his brother out of a street gang, and we've been together ever since."

"A street gang?"

"The Cobras. You'd know if you saw his shoulder. The kid got a snake inked there like a fucking idiot."

"Oh, he's an idiot, is he?"

"Yeah. That's what I said."

"Let me guess, you're *infinitely* smarter. That's why you got ink on your forearm instead."

I grab at my arm and pull it close. I guess it doesn't matter that he's seen my tattoo, but I've come to loathe the thing.

"No," I drawl, staring at it. "I'm just as stupid."

We cross the Joliet city limit, and the drizzle continues steady until we get into town. Rhett takes every corner sharp, speeds through yellow lights, and only slows for stop signs. That's cop driving for you.

"This isn't how I imagined arresting you," Rhett says. This guy has an odd train of thought.

"Tell me," I say. "How did all your arrest fantasies play out in your head?"

He purses his lips as he turns the car into the suburbs. "They aren't *fantasies*."

I stifle a chuckle. His buttons are easy to push. "I know you wanted me to lose it. That's it, right? You'd kick my ass?"

"I imagined you'd be more resistant."

"I'd hate to rough you up in front of Miles. He thinks highly of you."

"He does?" Rhett asks, a hint of surprise in his tone.

"Tsk."

"Well, he wasn't there when I arrested you in the hotel," Rhett replies, ignoring my dismissal. "No reason to hold back then."

I relax and stare up at the car ceiling, my one eye strained from the low lighting. "Sometimes a man has to follow through with his duty. You carried out yours, and I'm carrying out mine."

Maybe I don't owe Miles anything, but I feel like I *need* to do right by him.

We pull up into the driveway of my house, Rhett deep in thought. There aren't any cars in sight. We either beat Charleston here or we're far too late to do anything about the evidence.

I step out of the vehicle and hobble over to the front door. Locked. I don't have my keys. Instead I walk around to the back, open the gate, and shuffle over to the back door. We never lock it. Probably not a good habit, considering our questionable neighborhood, but it's not like we have much to steal, either.

With a forceful shove, I open the back door and walk inside. The darkness is still. Rain runs the length of the windows.

I walk to our room and switch on the light. The first thing that strikes me is that fact that someone has been in the room—someone not Miles or myself. My old case files from Shelby's office are open and scattered across the floor. Fuck, did they actually beat us here?

I kneel down and pick up the first file. The moment I catch sight of the name, I freeze.

McMillian.

The other files are closed and mostly undisturbed, but McMillian's is open with the police report clear as day, not to mention the terrible witness statement I took from Ms. Timo. Who would break into my room to read this?

I turn around and check the closet. Shelby's hard evidence waits under the floor, just where I left it. My breath goes short when I realize what must've happened.

Shannon got in here and rummaged around through my files. It had to be her. Who else would be so curious? But, then, if she read this, what happened?

I grab Shelby's evidence and throw it on the bed.

"Miles?" I hear someone call out.

With stiff movements I exit my room and walk to the back door. Rhett and Jayden are standing a few feet into the house. Jayden whips his attention over to me and then looks around.

"Where's Miles?" he asks.

I glare at the kid. "What's going on?"

"It's Shannon and Lacy. They ran off. They're gone."

CHAPTER TWENTY

"Explain," I command.

"They came over here to get something," Jayden says, the speed of his speech twice as fast and frantic. "And then Shannon ran off! Lacy came back and told us, but we couldn't find Shannon anywhere. And then, uh, Lacy disappeared, and—"

"How long ago?"

"I dunno. A couple of hours? It wasn't long after you and Miles left."

"And what have you been doing this entire time?" I shout as I take a step closer. Jayden cringes away.

"We called the p-police," he stammers. "They sent two officers. They've been out looking."

I catch my breath; dread replaces all other feeling in my body. "You called the cops?"

"Yeah. Ms. Timo did."

"Two officers showed up?" Rhett asks.

Jayden turns to him, confused, and then glances back at me. I motion for him to answer Rhett. Jayden inhales and says, "Yeah. They showed up quick."

"Fuck," I mutter aloud.

There's a real possibility that these two overzealous cops are getting Worldwide Decurion paychecks, which means they might find the girls, bring them in, and report they found nothing at all. This is a terrible neighborhood; maybe they think they can get away with it. What the fuck am I going to do if that's the case?

I head for the front door, and Rhett grabs my arm, stopping me midway and hurting my shoulder. I turn on my heel and glower. "What?" I snap.

"Where're you going?" he asks.

"To look for the kids, obviously."

"I need that paperwork."

"It's in my bedroom," I state, ripping my arm from his grasp no matter the pain it causes me. "It's on the bed. Take what you want."

He doesn't attempt to stop me a second time, and I storm out of the house—well, *storm out* as well as I can with a stiff leg. I enter the rain fueled by anxiety. Lacy and Shannon are young and no match for fully trained, fully grown police officers. Hell, I'm sure Lacy and Shannon would run into their arms, especially Lacy. They're "safe" and there to "protect" them. Proper authority.

I hope to God those two officers are just concerned men with nothing else on their plates.

"You're gonna walk around in the rain?"

I stop and turn, unwilling to glance over my shoulder. Jayden jogs after me. He comes to a halt at my side and wipes the water from his face with the back of his arm.

"You look fucked-up, man," he mutters.

I don't answer him. Instead I continue on my way, straight down the street, staring into the darkness with one eye, trying to catch sight of movement. There's a park a few blocks down—a terrible, seedy location for drug dealers and hobos—but they've got play equipment, trees, and shrubs. I imagine if I were eleven or twelve, I might head there to escape the rain.

Jayden shadows my trek, his shivering audible above the downpour.

"Lacy!" I call out as I lurch along. "Shannon!"

"They aren't gonna hear you through the weather," Jayden says.

"They might."

"We should go back."

"*You* go back."

I cross the final street to the park and sigh. The place seems larger in the dark of the night. I can't even see the play equipment from the sidewalk. Jayden runs around in front of me and I stop.

"This place is crawling with druggies. You never know what they'll do."

"All the more reason I need to find Lacy and Shannon," I say.

"We should let the cops do this."

I grit my teeth and take a breath. "Did you even look for them?"

Jayden shakes his head. "It's been raining. The cops said they'd handle it."

"Lacy is your goddamn sister and you never bothered to look? Your self-absorbed attitude never ceases to amaze me."

"You're one to talk." He steps forward and shoves me. I slip on the muddy grass, but I catch myself before falling. I clench my fists, more than willing to kick this kid's ass. Miles wouldn't like that, though, and I pull myself from the edge with a quick breath.

Jayden continues, "You can't lecture me about caring when you don't give a shit about Lacy! Or Miles, for that matter!"

Goddammit. Everyone wants a piece of me tonight. Every. Single. Fucking. Person. Either they're here to arrest me, torture me, kill me—berate me—it doesn't matter what, they think they've got something to drill into my skin.

I grab Jayden by the collar of his T-shirt and yank him close. "What the fuck is your problem?" I growl. "Get it out right now."

He leans away, all his posturing gone. I wait, because this is the only moment I'll give him, and I'm eventually rewarded with his ragged inhale of chill air.

"I don't trust you."

Wow. Profound. Was I really expecting anything different?

"You're everything from our old life," Jayden continues through short breaths, slow to get his confidence but quick to raise his voice. "In rehab they told us we had to separate ourselves from bad influences, or else we'd never get clean. You're like our father and our brother, Lawrence. Taking advantage of Miles. Using him. Only caring about what happens to you."

"I don't give a shit about what happens to me," I say, my volume matching his. "I thought I made myself clear, but obviously you're dense enough not to have picked up on it. I *only* care about Miles. But—and it's a big *but*—he cares about you and your sister, which means every time you fuck up, I'll be there to drag your ass back. And if your sister is missing, I'm gonna drag her ass back too. Understand?"

"That's not true."

"Really? You think I'm out here, arguing in the rain, because it's good for me? You think my master plan to screw you is to live in a tiny suburban house, sharing quarters with children, training to get a midrange-paying job? Fuck, kid—you must have a pretty damn low opinion of me. I'm not your shitty father and brother. I could do a lot worse if my goal was to fuck you all over and cut out at the last possible moment."

"Yeah, well…." He flusters a bit but frowns and continues regardless. "You're gettin' into fights, draggin' Miles around. I just…."

I shake him once, and he wipes away the water to get a better look at me. "I don't control your brother," I say. "He does what he wants, sometimes against my wishes. But as long as I'm still kickin', I'll take the bullet for him. Got it? He deserves that much."

"You'd…?"

"What the fuck do you care, anyway?"

Jayden doesn't answer. Maybe he doesn't even have the words to articulate what he's feeling. I remember him hating Miles for attempting to change him, for attempting to get him out of a gang. Perhaps Jayden has come to the realization—although maybe subconsciously—that Miles really *is* looking out for him, and he should do the same in return.

He's not a clever kid, but at least it looks like he might be trying to turn himself around.

"Get back to the house," I tell him as I release his shirt. "If something happened to you too, Miles would be upset."

Jayden wipes himself off and laughs. "Wow, you really are Miles's bitch, aren't you?"

Jesus Christ. The Pope himself would be tempted to kick this kid's ass. I swear he has the situational awareness of a cucumber. Just when I thought I might not hate his guts….

Jayden narrows his eyes, and in a voice low enough that it's almost lost to the rain, he asks, "Do you love him?"

"Get out of here!" I bark. "You're wasting my time!"

He jumps away and shuffles off. Once or twice he looks over his shoulder at me, but I ignore him. Kid needs to mind his own damn business.

I trudge forward into the park. There's a small piece of me that wants to spot someone milling about under a tree, someone with a puffy jacket capable of carrying plenty of supplies. I could ask if they have any prescription drugs for sale—OxyContin was popular not too long ago, and everyone knows it dulls pain like sleep dulls consciousness—but I don't want to deal with the chance of getting mugged. Plus, with the cops scooping people up and never bringing them back, I bet it's harder to find someone right now. I continue on.

The play equipment, soaked and dirty, already has multiple occupants. Three men and a woman have a makeshift tent set up under the grating. I wander up to them, and they give me questioning and apprehensive glances. I laugh to myself. I guess I look odd, everything considered.

"Have you four seen two kids lately?" I ask.

They shake their heads. I nod and walk by, unconcerned with pleasantries.

The picnic tables don't yield anything better. Nor do bikes paths or tennis courts. I stop at the swings to lean against the metal posts. It's only now that I realize how very drained I am. Anxiety isn't a long-lasting fuel source. And the more I look, the more convinced I am they aren't here. Where else is there to look? The tiny shrubs soaked in dog piss? No kid, especially two eleven-year-old girls, would want to subject themselves to that for any length of time. And Shannon was pretty good at hiding when she avoided her grandmother.

From the shadows of the storm, a man approaches me. I muster the energy to stand straight, if only to appear capable and not on the verge of a coma, but I relax the moment I realize it's Miles. The sight of him puts me at ease.

"Pierce?" he asks as he steps close to me. "What happened?"

"Ms. Timo lost the girls."

"Not that. What happened to you?"

"Eh. Some cops and thugs tried to rough me up."

"I think they succeeded."

Miles moves to my side and grabs my arm to sling it over his shoulders.

"*Stop*," I hiss. "Not that arm. The other arm."

He walks to the opposite side and takes most of my weight. I lean onto him, surprised by how warm he is, but I suppose it makes sense, considering I'm soaked in freezing water. We walk together out of the park and onto the street. I focus my attention on Miles.

He's quiet and doesn't look at me as we walk.

There's not much to say as we trek through the neighborhood and reach our house. Still, I wonder. He's not normally so distant.

We enter our house. Jayden paces the living room, and Rhett is at the kitchen table, sitting in a plastic lawn chair. Well, the *new* kitchen table—a flimsy fold-out thing—brings the whole place together in a unifying ghetto aesthetic.

Miles guides me to the couch. I lie back, soaking the cushions, and he unbuttons my shirt. Still, he says nothing, and I don't protest his actions. He takes my wet piece of clothing, walks into the bathroom, and returns with a towel.

"You're bothered," I say as Miles drapes the towel over my body. The room-temperature cloth is a pleasant change of pace.

"I'm worried about Lacy."

"Hm."

"Why'd you leave?" Miles asks as he tilts my head to the side and examines my busted eye.

"The gala?"

"Yeah."

"Rhett came to arrest me."

Miles furrows his brow. "What?"

"Someone tried to arrest you?" Jayden says, cutting into the conversation. "This guy?" He motions to Rhett. "Is that why he's here?"

Rhett stops leafing through paperwork and looks up.

"Pierce didn't do it," Jayden continues. "Whatever it is. He's been watching Lacy and Shannon. I know. I'd vouch for him. He's been busy every minute of every day."

"Now isn't the time for explanation," Rhett says. "But I appreciate how forthcoming you are with information."

"You can't arrest him."

"I have a warrant. But again, now isn't the time."

After his declaration, no one else speaks. Miles gives him a quick glance before returning his attention to me.

"Why?" he asks under his breath, keeping our conversation private.

I dry my hair off with my good arm. With the same volume, I reply, "Some asshole from the Vice family killed Shelby and pinned me as the one who hired him."

"So Jeremy can get you in jail? Is that it?"

"That's what I suspect."

He takes the towel from me and inspects the bruise across my gut. Deputy Chief Charleston did a number on me, for sure. I grimace as Miles grazes his fingers over the injury. For some reason, the feather touch hurts more than standing around did.

Miles gets up and leaves me on the couch. I can't help but feel like something is wrong, but what am I going to say? He returns with a second towel and a pair of tweezers. He kneels next to me, and again, tilts my head to get a better look at my swollen eye.

"Which officers came to look for your sister?" Rhett asks Jayden.

"Which officers? What do you mean?"

"Their names, son. What're their names?"

"Uh, Chal—or something. And Jones. I think."

"Challon and Jones?"

Rhett gathers up a few pages of his paperwork and walks over to Miles. When he flashes his information, Miles gets tense, his expression hardening. I don't need to see it to know what's going on. Both officers are on our guilty-as-fuck list.

"Stay here," Rhett commands, looking at me and then Miles. "I mean it. I need to turn over this evidence without delay, and after that I'll return."

"What if your buddies come to the house looking for said evidence?" I ask.

Rhett freezes midway through gathering up his paperwork. "Stay at a hotel," he answers. "Somewhere in town. Somewhere close." He drops the keys to Castor's vehicle on the table. "Use this. I called a colleague to come get me. I don't need it anymore."

"What about Lacy and Shannon?" Miles asks. "What're you going to do about them?"

"I'll send officers to deal with it. You two are to wait to hear from me."

"But—"

"Don't go looking for them yourselves," he states, a definitive tone to his words.

Miles nods once.

Rhett leaves. Before I can say anything, Miles grabs my chin and holds me in place. "Don't move," he commands.

Jayden walks over, his eyes wide, and I feel agitated by his presence. What is Miles doing? I'm not reassured when I see Miles pick up the tweezers and angle them toward my face. I close my one good eye. Miles grabs the twisted contact protruding from under my eyelid and pulls back, his movements slow, and the flimsy contact scrapes across my eye. The gradual pain builds with each drawn-out moment. Fresh blood runs the length of my face.

"*Sonofabitch*," I hiss. I have to hold myself back from punching the source of my agony.

The moment he pulls the contact from my eye, everything is better. The pain subsides, and I bring a hand up to quell the bleeding. The swollen eyelid still won't open, however.

Miles uses the towel to wipe up the blood.

"That was sick," Jayden says. "I should've recorded it."

Once the blood is gone, Miles leans down and kisses me—his mouth gentle against mine, like he's fearful of hurting me. I enjoy him close like this. I didn't even realize I craved it.

"Uh, seriously?" Jayden continues. "*This* is what you're into, Miles? A guy who's so messed up he's practically half beef jerky? You know women are pretty, right?"

Miles pulls away. "Weren't you defending Pierce a second ago?"

"Hey. He can be a good guy, or whatever, and still be a gross dude with an eye problem. You didn't have to make out with him *now*. You could've waited. That's all I'm sayin'."

"Jayden."

"Uh, yeah? I was just joking."

"Forget it. I want you to go get Ms. Timo."

"Get her?"

"Bring her here. We're going to a hotel."

"O-okay."

Jayden jogs out of the house and into the dying storm. Although I would say I like him a little more than I did yesterday, I still prefer silence over his commentary. The quiet that follows his departure is welcome.

"They wouldn't take two runaway girls to jail," Miles comments, his voice so neutral it borders on uncaring. But I know that can't be the case.

"*If* they found them," I say.

"Let's pretend they did. Where would they take them?"

"The Vice family is the one moving people, right? They'd take them there. For packing."

"And you would know where that is?"

"I haven't been in the loop for a while," I drawl. "But I know a few people. I could find out."

"Then that's what we're going to do."

I hold the towel over my eye and mull over the statement. Miles isn't talking to me like he usually does. It worries me, but I know for certain he's worried about his sister. Perhaps this is his way of not panicking. Unlike Jayden, who also had problems, Lacy is young, not yet a teenager. She shouldn't be left in the care of gangbangers for any length of time.

Nor should Shannon, for that matter.

"Didn't Rhett tell you not to do anything about it?" I ask.

"I don't care," Miles states, anger finally in his voice. "I know we can find her faster. You know everything about the Vice family. And even if your knowledge is a little out of date, you know all their friends and associates like the back of your hand. We have to do this."

I nod. "If that's what you want. I'll do it."

CHAPTER TWENTY-ONE

IT FEELS like an eternity ago that I stood in the Grand Noimore Waterfront Hotel. I glance at my phone and groan. 11:35 p.m. Fuck. It's still the same *day* as the gala, despite everything I've been through. Time sure does crawl when you're getting your ass beat.

Miles and I walk out of the Economy Motel and head for our car—well, Castor's car, but ours for the time being. He jumps for the driver's seat with enough energy for three men. I force myself to sit in the passenger's seat, my whole body protesting my every movement. I have my gun, but I know I'm going to be terrible in a fight. I touch the patch bandage over my eye and grimace.

At least the rain has stopped.

Before Miles peels out of the parking lot, Ms. Timo hobbles out of the motel. I roll down my window, and she stops once she can place a hand on the car door.

"Are you going to look for Shannon?" she asks.

The old lady has been crying for hours. Her voice is hoarse and her eyes bloodshot. You can't speak to her without the woman getting close to hysterics. I understand her concern, but it's hard to comprehend the level of panic, considering I'm not a father. Still, I feel for the crone, especially when her hands shake with every word.

"We'll be back," Miles replies. "Stay with Jayden. The police will call him when they find something."

"It's all my fault," Ms. Timo mutters. "I should've spoken to her sooner. I should've—"

"Save it," I say, curt.

She frets for a moment. "I came to say I'm sorry."

"For what?"

"Lacy's a good girl. She never would've run off if it weren't for her concern for Shannon. I didn't mean to harm your family."

Miles offers her a smile. "Everything will be okay. I'm sure the police will find them soon, and we'll all laugh about this later." He delivers the pep talk with an edge of genuine optimism. Ms. Timo doesn't know about the corrupt cops or the dubious plan to sell lowlife criminals and runaways to the body trade, so she accepts the reassurances without a second of thought.

"You're right," she murmurs. "You two hurry back. It's late."

I roll up the window, and Miles drives the vehicle out of the parking lot. The clouds part, revealing the starry night, and it's enough to remind me of my fatigue. I lean back in my seat and rest my uninjured arm over my face to block out what little light surrounds us.

"Where should I head?" Miles asks.

"Do you know the bar on South Street called Copper Town?"

"In Noimore?"

"Yeah."

"No, but my phone does."

I chuckle. "Head there. I know a few guys who frequent the place."

Miles nods as he pushes the gearshift into place. I guess he knows how to drive a manual as well. My mind dwells on the fact as I close my eye and drift into sleep.

"PIERCE. WAKE up. We need to find Lacy."

I jerk to the side and take in a ragged breath. Grogginess clouds my thoughts. I sit up, my head buzzing, and glance over at Miles. He zips up his jacket, concealing his shoulder holster and firearm, and he gives me the once-over.

"I need to find Lacy," Miles repeats, his voice hushed. "Here." He hands me a bottle of water and a Snickers bar.

When did he stop to get these? I must have been out like a light. No matter. I guzzle the water and consume the Snickers without thought. My gut grumbles a bit, but everything stays down.

I look at my phone. 12:05 a.m. That's record time. Miles must've been speeding like a lunatic.

With the last of my water, I splash my face. "All right," I say. "Let's go in. And let me do the talking."

"I don't want one night to go by with Lacy in their hands. Please, Pierce. We need to find out where they're keeping people, and we need to do it tonight."

There's no urgency in his tone—he sounds as calm as they come—but his words convey everything. I don't look like hot stuff, and he's worried I might blow this. Funny enough, I'm more comfortable handling this than I would be taking proper witness statements.

I step out of the vehicle and walk up to the bar. It's a simple building painted black and wedged between two larger businesses, practically at the end of an alley. The windows, plastered in neon signs that flash and blink, are covered from the inside with thick blackout blinds. I like this place. It's private. Not many people outside Noimore even know it exists.

Miles and I enter. A cloud of smoke wafts out into the night as we cross the threshold. Despite the fog, there aren't many individuals in the joint. The bartender, Sammy, doles out drinks at a slow rate, serving the three at the bar with no haste in his movements. The other four patrons—men I don't know and don't care to know—eye me and Miles as we stroll in.

"Where's your buddy?" Miles asks.

Having one eye makes it hard to glance around and my neck aches like a bitch, but I eventually get everything. The copper accents on the bar, tables, and chairs sparkle under the dim overhead lighting. My old associate, James "Chronic" Ward, is nowhere to be seen. I head straight back to the bathroom, certain he's there. I'm also certain Sammy won't like the fact we aren't ordering a drink, but I don't want the man to recognize me.

I get two steps into the men's room and spot Ward leaning against the sole sink. He's hard to miss, what with his tight black leather pants and open jacket. The guy sports a whole host of tattoos, and I suppose he wants to show them off, which is why he opts out of wearing a shirt. Despite his thuggish appearance, he smiles wide, a cigarette clamped in his teeth.

"Hey, friends," Ward says, a slick manner to his speech. "Lookin' to relax?"

I step up close to him, and he straightens his posture, his smile disappearing.

"Pierce? Is that you?"

"Last I checked," I say.

He grabs my upper arm and pulls me to him, half smiling. "Shit, really? I heard you were dead. And then maybe you were alive again. I haven't seen you in ages." I enjoy the smell of the smoke he exhales—it's my favorite brand of cigarette.

"I need to speak to you."

Ward tilts his head. "*Me*? Heh. All right. Let's get some privacy."

All of us walk out of the bathroom, and once again, we're given odd glances by everyone in the room. Sammy and Ward exchange a quick nod, and I know we won't be hassled by the bouncers while we're outside.

We step out into the cold, and Ward rounds the corner of the building, standing a few feet away from the grimy dumpster. There aren't any homeless druggies milling about, and I know why. Everyone's doing their business behind closed doors now.

"You wanna smoke?" Ward asks, withdrawing a cheap cigar from his pocket and twirling it around. I sneer. All the guys in this area empty those cigars and fill them with weed—and add their own "flavors."

I shake my head.

"You sure? It's got some embalming fluid."

"Like what you soak dead people in?" Miles says, interjecting himself into the conversation.

"He means it's got PCP," I reply. "Forget about it."

Ward stares at Miles for a moment before returning his attention to me. "What's this? Ya got yellow fever?"

"I'm not here to bullshit, Ward. I've been out of it for a while. I need information. I know you still work for the Vice family. This is your side gig."

"Yeah," Ward says. "Okay. What did you want to know?"

"What's Jeremy been doing since I died? Where'd he hole up?"

"Oh, wait, you want to reconnect?" He laughs, throwing his whole back into it. "*Seriously*? D'aww, you must miss him! That's adorable."

I wait for Ward to collect himself before continuing, my expression never changing. "Where is he?"

Ward chuckles once more. Then he says, "Man, I dunno. Operations have gotten weird since he got outta jail. He changed things up. Started spendin' money."

I suspected his time in jail had been the game changer. Jeremy must've spoken to Worldwide Decurion and then the crooked cops of the Noimore system.

"What about spending money?" I ask.

"On properties. He owns a lot of empty lots and such. I guess he's going to build stuff, like his old man, but now he also owns a bunch of trucks and boats and junk." The guy squints and smiles, like he's holding back another round of laughter. "Want me to give you Jeremy's number? I got it from one of his enforcers. You two could sext each other. Wouldn't that be cute?"

I glare at him. "Shut the fuck up. I'm not here to talk to him. I want to know where he stores things. Which one of these new properties has traffic going through it?"

Ward takes a long drag on his cigarette as he mulls over the statement. As he exhales he digs into his pocket and pulls out a half-used pack. "Want one?" he asks, shaking the pack of cigarettes.

"No," I say.

That's not true. I want one, but I shouldn't take it. Now isn't the time.

"You've changed," Ward mutters as he puts his pack away. "And not like you did with Jeremy, where you got ruthless. I mean, you're the shadow of Pierce. Some old man with one foot in death's door." He chuckles. "Or maybe you went face-first, huh?" He points to my eye and gets another solid laugh.

"Where does he keep things?" I repeat. "And then you can get back to your business."

"I dunno, Pierce. You're messin' with my livelihood. I don't get much from backroom dealin'. I need Jeremy if I'm gonna keep up my lifestyle choices, if ya get what I mean."

"A choice of bedpans is gonna be your next lifestyle decision if you hold out on me, Ward. This isn't up for discussion."

"Big talk for a guy with a busted face."

I grab Ward by his jacket and pull him close. "I'm the guy who was dead eight months ago, remember? I've got more than one card to play."

He jerks out of my grasp and glares. Before he says anything, he brushes himself off and slicks back his greasy hair. "Why'd you come to me? I don't want no part of this."

"You keep to yourself, you deal to all using members of the Vice family, and I've never had issues with you before. I'm not looking to put

Jeremy out of business. I'm looking to get something back from him, and he'll never suspect *you* pointed me in the right direction. Everything works out, right?"

Ward finishes his cigarette and snuffs it out under his boot. "What's in it for me? Or is your threat my only incentive?"

"Not his threat," Miles says. "It's mine."

He steps around me and slams Ward up against the wall of the bar. Unlike Miles, who has the cut of muscle to show for all his exercise, Ward is more a lithe guy with long limbs and scrawny legs. He reaches for something tucked into the belt of his pants, right on the small of his back, but Miles beats him to the punch and grabs Ward's .22 handgun. When Ward goes to take it, Miles decks him across the face, the genuine crack of knuckles on skin echoing throughout the alley.

"Hey," I bark. "Calm down!"

I don't go to intervene. Either Miles will listen or he won't. No need for me to get roughed up on Ward's behalf.

"Whoa, whoa!" Ward pleads. "Stop!"

"Are you going to talk?" Miles growls, his teeth practically clenched shut. He eases up a bit but keeps Ward pinned to the wall.

"You're lookin' for trouble if you ask around like this."

Miles cocks a fist. Ward flinches.

"All right," Ward says, his hands up. "Jeremy keeps stuff in lots of places, but I assume you want the bodies, right? He keeps his bodies in an old ambulance dispatch station before shippin' them out of town. The dispatch station's set up for keepin' people alive before a long trip, ya see?"

"Where, specifically?" I ask. The ambulance dispatch center rings a bell. And then I remember. It was on Shelby's list of locations. That's a good sign—there's a good chance Ward is telling the truth.

"On School Street and Oakwood Ridge," Ward replies. "It's next to an old retirement home. Both of them are closed, okay? Whole damn neighborhood is abandoned."

Miles goes to release him, but I stop him with a wave of my hand.

"What else?" I ask. "You're not telling us something."

Ward lets out a long exhale. "The place *was* abandoned. Jeremy uses it for storage. And his weird games. Guy's a kook."

Ah. The place will be swarming with hired guns. That could be a problem, but then again, we have surprise on our side. People underestimate what surprise can do for them.

I motion for Miles to let the guy go. He does so, and Ward jumps away.

"Can I get my gun back?" he asks.

Miles pockets the weapon. Smart kid. We don't want to risk Ward getting weird and shooting us in the back.

"What's Jeremy's number?" I ask as I walk up to him.

Ward cocks an eyebrow. "You're gonna call him?"

"Perhaps."

Ward pulls out his cell phone and begins flipping through his contacts list.

I snort. "You don't know it by heart?"

"Of course not. Who remembers phone numbers anymore, am I right? What's the fuckin' point?"

I grab Ward's phone and throw it to the cement, shattering the screen. For a moment he stands still, frozen with his mouth hanging open. I stomp on the device, turn on my heel, and head back for the car.

"What the fuck was that for?" he shouts after me.

I can't have him calling Jeremy to warn him. And if he can't remember the number, the only way he'll warn the man is personally driving up to him. This is my last guarantee, basically, to remain incognito. It's not 100 percent foolproof, but anything is better than nothing. At least Ward doesn't know what we're looking for. Jeremy would never suspect I was looking to save two little girls.

As we walk to the car, I spot Miles rotating his arm.

"Got a little physical back there," I say.

"Yeah," he mutters.

"You're worried. You've been on the edge of losing it since you got home."

"I've been on the edge of losing it since Jayden called to tell me what happened."

Now it makes sense. His odd behavior goes back to his bizarre need to mother his siblings. I guess I can't fault him for that trait. I knew about it going into this arrangement.

We both get into the car, and I feel the need to say something to him.

"Careful," I say. "You don't want to lose your head. It invites accidents."

Miles starts the car. "You're right."

"I never thought I'd have to give you advice like that. A year ago you'd be flailing about, asking for my help."

"Well, I've taken everything you've said to heart." He turns and stares at me, his dark eyes filled with a sort of energy I can't muster at the moment. "I want to be more like you, Pierce. You're… confident. And you know how to handle yourself."

Heh. It's a good thing he can't read minds. Self-doubt is like a fire—it'll consume you if you stand in it too long—and I burned myself earlier tonight. Of course, none of my problems are resolved; I've just tabled them until I have all these emergencies taken care of. I still need to deal with reality.

"Plus," Miles adds as he pulls away from Copper Town. "Don't you prefer men who are assertive? I mean, I know you liked me before, but you always seem to stare at men who are, well, *forceful* and *gruff*."

"You're doing this for me?"

"No, I just thought it was a nice benefit."

"Good. That's how it should be."

RETIREMENT HOMES give me the creeps. Not haunted houses, not dark alleys. Retirement homes. I don't know why—I've never been beaten in one and left for dead—but I've avoided them all my life until now. Something about the very concept of them gets under my skin. Men and women too old to live but not old enough to die…. It's like a hellish limbo on Earth.

This retirement home used to have a name, but not anymore. The sign sits in disrepair, the letters long gone and the lights dead. It's not small, however. Two stories and in the shape of a U—from the outside it looks rather massive. Adjacent to the retirement home is an emergency dispatch center. Probably a good choice for one, what with the old folks right next door.

There aren't as many thugs as I thought there would be, but there's enough to take note, and I can't see inside. Pairs of bruisers circle around the perimeter, shootin' the breeze. They must be moving bodies soon—why else have so many guys roaming the area? And that would explain why the crooked cops would opt out of the gala to work tonight's shift. It would also explain why two cops in Joliet would go out of their way to drop off runaways. They want them gone fast.

"How are we going to do this?" Miles asks.

I shift behind our broken-fence hideaway. The neighborhood really is abandoned, and I suspect it was scheduled for demolition and urban improvement until Jeremy got his hands on a few parcels of property. Regardless, I lean against the busted property division and think over the problem.

"I don't know much about this place," I say. "It's not a haunt I stalked before I left the Vice family. We could try finding a guy I know—but there's a good chance he won't be happy to see me. Or we could go straight for the holdings and search for Lacy, but if we're trapped in a corner with forty guns on us, we're not leaving."

"How long do you think we have?"

"What? I have no idea."

Miles motions to a cavalcade of semitrucks rolling down the far road, the roar of their engines dominating the area once they near. The three monstrous vehicles have grocery store advertisements across their trailers. Anyone with half a brain could see they aren't here to pick up cabbage, but I guess no one is around to see anything at all.

"I guess we don't have much choice in terms of action," I murmur as I watch the semitrucks come to a stop in front of the emergency center and retirement home. They really are moving bodies tonight.

CHAPTER TWENTY-TWO

THE SEMITRUCKS maneuver with the grace of a drunken bull. One by one they angle and turn around, forcing the back ends of their trailers to face the buildings. Only one semitruck can fit in the parking lot in front of the emergency dispatch center. The other two park in front of the retirement home. Once situated, the drivers jump out and open the trailers.

Another parade of three vehicles pulls up to the party. They're all black and sleek, one fancier than the rest and clearly a short limo. The other two are SUVs, and four men exit each one. The compact limo, on the other hand, has the one person I had hoped to avoid.

Jeremy Vice.

It's not hard to tell. He's shorter than the rest, wearing a much fancier charcoal suit, and his ears angle straight out. Miles spots him too, and his whole demeanor hardens in an instant. He pulls his gun and holds it at the ready. I place my hand on his arm and shake my head.

"We're not fighting all of them," I say.

"I know."

"Then don't act like we are."

Miles keeps his handgun out, but he relaxes his stance and takes a deep breath.

I sit and observe Jeremy and his men enter the retirement home. The bruisers outside, along with the truck drivers, open the trailers and prep the insides, like they're making room for the cargo, or perhaps making cubbies among legitimate goods.

"I'll handle Jeremy when the time comes," I mutter. "You focus on finding the girls."

Miles grits his teeth. "No. *I'll* handle Jeremy."

I give him a one-sided smile. "I think I owe him for a couple months of my life."

"He shot my brother," Miles states, venom in his voice. "He threatened to kill me. He took you away. Now he has my sister. I don't think his harm is exclusive to you."

I hadn't thought of it that way. "He'll have muscle with him at all times," I say, hoping to cast doubt. "We shouldn't go out of our way for a vendetta." Maybe *I* would go out of my way, but I've run on the streets for twenty years and know how vicious some people can get. Miles shouldn't face down Jeremy. I'm afraid he'll learn a lesson the hard way if he does.

Miles shifts his weight from one foot to the other, muttering things to himself. I look over, and he shakes his head. "Pierce, what're we going to do? Should we call the cops and hope we get some of the good ones? What if we call Rhett?"

They might not make it in time, even if we *did* call the cops. "Send Rhett a message. Tell him we're trespassing on private property."

"Why?"

"Because it's a crime, he'll have to do something, and he'll know what we mean without outright stating our activities."

"All right. But that doesn't solve *this* problem." Miles types away on his phone, one-handed, and gets a small paragraph out before I gather my thoughts. Tsk. He sure knows his way around a cell phone.

"We'll steal a truck," I say. "We'll get in the cab, take out the driver, pretend we're following their group, and then break off. They won't fight us once we reach public areas, and by then Rhett will have officers ready."

I hope.

"Do you know how to drive a truck?" Miles asks.

I open my mouth and then close it. Fuck. Are they really more difficult to drive? I don't want to find out in the middle of a getaway. I shake my head. "We'll force the driver to cooperate. A gun to the back of the head is a great motivator."

"We can't bullshit around anymore. We need to find Lacy before they load anything."

I motion to the paramedic station. Since everyone is busy inside the run-down retirement home, we should be able to investigate without much hassle. Miles picks up on my gesture and scouts ahead, darting from one shadowy location to the next as he heads to the emergency dispatch center.

I like the night, but the stillness isn't my ally. I hobble along, my injured leg and ripped-up calf preventing me from perfect stealth. The hard click of my shoes gets my heart rate up. All it will take is one thug to spot me and we'll lose any semblance of an advantage.

For a moment, I wonder why everyone is inside the retirement home. If the bodies are kept in the medical areas of the paramedic dispatch building, what is Jeremy doing one building over? I grind my teeth as I duck behind an overgrown tree on the opposite side of the parking lot—I know what they're doing. They're fuckin' around with the merchandise before it's shipped out. One last hurrah before it's no longer theirs. They aren't taking organs, obviously, not like some of the buyers, but I'm sure they're not keeping their hands to themselves.

Miles runs across the street and slams his back against the dispatch building. He glances around before motioning me to join him. I follow after, taking twice as long, and stop only once I reach his side.

"Where has everyone gone?" Miles whispers.

"Inside."

"Why?"

"I don't know," I say, keeping my deductions to myself. He doesn't need to hear any of my thoughts. It's best not to think of Shannon and Lacy in the hands of men like Jeremy and his goons.

I hope to God they're in the dispatch building, drugged and awaiting shipment or something. That's better than every other scenario I can think of.

"One of us should go around to the back," I say. "We enter both ways, get as much information as possible. If you think you'll get caught, leave and we'll meet up across the street."

"All right," he replies, an unsteadiness to his voice that betrays his fear. Still, he doesn't show it. He has his gun, he holds himself ready, and he takes off around the building. I guess I get the front.

I move over to the glass front door and see the name of the dispatch unit, along with the address, has been scraped from the building. The inside is dark. Nothing to see and no movement. I try the door and find it open. I'd say I'm lucky, but I know that's not the case. People are inside.

I enter.

Dust hangs on the air. I wrinkle my nose to stop a sneeze and continue forward. I didn't bring a flashlight, and I wouldn't use one, considering the situation, but I'd love to have the light. The reception desk is cast in shadow, the doors leading deeper standing ajar. I amble around and open the first one I come across, listening to the long creak as the door swings inward.

It's impossible to see more than two feet down the darkened hallway at any point. I scoot along, hesitant, and keep my back close to the wall. Twice I crunch down on what I think is glass. Bottles, maybe? I try to avoid them.

I come to a T intersection at the end of the hallway, and I only know that thanks to the light emanating from under some of the doors.

A loud bang—metal on metal, not a gunshot—echoes throughout the building. Adrenaline dumps into my system. I grab my gun, hold my breath, and continue to listen, my heart beating so hard it's difficult to distinguish the other sounds.

Men laughing.

I take a deep breath. Then exhale.

"Another, another!" someone yells.

One of the lit rooms erupts in a round of cheering. They're playing a game? I don't fucking know, and I don't want to think about it. Instead I glance down the opposite end of the hall. There are some other doors, but it's hard to make anything out.

The "party room" door opens, casting light into the hallway and destroying my dark-vision. I scoot back, hiding around the corner.

"One sec," a man says with a grunt.

The door closes, taking the light with it, and some lowlife wearing tough reinforced clothing staggers down the hallway at an uneven pace. He passes by me—*right by me*—and I remain unmoving. He never turns to acknowledge me, and I suspect his vision is impaired, even if it's not as bad as mine.

The thug bangs on a few doors down the other hall.

"Finish up," he says. "Boss called. It'll be time to move out in thirty minutes."

He repeats this process three times more. I get my gun ready, half tempted to shoot him right now, but what would I do then? Instead I wait as he stumbles back into the party room. The people tell him to take a seat, and I imagine most of them aren't drunk off their asses; it's just him.

I take the hallway opposite the party room and trace the man's steps. I have a choice of four doors—one secured shut with a chair posted under the handle. Keeping my handgun close, I shuffle over to the chair and push it aside. People stir behind the other three doors. They're "finishing up" whatever it is they're doing, and I know I need to hustle.

I enter the blocked room and find an unmoving body atop a medical table, though the silhouettes of shapes make it impossible to see detail. I flip the light switch, but nothing happens. Of course not. This place probably doesn't have power—any light I've seen is emanating from outside stuff brought in. Flashlights and lanterns, perhaps.

Whoever is on the table isn't Lacy or Shannon; that much I'm sure of, considering they're an adult. I do spot paperwork, however, and I'm reminded of what Miles said about gathering evidence. Perhaps this is information from Worldwide Decurion. I don't truly know, but I don't mind taking that risk. It's the least I can do for Shelby at this point. I should make sure these assholes are brought to justice, for him and his kid.

I fold up some of the paperwork and jam it down into my pants pocket.

Doors in the hall open and close, and I shuffle back to catch the shadowy shapes of individuals heading for the party room. Leaving the poor schmoe on the table, I return to the hallway and try another door. It's locked from my side with a chain, and I know it's a fixture added to the building long after it was closed down.

I unlock the door and step in.

"Get back!"

I catch my breath, caught off guard by the sudden command, and I lift my gun to answer. There's a portable lamp at the back of the room, shining bright behind the speaker. It doesn't take me long to piece together their identity, however, and I thank whatever God above is watching.

Lacy stands in front of Shannon, a syringe in her hand like a knife. She's dressed in a long white T-shirt—a man's shirt, hanging far enough to act as a short dress—and nothing else. No shoes, no socks. She glares at me with a determined passion I've seen in a few rare men, like she's ready to kill me if needed. Shannon, on the other hand, huddles near the wall, her long brown hair draped over her face as she hugs her knees to her chest. She too wears a long men's T-shirt.

"I said, get back!" Lacy says, holding the syringe high, her fingers tight around the glass and her thumb on the plunger.

I guess she doesn't recognize me in the shadows of the doorframe. I step up into the light and lower my weapon.

"Lacy, keep quiet."

Her eyes go wide, and her mouth hangs open. "Pierce?" she whispers. "How did you—"

"Shh," I hiss.

I walk over to her, and she hesitates. After fidgeting with her long black hair, she hands over the medical instrument. I pocket the thing in my jacket, keeping the needle tucked into the corner, unsure of where she got it. I flinch as Lacy throws her arms around my torso in a tight hug.

I don't think she's ever touched me before, let alone embraced me. I pat her shoulder, awkward about the whole situation. I feel her hands twist into my jacket, like she doesn't want to let go.

My gut hurts. I'd push her away, but I can't bring myself to do it. Instead I wait.

Finally Lacy releases me, her expression one of mixed emotions, unlike a few seconds ago. I kneel down and rest my weight on one knee.

"Are you hurt?" I ask in a hushed voice, glancing from Lacy to Shannon. "Can you both... walk?"

I don't know what to ask them, or even say. I swear I'll kill the son of a bitch who hurt them, but that won't change whatever's happened.

Lacy grabs my jacket sleeve, her grip tight. "There were police officers. They got in their car. They took us here, all the way from Joliet. They wouldn't talk to us. I thought we were in trouble."

She speaks fast and takes quick breaths between short sentences. I listen, keeping my attention on her, but she won't meet my gaze. She stares off to the side.

"They said we had to wait here," Lacy continues. "And then other people came to see us. They had guns. They told us to take off our clothes. I told them no. Shannon did too. But they didn't listen. They had guns. We didn't want to. We told them no."

"I understand."

"We didn't want to," Lacy repeats, this time staring at me with glassy eyes.

"I believe you," I say.

"Shannon cried, and... and then they gave us shirts. And then a man asked us a bunch of questions. He had so many needles. He took our blood."

I grit my teeth. At least these assholes had some humanity. When two little girls started crying, they handed over shirts.

Shit like this never happened when I worked for Big Man Vice. Jeremy's brought the bar down a few notches if I'm thanking his men for showing shreds of decency.

I know we were all criminals—it's not like we were good guys worth emulating—but we fought and killed other criminals back in my day. Decency meant keeping hardworking stiffs out of the equation, and Big Man Vice never targeted children. He was a church man and thought God wouldn't forgive certain acts of violence, no matter how much you pleaded.

"They didn't hurt you?" I ask.

Lacy shows me the crux of her arm. The red spot, illuminated poorly by the sole lamp, indicates where they drew blood. "He just left."

As though talking about this thug brought him back, I hear movement in the hall. I stand, tense, and glance around. It's a square room with counters lining two walls, but otherwise barren. No windows. Nothing in here to hide behind. Nothing in here to use as a silent weapon.

Except the lamp. It's made of three metal rods attached to a thick metal base.

I motion for Lacy to give it to me, and she complies with my nonverbal command. Once it's unplugged, the room goes black, but at least that adds the fun element of surprise.

The door opens. I step forward, not giving a shit about my limp, and the man in the doorframe takes a step back.

"The fuck's going on here?" he asks, squinting.

I bash his face in with the base of the lamp. It's dark, even in the hallway, but the wet crunch of teeth is distinct. He hits the floor and I stomp down on his nose, busting up what's left of his mug. He lies motionless. He could be dead, but I doubt it. The scrape of glass draws my attention away from his body.

"Juan? The fuck?"

Another thug stands at the T intersection. He points his gun but doesn't fire, his uncertain movements betraying his lack of sight. He steps forward, sure to see me at any moment, and my mind goes blank. What am I going to do? Gunfire will get us caught. It has to be my last resort.

More glass crunching.

Someone runs up behind the guy and gets him in a rear naked choke—one arm around pulled across the neck and restricting his airflow—while the second hand rips the gun away and throws it to the floor before aiding in the choke with a powerful torque. Despite my impaired visibility, the skill in the technique is clear as day. Two moves and the thug was disabled. The newcomer knows his stuff.

After twenty seconds, the thug collapses to the floor.

"Miles," I mutter the moment I get a good look at him. I don't think I've ever found the man quite so fucking attractive. He walked over and knocked that guy out without a second's hesitation. It gets my blood going.

Miles jogs to me, the hallway a mild obstacle course of bodies at this point, and he grabs my shoulder. "Have you found them?"

I back up into the room. Lacy runs into her brother's arms the moment he rounds the corner. The siblings share a tight embrace, and I turn away, not wanting to intrude on their moment.

"Miles, I knew you'd come," Lacy says, practically breathless.

"Of course. Always."

Shannon sits against the wall in the same position I saw her last. I shuffle over and motion for her to stand, though I doubt she sees.

"Get up," I command. "We need to leave."

She doesn't move.

Fuck. Now isn't the time for this.

I bend down and scoop her up into my arms, my shoulder burning in protest. I half stumble forward, and I almost go face-first into the wall, but I catch myself and keep her close. She struggles for a moment, like she doesn't want to be taken from this place.

"I'm getting you out of here," I growl.

I hear a stifled sob and then nothing. Shannon quiets herself and goes still. I walk with her back to Miles. She's not heavy, but my body isn't in perfect shape.

"Hurry," Miles says, urgency in his tone and movements. He picks up Lacy and leads us out the way I came, to the front door. I'm slow, but I know where I'm going. When we reach the glass front doors, I get a good look outside. At least ten guys are there, prepping the semitruck. Miles backs up into me, keeping us on the border of the darkness and just out of sight.

"We need to go out the back," he says.

I turn around and follow him through the medical building, avoiding the hallway we littered with unconscious goons.

We don't have much time. The guy I hit and the guy Miles choked out will both wake up soon, I'm sure of it. When we reach the long hall to the back, Miles once again freezes. More guys are waiting at the back exit, at least six of them. They smoke and exchange small talk.

Miles turns around and pushes me down another hall.

I'm lost now. Miles is the one running things. I follow him as best I can.

We reach some sort of side door exit, and he throws it open without a second thought. We step outside—into a shadowed alleyway between the retirement home and the paramedic building—and I see the lights of cars at both ends. Lowlifes mill about the parking lot and the back area of the building, blocking both our exits. What're we going to do now? We're out in the open and carrying two little girls. It's only a matter of time before we're caught.

Miles rushes over to the retirement home. He stops in front of a side door and motions me with a jerk of his head. I walk over but step in front of the door, blocking the handle.

"What're you doing?" I ask, incredulous. "We can't go in there!"

"It's our only option. The place is huge. We could hide, or find another way out."

"No. There are more guys in here than the dispatch center."

"What else are we going to do?"

Damn. This plan reeks of uncertainty. But there are goons everywhere. Lacy and Miles stare at me as though I need to ultimately decide. I curse under my breath and step out of the way. I guess we're going into the retirement home.

CHAPTER TWENTY-THREE

THE DOOR shuts behind us, cutting off all moonlight.

Darkness.

Shannon shudders against me and takes in ragged breaths. My shoulder burns, and I kneel to set her down, but she tightens her grip and refuses to let go.

"You're okay," I tell her, trying to be gentle. My gruff voice isn't built for it.

"Nobody came for me," she replies, her words so distant they could belong to a ghost. "Nobody...."

"What're you talking about, girl? I'm right here. Miles and I came for you."

"You came for Lacy! I'm not... not...." Shannon's voice cracks, and she presses her face into my jacket. After another ragged breath, she continues, "Nobody.... They don't want me. Nobody cares."

Miles sets Lacy down. "We really don't have time for this. I'm going to look around and—"

"Don't go far," I command. "We'll end up shooting each other if you get out of sight. There are too many variables here."

Through the gloom I can hear him exhale and run a hand across his neck. "Okay. I'll stay close. But we need to hurry. I don't want to get caught in a firefight."

I don't want Miles to leave. I don't want him to get more than a few feet away, if possible. He's my only real companion here—the one I trust—the one I'm most concerned with. Even separating to search the emergency dispatch center got me nervous.

But Miles walks a few feet around the retirement home, in the nearby area, and I strain my ears to make sure he's nearby. This place is cold and dreary. The open echo of Miles's steps tells me we're in a large room, perhaps a cafeteria, and I wait for my one eye to adjust to the low lighting offered by distant windows.

"Shannon, let go," I say.

She doesn't respond, and she doesn't move.

Lacy takes a step closer and places a hand on her shoulder. "I'm here."

Still, Shannon says nothing.

There's a small piece of me that wants to shake her and tell her that now isn't the time for existential dread. We've all got problems, and we've all got shit to deal with on our own time.

Lacy grabs my arm. "Say something," she pleads. "You knew about her mother."

Goddammit. *I* didn't make the choice to hide it from her.

Of course, I understand why she's upset. Her mother is dead, her father isn't going to be in her life anytime soon, and her grandmother keeps secrets from her. Who is she supposed to turn to? Who's left?

"We weren't going to leave without you," I say. "You need to pull yourself up by your bootstraps and help us. Okay? When I was young, my father died, and my mother went to jail shortly after. I can take care of myself, right? Sometimes life kicks you in ass, but you're strong enough to kick back. I know, because I did it. You can too."

"Your father died?" Lacy asks, surprise in her tone. "And you don't have your mother?"

"I'm fine. A little secret—sometimes you make your own family."

Of course, what I *don't* tell them is that I made a mob family my family. I went from not having a home to breaking skulls for living. Not really Hallmark movie material, but they don't need to know the details, right? Hell if I know.

"I'm cold," Shannon whispers.

Better than her staying silent. "I'll give you my jacket."

She lets go of me, and I stand in order to shuffle off my outer layer. I wrap it around her and zip up the front.

A door slams open. Everyone jumps, but it's an echo of a far-off door somewhere in the retirement home. Miles rushes back to us and motions to the opposite end of the room.

"C'mon. We need to go."

I follow Miles, and the two girls stay by my side, both of them with a grip on my shirt. We exit the large cafeteria and enter a nurse's station. It's long been abandoned. All that remains is the desk and metal filing cabinets. Miles takes us to the other end and cracks open the door.

"Boss! Boss!"

We all freeze. The front lobby hosts a crowd of people. There's a commotion. I can taste the tension in the air, just from the bated breath and silence that follows the cries of *boss*.

"We've got a problem," the same man continues, his voice a mixture of smoker and stoner. "Juan and Guerrero were cleanin' up, when they were attacked."

"Attacked?"

Jeremy's voice. I'd bet my life on it.

"Dropped in the hall. Guerrero says there were multiples of 'em. I don't know what they're doin', but they took two of the merchandise."

"Someone specific?"

"Two little girls the cops brought in. Maybe they're family. I dunno."

"We shouldn't be picking up anyone important," Jeremy shouts. "None of these plebs should have any connection to anyone of significance!"

"They didn't. They *don't*. They're runaways. Just some Asian and white trash. Cops said both had fathers that were in jail and—"

"An Asian?"

"Yeah. That's what I said."

I don't even need to see the man to know he's put one and two together. I nudge Miles and motion to enter the room. Change of plans. The lobby is huge, and there's only light near the front door—we're not leaving that way, which means there's little option to get to the trucks. We can slip through the sidelines if we're quiet, and we need to leave *right now*.

"Search the place," Jeremy commands. "And open up windows. You never know when they'll have something chemical." He waits a moment. "Well? I said search the place! Not you two. You stay with me."

The hired guns take off, scattering to cover the most amount of territory.

Miles shuffles into the lobby, keeping to the shadows, and I trail behind with the girls. They aren't wearing any shoes, which gets me worried, considering the condition the building is in, but I don't have anything to give them, and it's not like I can carry them both.

Miles takes the first hallway he comes across, and we're met with a flight of stairs. Gunmen swarm around the lobby behind us—I hear one enter the nurse's station and head for the cafeteria—so it's not like we have much choice, but I feel like an animal boxing itself into a corner.

Lacy, Shannon, and Miles take the stairs without difficulty. By the time I reach the second story, I'm running on fumes. Thankfully, or perhaps to my disadvantage, moonlight floods through the windows, illuminating the hallway before me. The place remains furnished, and I suspect it is all thirty-plus years old. Sheets cover everything, like the place is inhabited by furniture in ghost costumes.

I slink along the hall when I spot movement ahead. Miles ushers Lacy and Shannon into a room, keeping them ahead of him while he brings up the rear. Another silhouette emerges from the door across the hallway opposite Miles. The man creeps closer, his handgun at the ready, and I act on instinct. I pull my firearm and—fearing I'll miss—unload the clip. I hit the man a handful of times, but the cacophony of shots is what worries me the most. He hits the floor with a wet thud.

Miles rushes over and offers his shoulder for support. He half carries me down the hall and shoves me into the room with Shannon and Lacy. Once inside, he blocks the door by knocking over a heavy filing cabinet and pushes us to keep going. The sound of men running up the stairs gets my heart rate up and my palms sweaty.

Shannon and Lacy run to another door at the far end of the room. They open it and rush forward, into a giant dining hall or lobby, I don't truly know.

Miles returns to me and again offers his shoulder. I lean on it and tuck my gun away. Without bullets, it's worthless.

"Thank you," Miles says. "I didn't even see the guy."

"I got your back."

He grips me tight. "I love you too."

The statement catches me off guard. Is that what we've been saying to each other this entire time? Miles doesn't hesitate, and he helps me enter the dining hall with little effort, his focus on the task at hand. Now isn't the time to dwell, and I bury my thoughts, saving them for later.

The floor sags as Miles and I walk out onto it. We both stop, and I take a step back—the whole room is sunken down, like a crater. It'll cave at any second.

Shannon and Lacy must not have noticed. They're halfway across the massive room and weaving between cloth-covered tables.

"Find them!" I hear Jeremy yell, even from the floor below. "Absolutely no one leaves this building!"

Banging drowns out all other commands as men attempt to slam open the door Miles blocked. Shannon and Lacy wait at the far end of the room, their nervous restlessness apparent as they pace back and forth, motioning for us to hurry.

Run across the weak floor or take our time? I let go of Miles and urge him forward. "C'mon," I say. "We both shouldn't go at once. Get to your sister."

He must know we don't have time to bicker. He runs along the wall and jumps over a table in the process, deepening the floor with his landing, like the supports under the room have been removed. Chairs slide down the curve toward the center point. Miles reaches the girls in record time, but not before thugs break past his file cabinet barrier.

I wait at the door, my back pressed against the wall, and I trip the first one through. The second guy rounds the doorframe, and I punch him across the jaw. He staggers back, I grab him by the jacket, and then I throw him into the first, knocking them both down.

The floorboards snap but don't outright break, and the room sinks another three inches. Everyone holds their breath—both gunmen wide-eyed with realization—and I attempt to back away, but my stiff leg isn't capable of soft steps. Five more chairs slide into the center of the room, along with a table, and finally a metal shelf tips forward, crashing onto the crumbling floor with a tumultuous slam.

Everything happens in slow motion, like my mind lags from information overload. The floor gives out, I'm falling, and dust whooshes up from below, filling the air. Glass shatters. Wood splinters. The groan of metal twisting against its will finishes the chorus of destruction. I'm on my back, blinking away the debris, when reality returns to its normal speed. Needles of wood puncture parts of my body, but I can't feel a damn thing.

"Pierce!"

It takes me several seconds to gather my strength and roll onto my side.

Well, I think everyone knows where we are now.

To my surprise, Miles yanks me to my feet. Did he jump down after me? I stare up at him, squinting, and he smiles back, like he's got the situation under control. I wish that were true, but there's something to be said about confidence.

"Miles!" Lacy screams from the second story. "Pierce!"

"Keep going," Miles commands. "To the stairs. We'll meet outside."

He doesn't have time to give any more instructions—both men who attacked me rise from the broken floorboards covered in dust, debris, and blood. Miles whips out his handgun and fires, his aim on par with Rhett's. After two shots, he's done, but the loud bang of firearms continues. Jeremy's men fire at us from a room over, and Miles pushes me behind a pile of wood and metal. I hit the floor on my stomach and lament the fact I have no bullets.

What am I going to do in this situation?

"*Pierce!*"

The shout belongs to Jeremy. He's somewhere in the building, no doubt behind his myriad of goons.

"*I know it's you!*" His anger borders on incoherent rage, and even some of his words seem slurred. "I'll see you suffer for this! *How dare you turn against me!*"

The gunshots stop. Miles takes a deep breath, coughs, and then helps me to my feet again. The cloud of settling particles mixed with darkness makes everything a clusterfuck. Rays from flashlights attempt to pierce the quagmire, but they flail about with little effectiveness. Miles and I duck when a beam streaks by, however, just in case.

"Go," Miles says. "The stairs are that way. You should get to the girls. I'll be right behind you."

"He wants *me*," I say between stifled coughs. The building settles, creaking all around us, but I know the men are searching for sounds. It's a deadly game of hide-and-seek at this point.

"I won't let him have you. Go. You know I'm the one in better condition for this."

"What're you doing?" Jeremy hisses. "Smoke him out! *Burn him*! I don't care! Don't let him get away!"

I nod and head in the direction he pointed, crawling over broken floorboards. Miles fires his gun—no doubt at random—in what I suspect is a ploy to draw people to his location. It worries me, but I know we can't make a stand together, not if we want a chance at living.

Molotov cocktails shatter across the floor all around me, bursting into flame. I wouldn't be concerned if I were agile, but as it stands I have to walk through this bullshit. To make matters worse, the cocktails aren't just made with alcohol and gasoline, they have something else— something added to create thick clouds of choking black smoke.

Perfect.

Gunshots fill the air. Like a nightmare, I run forward, anxiety gripping my every thought. I stumble through the thick smoke, coughing incessantly, until I hit the door and stagger beyond. The sound of running and the hushed orders of men looking to find me mix together. Then I notice there are bodies in this room. Unconscious bodies.

"Pierce!" Jeremy shouts, closer than before. "No matter where you go, I'll find you! I'll make you regret running!"

I keep moving forward until I reach the stairwell, gritting my teeth the entire way. Jeremy will burn this whole place to the ground, no matter the cost. Money. Resources. *Lives*. The kid is fucking insane.

"Pierce!" Lacy says with a gasp as I put my foot on the first step. She and Shannon bound down. They wrap their arms around me and grip tight.

I usher them toward the exit. "We're going to the back," I say.

"Try the exit!" I hear a man shout from the darkness of the hall.

The girls look at me, fear in their glassy eyes.

"Get behind the stairs," I command. "And don't come out for any reason."

They rush to comply, and I take a moment to make sure they're hidden well enough. When the bruiser rounds the corner into the stairwell, I lunge, taking us both to the floor.

Big mistake.

He effortlessly flips the tables and gets me on my back. I'm weak and struggling to breathe. He punches down, busting my lip, creaking my nose—I should've known I can't grapple with someone at their full strength when I can barely muster a run.

The taste of copper fills my mouth on the third punch. Still conscious but limp, I figure it is better he gets me than finds the girls. He grabs me by the collar of my shirt, searches around for his dropped gun, and upon finding it, brings it up to my neck.

"Where're the others?" he growls as he buries the barrel of the .22 deep into my jugular.

I don't answer. I'd never answer.

Shannon exits her hiding spot, walks over with the stealth of a shadow, and stabs the man with Lacy's needle, right in the soft of his back. I'd be willing to bet—based on the man's unbridled scream—she hit his kidney dead on.

I twist the man's gun around and fire, the muzzle flash a momentary bright spot etched into my eye as the bullet rips through the guy's cheek and head. Shannon jumps back, both hands over her ears, and I throw the still-bleeding corpse off my body in order to stand.

Taking the gun, I motion for the girls to run. "C'mon!"

Lacy and Shannon bust out into the glory of the moonlight. Hot on their tail, I exit to find the beam of a helicopter spotlight rushing down on me. The beat of the propellers muffles all sound as it drops near the retirement home. The symbol for the Illinois State Police adorns both sides of the vehicle—a star over the silhouette of the state.

I have never been so happy to see the cops in my entire life.

Took Rhett fucking long enough.

"Miles!"

Lacy's excited shout is almost lost to the helicopter. I whip around and spot Miles exiting the building. He's covered in grime, splattered with speckles of crimson, and jogs over with heavy steps, but otherwise he appears unharmed. Once together, we move away from the building and cross the street. The sirens of police vehicles screech into the area. We'll be swarming in blue uniforms before the dawn. It's no wonder the hired guns fled.

"There were people inside," Miles says between heavy breaths. "And I'm sure they'll try to leave."

"The trucks aren't going anywhere now that the cops are involved," I state. "Leave them."

"What about the other vehicles? We should try to stop them."

Of course Miles wants to save them all, but we're lucky to have made it out with our lives. Orange flickers of flame lick out the windows, and black smoke blots out the last of the stars. It's not the people in the trucks who need rescuing.

Miles glances off toward the building. His sister takes his arm. "Don't go," Lacy says.

Shannon nods. "You both should stay."

I'm sure some of these assholes are going to escape. They still have cop buddies on the inside, at least tonight, and the smaller vehicles can, and have, escaped from the police in the past. Not the trucks, and not everyone, but that's better than nothing, right?

I turn to Miles, who stares at the building with a look of conflicted desire. "When the fire engines get here, tell the firefighters," I say. "You know they're more capable of handling the situation than you are."

Miles holds Lacy close. "You're right. I… I'll stay here."

Shannon sticks to my side. "What's going to happen?"

"The cops are gonna take us home."

"But they brought us here!"

"These ones are good guys."

Shannon rubs at her eyes. "And if they're not?"

"I guess we'll have to fight them too," I say with half a laugh and half a sigh.

Miles gives me a one-sided smile before regarding Shannon. "Don't worry. We won't let anything happen to you two."

CHAPTER TWENTY-FOUR

NOTHING FEELS better than ice on my face.

I rest back in the chair, staring at the ceiling, as the ice melts inside its plastic baggie. Water pools, but I don't mind. It's still cold, and that's all that matters. It soothes the pain.

The door to Rhett's office opens. For the short period of time before it closes, I catch the cacophony of typing, talking, hustling, and shouting. Despite everything happening in Noimore, the Joliet City Police Department is just as swamped. Reporters want answers for the dozen crooked cops. It's a scandal unlike the city has ever seen.

Miles sits up in his chair and places a hand on my leg. I straighten my posture and toss the half-melted bag of ice onto Rhett's desk. The man looks overworked and stressed, like someone who patted themselves down after nearly burning to death. He doesn't give my ice bag a second glance.

"Did you find anything about Worldwide Decurion?" Miles asks.

"The man I apprehended in the boathouse is willing to testify that they're involved," Rhett says as he paces back and forth. He stares down at the mess of paperwork on his desk and frowns. "And thanks to the evidence Shelby supplied us, I have most of the collaborating police officers under arrest, including Deputy Chief Charleston."

I finger the paperwork in my pocket but remain silent. It's good to hear the man Rhett spared will talk. I know Worldwide Decurion is behind the trafficking—the stuff I gathered from the dispatch center says enough—but I can't hand over illegally gained evidence. Well, I'm sure Miles can find a loophole, but for now, I keep the information close, just in case it's needed in the future.

"Did you save the people?" Miles asks. "The ones inside?"

"As far as I know, there were seven dead bodies found once the fires were taken care of. We're still identifying them, but everyone else we found was taken to the hospital and is expected to make a full recovery."

Miles breathes easier.

"How was your sister?" Rhett asks. "And the other little girl?"

"They seemed okay once they got away from the building. I intend to pick them up from the hospital on the way home."

"Do you think they'll keep at it?" I ask, my voice a grate to the ears.

Rhett lifts an eyebrow. "Who?"

"The traffickers. Their whole operation."

"Without the cops? And with us hot on Worldwide Decurion's trail? No. I doubt they'll even have the option."

Miles scoots to the edge of his chair. "What about the Vice family?"

"They were co-owners of the property," Rhett replies. "So they're under investigation."

"But you didn't arrest any of them? Jeremy was there in the retirement home."

"None of the men we arrested admit to seeing him, and he wasn't picked up by any of my officers."

Miles curses under his breath, but I offer a weak laugh. That's my luck. Of course he would get away. He's made of slime, after all. He'll slip through any crack available. It makes my life ten times worse knowing he's out there, though. Especially now that he knows I'm back from the grave.

"Why are we still here, then?" Miles asks, his fingers gripping my pants tighter. "We gave you our statements."

"I'm charging you both with trespassing," Rhett drawls. He picks up a few pieces of paper and tosses them over. Miles takes them and skims over a few lines before returning his gaze to Rhett's.

"Really?"

"You *were* trespassing."

"But—"

"And this way you'll both be in our system with fingerprints and mug shots." Rhett looks away from Miles and gives me his full attention. "Which means your fingerprints won't be mistaken for anyone else's. They'll be on file as Percy Adams and Miles Devonport. No one else's."

Miles goes quiet, and I shift in my seat.

"I thought—" I begin, but stop to gather my thoughts. "Didn't you have someone in custody claiming that I hired them for a hit on Shelby?" Why help me by getting my new identity solidified in the system?

"It turns out Donny McCoy is a pathological liar," Rhett says with a sigh. "We've caught him in a few inconsistencies, and he's flat-out admitted to stretching the truth. It seems he isn't a reliable source of information. Plus, officers have a bit of discretion. After everything I've come to know of you, I doubt you'd hire someone to kill Shelby."

"I definitely didn't," I state.

"Yeah, well, maybe Nicholas Pierce would have. But he's dead, so says the paperwork. Just like the paperwork says Percy Adams once trespassed into gun-infested territory to save a couple of kidnapped girls. If I had to go on record for a crime, I wouldn't mind having that one."

For a moment, we regard each other.

Damn. Rhett's not such an insufferable asshole after all. Almost makes me want to apologize for fucking with him in the boathouse.

Almost.

Miles lets out a long exhale. "Is there anything else?"

"There is one thing."

Rhett shuffles through the mountain of paperwork and snatches up a bundle of time receipts. He hands them over, and I stare at them for a few seconds to allow for my busted eye to focus. They're handwritten time cards, basically. All in Shelby's handwriting. All three years signed off as though I had worked for him for some time.

"I found that in the stack of evidence you gave me," Rhett says. "I figured you'd want it back."

I nod. "Thank you."

A woman in a tight blouse enters Rhett's office. It's the secretary—what's her name?—Monica. She walks over to Rhett and hands him a mug of coffee. "Anything else I can do for you?" she asks with a smile.

"I'm swamped, Monica," Rhett says. "I appreciate the drink, but—"

"If you need anything else, I'd be more than willing to help!"

"Yes, I understand."

She places a hand on his arm, and I almost feel for the guy. Too polite to tell her no, too stressed to deal with it properly. And Monica drools like a puppy. Her fingers are gonna be so wet I'll be afraid to shake hands with her the next time we meet.

"I think we need to go," I say.

Miles stands and offers me a hand up. I take it, despite feeling like a useless pile of jelly, and I lean on him in order to walk.

"All of us," I say to Monica. "Rhett needs to do some paperwork."

She gives me an odd look, almost like she's saying *who the hell are you?* but Miles backs me up.

"Yeah, isn't that right, Rhett? You were just telling us how you needed some peace and quiet."

Rhett nods. "Yes. I have enough work for thirty people on my plate."

Monica forces a tight smile. "All right. Call me if you need me." She walks out with me and Miles, never regarding us in the least, and heads off toward her desk at the first possible moment.

"You sure you want to be carrying me like this?" I ask with a half smile as Miles and I continue our way through the police department. "These all might be your future coworkers, and I'm some random sad sack getting blood on your clothes."

"I'd rather have them know where my priorities are," he replies, holding me closer. "I've got your back, Pierce."

I love you too.

The words hang in my mind for a moment, but I can't bring myself to say them, or even bring up what Miles said. The phrase *I've got your back* will literally never be the same for me again.

How long have we been saying it to each other? Forever, it seems. Even thinking about it gets my chest tight. Has he always known that's what we've been saying to each other? Am I the one oblivious to what's been going on, or have I been denying it to myself?

I hold Miles tighter, despite the stares of passing officers.

All I want is a little while longer....

WHY DID I ever think I could handle a garden?

Dead. They're all dead. After one week too. Obviously something I'm doing is incorrect. I couldn't even handle this one thing—this one simple thing.

I plunge the shovel into the garden box and throw the soil across the yard. The tiny husks of my pre-plants disappear amongst the grass and dirt. I scoop another shovelful, and then another. I stop when I reach the radish, however.

Unlike everything else, it's still alive. I'm not even sure how, but I know this garden box can't possibly be good for it.

I walk over to a part of our lawn with green grass and dig a hole, careful not to disturb too much. Then I return to the garden box, dig up as much of the radish and its miracle dirt as possible, and replant it with the lush grass. Hopefully this part of the lawn is over a vein of plant resources or something. The radish will do better here, outside my care. This is for the best.

"Thank you."

Ms. Timo stands between the missing fence posts. I regard her with a quick nod.

"Shannon talks about you nonstop," the woman continues. "She wants to know if Lacy will come to visit again, and if she can spend time with you all."

"I don't know," I say. Lacy's mother didn't appreciate her kids getting caught up in criminal affairs. On the other hand, she hasn't said a bad thing about me since the report of my assistance in saving her daughter.

"Think about it? She'll be heartbroken if you say no."

"I will."

Ms. Timo nods and shuffles back to her house. Miles will have to deal with it all.

Once my box is long gone, I throw down the shovel and head back for the house. I stop the moment I lift my gaze and catch Miles standing in the doorway. The late afternoon sun shines down around us. He shouldn't be home at this time. He should be at class.

"Pierce, what're you doing?"

I brush my palms together and remain silent.

Miles walks out into the backyard, his hands in his pockets, and steps up next to me. "Well?"

"I'm cleaning up," I reply.

"That's it?"

"Yeah. Gotta keep busy."

Miles sighs and looks away. His gaze hardens as he stares at the garden box. "You've been different lately. Don't deny it. You keep trying to avoid me—to avoid telling me things."

I don't offer any commentary.

"You didn't tell me everything about Shelby," Miles continues. "And you go off on your own more often than not, even if I tell you I want to be there with you."

"I have to do everything you say, is that it?" I ask, more edge than sarcasm in my voice.

"No. I just want to know why."

Again, I get quiet.

Miles takes his hands out of his pockets and crosses his arms over his chest. When he looks up at me, I swear he's on the verge of anger. "Are you trying to leave me?" he asks. He's so direct and to the point that there's no sidestepping the question.

He must have seen that I cleaned out most of my stuff from our room, and that I've taken money out of the bank account.

"You don't need me," I drawl.

It's true. He can't deny it.

"So?" he asks as though that isn't a factor.

"I'm holding you back."

"How can you say that? It's not true."

"Isn't it?" I shout, hitting rage faster than I suspect Miles is prepared for. He flinches at my outburst, and I throw an arm up in the air with heated movements. "Don't you hear what everyone says, kid? You have a future! When they talk about you, they talk in what-ifs, like they have no idea how far you'll go. *This* is how far I'll go. Right here, right now. There's nothing else I'm good for. I've proven that time and time again."

Miles matches my anger with his own. He steps up to me, like we're about to rumble, and hardens himself back to a glare. "What does it matter, Pierce?" he shouts. "It doesn't."

"Think long-term! You need someone who'll go the distance with you, Miles. Hell, I'm gonna die twenty years before you, regardless. You deserve a partner who won't cut out at the end of the race."

"Pierce, if it weren't for you, I wouldn't be alive! I'd be dead at the bottom of a river after a lengthy warehouse beating!"

I shove him, much to Miles's surprise, and he almost falls flat on his back. He catches himself and recovers, confusion written across his face.

"You owe me nothing," I shout, unable to control my volume. I don't care if the whole goddamn neighborhood hears what I'm saying, so long as it sinks into Miles's head. "You paid me back! You saved me from Jeremy, and now I have a life again. We're even. You're duty bound to nothing!"

"Everything I do—" Miles walks up close and returns the shove, both his hands on my shoulders. "—I do for you!"

I stagger a moment and grit my teeth. "What're you talking about?"

"All those awards? All my scores? All my success? It's to show you that I can do it! I can be the man you depend on! Someone you can trust!"

"You said you were doin' it for you."

"I am!" He grabs my shirt and twists his knuckles into the fabric, keeping me close. "I want to be the man you can depend on!"

"You're confused," I practically hiss. "You could have anyone you wanted if you stopped being naïve and thinkin' with your dick."

"Tsk. I'm not confused—*you're* confused! I know exactly what I want, Pierce!" He half laughs while grinding his teeth. He collects himself with a few short breaths. "I want… I want you to live as long as possible. I want to give you everything you've ever wanted. I want you to see all the things you've been missing in life. And then, when you're gone, I'm gonna spend those last twenty years counting the days until we're together again."

Miles pulls me even closer and slams his forehead down on my collarbone. I feel his breath come out in short, ragged bursts. I stand still, mulling over his statements, unable to move or respond.

I wish I was half the person he thinks I am. I'd be a goddamn superman.

With an unsteady hand, I trace the length of his spine. Miles must take my motion as acceptance, because he releases my shirt and wraps his arms around me. Together, held tightly by Miles's grip, I relax a bit. He smells good.

"Tell me why you're really leaving," he demands in a hushed tone.

"I don't want to see you hurt," I reply, all anger gone. "At first I thought my past would haunt you…. Now it's my future. What if someone comes looking for me? And they will. What if you're caught up in it?"

"I want to be caught up in it."

"What if your family is caught up in it?" I ask, serious and cold. "Jayden already got shot. Lacy abducted. How much more will have to happen before you realize it's me that's the cause?"

His nails dig into my back. "I'm not going to let them dictate how I live my life. We can beat them, Pierce. And even if you leave, I'm going to go after them, so there's really nothing you're saving me from."

"Them?" I ask.

"Jeremy. His mob. All of them. I want them gone, and come hell or high water, I'll do it."

I return his embrace, unable to stop myself from smiling. "Pretty ballsy."

"Yeah, well, stop trying to ditch me," Miles states. "No dying. No leaving in the middle of the night. It won't change what I'm going to do—and I'd rather have you with me. I… I want to be more confident. Like you. And when you're around, I feel like your conviction rubs off on me."

"Heh. All right. You have me. But I can't promise anything about dying, except that it'll happen one day."

"So we'll do this together?" he asks. "I don't need to worry about convincing you ever again?"

It's his conviction that gets me. He wants to do it together. No hesitation. And he wants to right the wrongs of my past. No reservations. Even I wasn't that sure when I mulled over the possibilities of the future. Maybe he's right. Maybe I *was* the one confused about what I wanted.

Marry me.

It's what I want to say, but even in my mind, it feels awkward—something I never considered right for me. The crimson orange of the setting sun lights everything in a passionate way, and I blame the atmosphere for my sudden swell of emotion.

I don't need any formal paperwork or ceremony to know that I'd die for him, or that I'll never contemplate leaving him again. Still, he waits for my response, and I know he wants to hear my deepest thoughts.

"I love you," I say. Words I haven't uttered since childhood.

His voice is thick with emotion when he replies, "And I you."

"Heh. Don't get weepy on me."

Miles breaks our embrace and smiles, a sort of mirth about him that I enjoy. "We have to move, by the way. My mother thinks our neighborhood is to blame. She won't let me see Lacy again until I find a better place."

"Fine."

"Really? You don't mind?"

"The kid next door won't like it, but we can go anywhere you want."

Miles rubs at his neck and stares at me. He lifts both eyebrows, like he wants to suggest something, and I wait for it, knowing it's something preposterous.

"We could ask them to move too," he finally says.

"Yeah. The old lady really has the funds for that."

"We have the funds for that."

Eh. I think back to Shannon in the retirement home—about how she said no one would come for her—and I know I can't stand the thought of up and disappearing on her, especially when she and Lacy became fast friends. Then again, we aren't made of money. We're bound to burn through most of my mob money helping people out. You'd think half a million goes a long way, but shit isn't cheap.

"We don't have to do it unless you want to."

"Fine," I drawl. "Talk to her. Let's see what we can do."

Miles taps me on the arm. "I knew you'd come around, Pierce. You're a good guy."

S.A. STOVALL grew up in California's central valley with a single mother and little brother. Despite no one in her family having a degree higher than a GED, she put herself through college (earning a BA in History), and then continued on to law school where she obtained her Juris Doctorate.

As a child, Stovall's favorite novel was *Island of the Blue Dolphins* by Scott O'Dell. The adventure on a deserted island opened her mind to ideas and realities she had never given thought before—and it was the moment Stovall realized that storytelling (specifically fiction) became her passion. Anything that told a story, be it a movie, book, video game, or comic, she had to experience. Now as a professor and author, Stovall wants to add her voice to the myriad of stories in the world, and she hopes you enjoy.

You can contact her at the following addresses:

Twitter: @GameOverStation
Email: s.adelle.s@gmail.com

S.A. Stovall
VICE CITY

Vice City: Book One

After twenty years as an enforcer for the Vice family mob, Nicholas Pierce shouldn't bat an eye at seeing a guy get worked over and tossed in the river. But there's something about the suspected police mole, Miles, that has Pierce second-guessing himself. The kid is just trying to look out for his brother any way he knows how, and the altruistic motive sparks an uncharacteristic act of mercy that involves Pierce taking Miles under his wing.

Miles wants to repay Pierce for saving his life. Pierce shouldn't see him as anything but a convenient hookup… and he sure as hell shouldn't get involved in Miles's doomed quest to get his brother out of a rival street gang. He shouldn't do a lot of things, but life on the streets isn't about following the rules. Besides, he's sick of being abused by the Vice family, especially Mr. Vice and his power-hungry goon of a son, who treats his underlings like playthings.

So Pierce does the absolute last thing he should do if he wants to keep breathing—he leaves the Vice family in the middle of a turf war.

www.dsppublications.com

ANNE BARWELL
COMES A
HORSEMAN

Sequel to *Winter Duet*
Echoes Rising: Book Three

France, 1944

Sometimes the most desperate struggles take place far from the battlefield, and what happens in secret can change the course of history.

Victory is close at hand, but freedom remains frustratingly just beyond the grasp of German physicist Dr. Kristopher Lehrer, Resistance fighter Michel, and the remaining members of the team sent by the Allies—Captain Matt Bryant, Sergeant Ken Lowe, and Dr. Zhou Liang—as they fight to keep the atomic plans from the Nazis. The team reaches France and connects with members of Michel's French Resistance cell in Normandy. Allied troops are poised to liberate France, and rescue is supposedly at hand. However, Kristopher is no longer sure the information he carries in his memory is safe with either side.

When Standartenführer Holm and his men finally catch up with their prey, the team is left with few options. With a traitor in their midst, who can they trust? Kristopher realizes he must become something he is not in order to save the man he loves. Death is biding his time, and sacrifices must be made for any of them to have the futures they want.

www.dsppublications.com

DAVID C. DAWSON
THE DEADLY LIES
a Dominic Delingpole Mystery

SOUTHERNMOST MURDER

C.S. POE

Aubrey Grant lives in the tropical paradise of Old Town, Key West, has a cute cottage, a sweet moped, and a great job managing the historical property of a former sea captain. With his soon-to-be-boyfriend, hotshot FBI agent Jun Tanaka, visiting for a little R&R, not even Aubrey's narcolepsy can put a damper on their vacation plans.

But a skeleton in a closet of the Smith Family Historical Home throws a wrench into the works. Despite Aubrey and Jun's attempts to enjoy some time together, the skeleton's identity drags them into a mystery with origins over a century in the past. They uncover a tale of long-lost treasure, the pirate king it belonged to, and a modern-day murderer who will stop at nothing to find the hidden riches. If a killer on the loose isn't enough to keep Aubrey out of the mess, it seems even the restless spirit of Captain Smith is warning him away.

The unlikely partnership of a special agent and historian may be exactly what it takes to crack this mystery wide-open and finally put an old Key West tragedy to rest. But while Aubrey tracks down the X that marks the spot, one wrong move could be his last.

www.dsppublications.com

www.ingramcontent.com/pod-product-compliance
Lightning Source LLC
Chambersburg PA
CBHW070445120726
47910CB00003B/931